By Aya de León

Queen of Urban Prophecy

A Spy in the Struggle

Side Chick Nation

The Accidental Mistress

The Boss

Uptown Thief

QUEEN OF URBAN PROPHECY

AYA de LEÓN

www.kensingtonbooks.com

DAFINA BOOKS are published by

Kensington Publishing Corp.
119 West 40th Street
New York, NY 10018

All Kensington titles, imprints, and distributed lines are available at special quantity discounts for bulk purchases for sales promotion, premiums, fund-raising, and educational or institutional use.

Special book excerpts or customized printings can also be created to fit specific needs. For details, write or phone the office of the Kensington Sales Manager: Kensington Publishing Corp., 119 West 40th Street, New York, NY 10018. Attn. Sales Department. Phone: 1-800-221-2647.

The Dafina logo is a trademark of Kensington Publishing Corp.

ISBN: 978-1-4967-2862-3
First Trade Paperback Printing: January 2022

ISBN: 978-1-4967-2864-7 (e-book)
First Electronic Edition: January 2022

10 9 8 7 6 5 4 3 2 1

Printed in the United States of America

For Pam, the fizza-fizza-Funkstress

Acknowledgments

I would like to thank all the women in hip hop who have gone before me and before Deza. I have shouted many of them out in the book. And thanks as always to my literary crew: my agent Jenni, as well as my Kensington team, Esi, Michelle, and Vida. My family—blood and chosen—Dee, Stuart, Anna, Larry, Paci, Neens, Coco, Pam and Carolina, and especially my newfound *Familia from Scratch*. Thanks to FFS and particularly Kris for all the in-person (masked and outdoor) schooling and childcare that made writing a book during the pandemic possible. For the hip hop specific shoutouts, please see Author's Note. And thanks to all the leaders in the climate justice movement and the Movement for Black Lives for inspiring us toward a totally different society where we invest in the more just and humane and sustainable world we all deserve and are calling into existence.

Book 1

Chapter 1

Manhattan

"We'll be starting in thirty seconds," the producer's voice came through clearly in Deza's ear. She was sitting across from Dell Ballard, the host of CNN's *National Current*. She had on a plain black cotton top, but she was sweating. She sometimes did a Hands-Up-Don't-Shoot gesture when she talked about police violence, but with the massive rings of moisture under her arms, she would not be doing that today.

Every media outlet wanted her as a guest right now. First there was the *New York Times* arts section article. That interview was nothing like being on camera. She had been able to stumble through it. The reporter had noted in the article that she had been a little awkward, but he smoothed out all the quotes.

She had done in-person radio interviews—two of them on New York's Power 105.1. She spoke with "The Voice of New York," Angie Martinez, and was also on *The Breakfast Club*. On New York's Hot 97, she had done *Ebro in the Morning*. She had called in to the LA station REAL 92.3 on *Big Boy's Neighborhood*, and *The Sana G Morning Show* on KMEL in the Bay Area. But those were hip hop shows where the DJs spoke her language.

As for TV, she had initially only agreed to do interviews with Black journalists. Folks like Joy-Ann Reid, who understood politics *and* hip hop. She turned down *The View* because there was too much arguing and too many white women.

Her promo team agreed that she should warm up with Trevor Noah. His format would not only include the interview, he would let her perform the song first. Deza was a rapper. That was what she knew how to do. It gave her the chance to loosen up before she did her first TV interview since the girl had been shot and killed.

She had done plenty of interviews before—print, radio, and TV—but up until now it had always been about the music. She knew how to talk about her work in a way that sounded both humble and confident. She knew how to deflect the attempts to pit her against other female rap artists or to box her in to one style. But now she was suddenly out of her depth. How was she, a rap artist, supposed to know the answer to police brutality in the US, a problem that had arguably been going on since before slavery? Deza knew that the name of the girl in her song was, more than anything, a coincidence. But she also knew that the label had gotten this prophecy thing in its jaws and was locked down on it like a pit bull. She would need to play along.

The Trevor Noah interview had gone great. He was warm and had cracked jokes with her at the break. He could probably see she was scared shitless. He did everything possible to put her at ease. He started with the music and basically fed her the cues for her talking points.

She felt great after *The Daily Show*. She had green-lighted CNN with the publicist at Paperclip.

"This will be amazing," the publicist said. "It'll get you in front of a whole new demographic."

CNN had its New York studios in the Time Warner Center. On the way in, Deza had gone live on Instagram. She stood in front of the bright globe and gleaming buildings that rose out of the ground like stalagmites of platinum. She had started with her signature salutation: "Bring it to me, y'all." It was the title and hook of an early rhyme of hers. "This is ya girl, Deza," she continued. "Walking into the studios at CNN. I'm news, y'all!"

But now, she was in a cavernous CNN studio with a huge camera in her face, far from the host, Dell Ballard, who was in a studio in Atlanta. She could see his pale, square-jawed profile on a monitor. He was paying her no attention, rather ordering an assistant to get him a new jacket because he had spilled water on his lapel.

The producer counted "Three, two, one," in her ear. In a split second, the host went from adjusting the fresh jacket to talking.

"Our next guest is Deza Starling," Ballard began. "Whose debut album took an unexpected turn when . . ."

In the end, it all came down to the name Shaquana.

As a writer of rhymes, Deza wanted to use an economy of words. She didn't want to say, "the girl shot by the cop was Black." She wanted it to be implied in the name. Clear. Undeniable. Only an African American girl would be named Shaquana. She had toyed with Neisha and Kimani and Za'Niya, but landed on Shaquana. Later, she would wonder if she'd picked it partly for the sound. The alliteration of "shot" and "Shaquana," or the way she could rhyme it with "grieving mama." Whatever the reason, that choice was the direct cause and effect of her becoming the Queen of Urban Prophecy.

As it turned out, the spelling wasn't the same. The girl's mother had spelled it without the u. But ultimately, it didn't matter that much. It is not the writing, but the speaking of the names of the dead that carries the most power.

The difference was negligible. Because it was an undeniable fact, later corroborated by the footage from the officer's own body camera, that Shaqana was walking home from school with just one friend, when Officer Bob O'Brian, who was in pursuit of a suspect, shot and killed her.

A bystander had pulled out his phone to film the chase when the officer unholstered his weapon. The bystander later said in an interview that he was afraid the suspect, a young Black man who was never identified, would be shot. The clip of his video, which went viral, was the unsteady view of the running officer, with the sound of the shot, and the friend screaming her name, "Shaqana!" as the camera swerved to capture the young woman who had fallen onto the sidewalk.

In the final analysis, no one could deny that a girl named Shaqana had been shot on the way home from school by a white police officer chasing someone else. An officer who had so little regard for any of the Black residents of that neighborhood that he would run, gun drawn, down a busy block, and shoot while running, heedless of who else he might hit.

And there it was, Deza's album, the latest ode to hot girls, a debut album by Paperclip Records' new female rapper. Twelve tracks about money, sex, love, and heartbreak, and living that sexy rapper girl life. And a thirteenth that didn't quite fit called "Almost Home." About police brutality, and the story of a girl named "Shaquana" who got shot by a cop on the way back to her neighborhood from school.

A week after the album debuted and the first single, "Deza Daze Ya," was getting airplay, Shaqana was killed by police in Shelton, a small town outside Oklahoma City.

Chance the Rapper had been the first one to use the word "prophet." In a tweet claiming Deza as one of many prophets to come out of their shared hometown, Chicago. #AlmostHome.

And Deza suddenly rocketed to the top of the charts.

* * *

CNN's Dell Ballard tossed his first question to Deza.

"What was it like for you to realize that you had literally predicted a police shooting, right down to the girl's name, and the fact that she was walking home from school?" Ballard asked.

"It was like, horrifying," Deza said. "I'm scared to name any names in a rap again."

The host raised an eyebrow. "Are you saying you think it could happen again?"

"No!" Deza said quickly. "I just—I wouldn't want anyone with the same name to feel some kind of way about it. To worry, you know? From now on, my rhymes will contain anonymous victims of police brutality or whatever."

"So you don't think you predicted anything here?"

Deza said the line she had rehearsed, the line that would satisfy the camera and make a great sound bite. "I think that the Bay Area hip hop journalist Davey D said it best on KPFA's *Hard Knock Radio* yesterday, 'it's a shame that police violence is so prevalent in this country that eventually a rapper would write a rhyme about a young Black person getting shot, and the name and circumstances would coincide with reality.' That rapper just happened to be me. But it shows that decades of trying to reform the police have failed, and like the Movement for Black Lives has been demanding, we need to defund the police."

There it was. Perfect.

"So you favor the complete elimination of the police as an institution?" Ballard asked.

"I think a lot of that money needs to go to other services," she said. "If not all of it. For the simple fact that for me, as a Black woman, I've never been in a situation that I thought a police officer would make it better. There have been lots of times I've been in dangerous situations and wished I had someone to help me out. But when I thought about who I wished would show up, it was never the police."

"Isn't it true that members of your family have found themselves on the wrong side of the law?" Ballard went on. "Isn't it true that you have relatives in prison?"

"I'm not here to talk about my family," Deza said. "I'm here to talk about police violence."

"But you have a bias against police," he said. "Don't you?"

"Where did you even hear that?" Deza asked.

"It's part of the public record," Ballard said.

"You dug into police records?" Deza asked.

"Your own words," he insisted. "As a rap artist."

"I've never recorded anything about my family," she pushed back.

"Not in a studio," he said. "Can we roll the clip?"

Deza saw an image of herself, grainy and dark, on a stage in Brooklyn.

She was battling a male emcee who had accused her of not being "real." Of being an out-of-towner, who was soft compared to New York.

> Being from out of town and being soft ain't the
>   same
> I got family members all caught up in the game
> Southside Chicago is the hood that I rep
> And if you knew what it was like then you
>   would back up a step.

Ballard went on. "So my producers assure me that 'caught up in the game,' refers to illegal activity and the legal system. Are you referring here to the fact that two of your brothers are incarcerated?" Ballard asked.

"No," Deza said. "I'm—I'm just—just referring to the general situation of my neighborhood in Chicago. Where police brutality is an epidemic." Which was a lie. Not about police brutality. That was definitely true. She was referring to the fact that her father was a known drug dealer in Chicago.

But of course, there was no way she was going to say that on national TV.

"And my family has had a whole—a whole lot of different negative experiences with the police," she said. "Like my aunt was killed in a drive-by shooting in Chicago," she said. "And the police never solved the case. So you can see why I have no use for police."

She also didn't say that everyone in the neighborhood suspected that the police might have been behind the shooting. Since her aunt was an activist fighting against police corruption. But she wasn't going to say that on national TV, either. In this land mine of things she couldn't say, she stammered her way through the rest of the interview, wishing she had stuck to her original resolve only to do interviews with Black hosts.

Chapter 2

Brooklyn

Wearing shades in the club was corny, Deza knew that. But she needed the anonymity. She needed a break from being an urban prophet. It had been six weeks since the disastrous CNN interview.

Paperclip Records had put together a tour of their women artists, and the headliner had pulled out at the height of the Shaqana news cycle. Deza was contracted to tour to support her album, and they had a dozen appearances set up in mid-sized venues around the country. But they canceled those dates and replaced the other headliner with Deza. She wasn't sure she wanted to go on this thirty-city stadium tour. But the label didn't really ask. They informed her.

"This is an incredible opportunity," her manager said.

"I know," Deza said. "But . . ." How could she put it into words? These people were coming to see some urban mystic. But the label also wanted her to promote her album. Which was mostly songs about sex and romance. How was this going to work out?

With her manager's encouragement, she sent a fake-enthusiastic email to the label with lots of exclamation points! And then sank into a funk for the next week.

Now the tour bus would leave in the morning, and this was her last night in New York. Her last chance to really hear music. She grabbed her widest shades and went to her favorite club from back in the day.

Her driver walked to the front and told the doorman who she was. She took a selfie in front of the place and promised she'd post it on Instagram if they let her in. All the folks in the line gawked to see who was the nondescript brown girl in the shades with the big ass in the leggings and the Chicago T-shirt. Who was that bitch getting in all special? She wore no makeup. Nails not even polished. Had her hair cornrowed back in about thirty slender braids with no special style. They would dismiss her as the owner's daughter or niece and go back to their phone calls and conversations. No one would be tweeting "Deza just walked up to the club!!" because Deza was sexy and glamorous and now also sort of deep and magical. This year, Dilani Mara had created a Red Chocolate lipstick shade just for her. And these days there were people who counted the number of words and letters in Deza's Instagram posts and used them to predict lottery numbers. Deza had long, human hair weaves down to her ass, not cornrows that barely touched her shoulders. This girl was basic.

Deza danced alone. Sipped a few cocktails and drank in the music. An hour later, she was drenched in sweat. Yes! This was how it used to be. She would perform, then stay for the DJ set to burn off all that adrenaline. She missed the days when the music was something to make her feel elated and sexy. Some of her friends took Ecstasy to recapture the feeling, but the one time Deza took it, she ended up crying on the couch for three hours. No more Molly for her.

A good DJ could give her that all-over, sexy body sense if the music was mixed right. A good DJ knew how to work women with music. Her ex was a DJ. She caught him working some other chick after he'd moved in with her. She came home early to a remix of Marvin Gaye's "Let's Get it On." Fool that she was, she had assumed it was for her, that somehow he had known she would be home early. She had stripped off her clothes on the way into the bedroom, turning her own self on. And then she had appeared in the doorway, ready to see him licking his lips in anticipation. But his tongue was occupied in the mouth of some girl, his hips between her thighs, deep on the upstroke.

Deza froze. Her smile fell. The rain forest between her thighs abruptly turned to desert.

That's why she'd had three rum and gingers in the club tonight. She didn't want to remember his cheating ass. On the night that would have been their first wedding anniversary. If she had married him on the date they'd set. If she hadn't thrown that pathetic little girl out of their house in a dress with one shoe and no drawers. If she hadn't pulled off the ring and thrown it at him, along with all his clothes.

And the records. Every. Single. One. He mostly used Serato Scratch, but at home he had a single turntable and two crates of vinyl. She had peeled the records out of their sleeves and dust jackets and thrown them out the window. With him standing there saying, "Fuck! Deza! Not the original Wu-Tang twelve-inch!"

The record was precious to him. A pristine copy that he could never replace.

As it sailed out past him onto the Chicago street, the cab containing the irrelevant little girl also pulled away.

Deza tossed all his stuff down two stories of the apartment building. Other than the records, it wasn't much. She tossed the turntable as well. It burst on the sidewalk like a bomb.

Sexy. That was what everyone had wanted from her for the last few years. Back in the beginning, she had felt it when she performed. Had felt sexy. First with her ex. Then when she was single. She spent night after night in the club dancing with different guys, getting heated, and would maybe perform once a week. Sometimes, she would look out at a hot guy in the audience and fantasize. Maybe he would end up being her man.

But she never did anything about it. She had sworn off fuckboys to focus on her artistry. The performance was her chance to get off in the music, feel the surge of the audience's attention on her. Prowling around the stage, rapping, singing, gyrating. It was magnificent. Her streams did well, but for the first couple years, everyone said she was even better as a live performer.

Deza stayed focused on her career. But then she got so well-known in Chicago that she couldn't go to clubs anymore. She burned out on the performing. All those nights giving everyone else a show. No time to soak up the music and the energy in the clubs. She was always giving. She had to fake sexy when she didn't feel it. She hated it that most of the fans didn't know the difference.

All those years, hustling for her big break. But when success finally came, it didn't feel the way she thought it would. Like the feeling of joy that could be captured in an Instagram post. It never seemed to be enough.

And now, in the last several weeks, the audience had wanted something even more complicated. How do you replicate a freakish coincidence? How can you end up being anything other than a disappointment?

She went to the DJ and asked him if he had "Earth on Fire," by Nashonna.

"Actually, my set is done," he said. "But I'll ask the next DJ." He was a light-skinned guy with his long hair pulled back in a puff, faded in the back and on the sides. A slight scattering of freckles on his skin that she could see as one of the bright club lights panned across his face.

He smiled at her. "I always appreciate the folks who come to really dance," he said, taking off his headphones.

Deza nodded. Resisted the urge to smile back. She didn't come here for boys.

A woman stepped up to the DJ stage and began setting up. She saw the guy DJ lean in to talk to her. The lady DJ smiled. She had short, spiky hair. She looked kind of tomboyish, but the smile was wide and warm.

Deza felt a wave of jealousy. Which was ridiculous. She didn't feel any way about this DJ. Probably just leftover jealousy from her ex.

What was she wasting time for? This song was half-decent. This was her chance to dance. So she went out on the floor and began to spin and twerk.

Five minutes later, she was already lost in the music when her song came on. "YAAAASS!" Deza turned to the girl DJ and blew a kiss.

The thudding bass got Deza's hips shaking, and she was lost in the burning planet Nashonna was describing, one where the people rose up like fire to defeat an evil empire.

Deza shook her hips like she was rubbing flint against stone to make flame.

She was caught in a reverie when the guy DJ walked toward her. He nodded slightly and stood facing her, dancing outside her circle for a minute. She liked that. Didn't push up into her space. He showed respect. Hovered nearby. She leaned forward and took his hand.

He could dance. Most DJs couldn't really. They liked to stay in the booth, just nodding their heads to the music. Then there were guys who wanted to dance with you, but they really wanted you to do all the work, bring all the energy. They just put their hands on your waist and ground against your ass in a lackadaisical rhythm. Some brothers put in the effort. They had the moves. But they were rare. This guy was one of those. He put his whole body into it. His shoulders, his hips, his ass.

He put his hands in the air, and his sleeve slid down. She could see the Puerto Rico tattoo on his arm. Right. Latin guys could move for real. They'd been dancing with the aunties at the family parties since they were toddlers.

The two of them began to sink into a deep groove of call and response. Her body, his body, their sweaty limbs occasionally brushing against each other. His hands trailing gently around her waist every now and then, never holding, gripping, groping. His touch was all invitation, no invasion, no possession.

She liked it.

He seemed to like it, too. Some moments she would be so deep into the music, but other times she would look at him, and he was smiling. She could see his eyes, but he couldn't see hers behind the shades.

Then, at some point, their faces got close. She could see the sweat on his upper lip. Droplets among the stubble. He had a wispy soul patch. Those lips. Full. Inviting. Suddenly, she wanted to kiss him. Began to lean forward a bit. No one knew her in this Brooklyn club. In this city that had never quite become home. It was her last free night before she hit that tour bus. She leaned in even closer.

Then the music changed, and it broke the spell. She caught hold of herself and twirled back away. Not too far, but inviting him to chase. He followed.

The DJ mixed into a gritty, old-school dancehall song, and it was just the excuse they'd been waiting for. They started a slow wind, him behind her, his hands on her hips. Light at first, but with more grip as the song growled on. She turned around and he kept his eyes on hers. Making sure she was enjoying it. She was. She definitely was.

"Last call," the DJ said as she mixed into the next song.

Last call? Shit. How had it gotten that late? She had a bus to catch in the morning. Deza needed to get out. She had dismissed the limo driver, and she couldn't be stuck on the curb waiting for a Lyft with all the end-of-night patrons.

She squeezed his hand. "I gotta go," she said.

He held her hand for a minute. "What's your name?" he asked.

"I gotta go."

"Lemme walk you out," he said over the music.

Normally, she would have turned him down, but his manner had been so respectful. And it could be a little sketchy out in front of the club at this time, when they were closing down. Sometimes the bouncer stepped away from the door.

She pulled out her phone and ordered a Lyft. By the time she got to the door, her driver was one minute away.

"So you gonna tell me your name?" he asked. In the streetlight, his face was even better-looking. Big brown eyes. A half-smile that conjured a dimple. Tan skin with those reddish freckles.

"Call me Dee," she said.

"Okay, Dee. I'm Damián."

"Nice to meet you, Damián."

"Any way we can stay in touch?" he asked. "Or maybe you come here sometimes, and we might dance another night?"

"I'm about to leave town," she said.

"Too bad," he said. "But what if our paths don't cross again?"

"I'll just have to leave that to chance," Deza said.

"Okay," he said. "Fate, huh?"

"Sure," she said. "You could call it that."

A silver car pulled up and her phone chimed a Lyft alert.

"That's my ride," she said.

"Bye, Dee," he said. "Hope fate brings us together again." He opened the door for her. "You get home safe, okay?"

Deza slid in. The driver was a middle-aged white guy.

"Deeza?" the driver asked as she buckled in. "Dezzah?"

Damián's eyes flew open wide.

"Deza?" Damián asked.

She gave him a little wave as she closed the door and the car sped off.

Deza had stayed out way too late. She'd danced off the three drinks but been buzzed from the dancing and the chemistry with Damián. By the time she got up to her hotel room, she was crashing. She forgot to take an aspirin or drink a glass of water before she fell into bed at five in the morning.

Her phone alarm went off at eight, but she groaned, turned it off, and rolled over. At nine fifteen, there was a knocking at her hotel room door.

Deza's head was pounding like a Drumma Boy instrumental track. She was rolling over in bed as her phone lit up. It was a text from Thug Woofer, her mentor.

Where you at, girl? Why am I getting a call that you're not on the tour bus that was supposed to have left fifteen minutes ago?

"Deza?" a perky woman's voice asked through the hotel room door. "It's Claire, the tour manager. We really need to get out on the road."

Deza dragged to the door and let her in.

Claire was about thirty, with a neat ponytail and a plump figure. She looked around the unpacked room and at her bleary-eyed headliner. The tour manager's smile dimmed a bit, but she handed Deza a cup of coffee.

"Okay," Claire said. "Why don't you wash your face while I just dump everything into your suitcase, okay?"

Deza shuffled into the bathroom and splashed her face with water as she heard Claire pulling clothes from hangers and opening drawers.

By the time Deza had peed and shuffled out, Claire was

behind her, sweeping all the cosmetics into a laundry bag and adding it to the luggage set. Large and medium suitcases, a garment bag, and a carry-on.

"Let's do this," the blonde chirped.

Deza took a swig of the coffee and put on the shades.

In the alley in back of the hotel, artists milled around two buses. Some talking, some smoking, some on their phones. Nashonna's latest single had just dropped, and someone was playing it out loud. It sounded good, even through the tinny smartphone speakers.

Deza arrived. She wore the wig she kept for days like these. When she'd had her hair cornrowed but hadn't sewn the weave in yet. This one was wavy and honey brown, hanging past her shoulders.

A knot of women artists stood behind her. "The diva arrives," one of them muttered loud enough for Deza to hear. She couldn't see who said it, so she ignored them. Plus, her head was still aching. She didn't think she could withstand the sound of her own voice yelling.

A light brown woman with auburn dreadlocks and a guitar case walked up to her. "I'm Anasuya," she said. "It's great to meet you."

Deza shook hands with her and mustered a smile. "Same here."

"Okay, everyone," Claire said brightly. "Let's climb aboard. Vienna, Anasuya, you're with Deza and her DJ. And me. The rest of the band is on the second bus."

Vienna was a dance music artist who played with both a DJ and a live band. She was a wisp-thin white girl who sang through a vocoder.

The other girl wasn't really Deza's DJ. The two young women had only met once, at the label offices. Deza's DJ had been Yolanda Gutiérrez, a Brooklyn DJ who was laid back, but sociable.

Deza was thrilled to call and invite her to join the tour. Deza had expected Yolanda to scream with excitement, but she didn't.

"Girl, I can't," she'd said. "I did an audition a while back for a spot on Funkmaster Flex's show. I didn't think I would get it, but I did. I'm so sorry."

"You got a fucking spot with Flex??" Deza said. "Don't be sorry. I'm happy for you. We're both doing it big."

In Yolanda's place, the label had provided a sullen Black girl DJ with a high-quality weave down past her ass—and an attitude. They had played a couple of gigs together and had no chemistry.

The rest of the artists stood around. Deza wondered what they were waiting for. Then she realized they hadn't yet loaded their equipment. A woman with short hair and thick arms easily lifted Deza's suitcases into the compartment on the bottom of the bus.

"Hold up," Deza said and pulled the medium-sized suit- case. It was a wheeling bag just for her hair supplies. She had three wigs and a pile of jet-black human hair tracks. Bone straight and thirty inches long. She'd put it in on the way to the New England gig. She also had several brightly colored bangs and other long tracks to change it up in different cities. She would coordinate the colors with her outfits.

"Deza," Claire said. "Why don't you go ahead and board? We'll handle the rest of your luggage."

"Why didn't they already load their stuff?" Deza asked.

"Electronic equipment goes on top," Claire replied dis- creetly.

It was awkward. Everyone else was handling their own luggage. Deza boarded with only the hair suitcase, plus her purse and her coffee. She gave the barest of nods to the driver, a Black guy in his forties with a bored expression. The nod was a mistake. It made her head hurt more.

Deza had seen the layout of the bus among the ton of

paperwork they had given her at the music label. It was like a super-narrow apartment with an aisle down the middle. A kitchenette on one side in the front, and a lounge with a minifridge, couches, and chairs on the other. Past the lounge was a compartment with a double bed. Across from it were three compartments with double bunks.

As headliner, Deza got the double bed compartment all to herself. She put her purse on a hook and lay down on the bed. It wasn't even close to the worst place she'd ever slept. She closed her eyes for a moment. The headache dulled slightly.

She hadn't been stationary for more than a few minutes when she realized the coffee was going right through her. She had to pee.

She stood up slowly. The headache seemed like it might go away. As she crossed to the bathroom at the rear of the bus, the door opened and the roadie woman stepped out, zipping up the fly of her jeans. As Deza walked toward the back, she passed Melissa, the DJ girl, who was leaning over, murmuring to Vienna.

"Who the fuck does she think she is?" Melissa asked. "Making us all wait an hour for her? She can predict the fucking future, but she can't tell time?"

Deza could feel the hairs on the back of her neck stand up. She turned around and faced Melissa.

"A real bitch would say that right to my face," Deza told her.

"Okay, then," Melissa said. She stood up and faced Deza squarely. "How is it that you were the only one right here, staying at a four-star hotel in Manhattan, while the rest of us woke up in our apartments in the boroughs or sleeping on friends' couches and took the subway down here?"

"Hey, girls," Claire yelled up through the window. "Let's not start any conflict so early in the tour."

Deza ignored her. "First of all," she said, "If you got a

problem with your accommodations, take that up with the label."

"I don't think that's what she means," Vienna said. "I think she means that you were right here, but you were the only one who couldn't get to the bus on time."

"Why don't we all just take five?" Claire asked.

"Seriously?" Deza said. "Are you acting like no other artist has ever been late?"

"Can you help them get settled in their separate compartments?" Claire asked the roadie, who nodded and re-boarded the bus.

"This is stupid," Melissa said. "Your big claim to fame is writing the name of a girl who got shot? You're not a professional. You're not ready to headline this tour. The only reason you got this gig is because the real headliner dropped out. Isn't Woof dating your sister or something? This is some nepotistic bullshit."

"Fucking bunch of jealous haters," Deza spat, and tossed her sunglasses on a side table. Then she proceeded to take off her earrings.

"Whoa!" the roadie said, taking Deza's arm.

"Are you serious right now?" Melissa asked. "You're gonna fucking try to *fight* me?" She backed away from Deza. "Claire!" she called. "I can't fuck with this train wreck of a tour. I'm outta this shit."

"Wait! You can't leave," Claire said, coming up behind Melissa. "We're finally ready to head out. All your equipment is loaded up."

"Call my agent," Melissa said. "I'm sure being *threatened with violence* by another artist voids my contract."

"Let's all calm down," Claire said. "I'm sure Deza is sorry."

"No," Deza said. "I ain't fuckin sorry. She wanna act like I don't deserve to be here?"

"I'm sure that's not what she meant," Claire said.

"That's exactly what I meant," Melissa said. "And she proved me right. She wants to fight, like this was some high school beef, not a professional issue? She threatened me in front of witnesses? I'm not staying on some thirty-city tour that comes complete with ghetto mean girls' bus drama from this bitch."

"Oh hell naw!" Deza said, and lunged for Melissa.

The strong-armed roadie jumped up and held Deza back. Claire jumped in between Deza and Melissa.

"Good fucking luck with this disaster," Melissa said, striding off the bus. As she turned to descend the steps, she swiveled her torso to face Deza, with both middle fingers extended.

"Get the fuck offa me," Deza screamed. She struggled to free herself, but the roadie's grip was iron.

"This is fucking crazy," Vienna said, and followed Melissa off the bus.

"Breathe," the roadie said in Deza's ear as Claire ran after the other artists.

Deza tried to pull in a breath through a tight throat. She tried to block out the sound of Melissa's voice outside the bus: "Did you all see that? She was on some Nicki and Cardi at the Met Ball–type shit . . ." She finally managed a slower inhale and exhale, and the hammering of her heart began to slow a bit. But now she could feel the renewed throbbing of her head. Through the open door, she could also hear Claire on her own phone.

"The DJ just walked off the tour," Claire said. Her chipper façade completely gone. "I don't know . . . Okay, then make that call."

Ten minutes later, when Claire came back on the bus, Deza had her shades on and was drinking her now-cold coffee while trying not to move her head.

"Soo . . ." Claire said. She wasn't upbeat anymore, but the

note of panic had drained from her voice. "We're getting a new DJ. Also, Vienna says she doesn't . . ." she made air quotes, " 'feel safe' on the same bus with you. Anasuya followed suit. They're gonna double up on the other bus. I don't know. The label said they'd work it out."

Deza just nodded. She had gotten this big break, and they hadn't even left New York before she had shown her ass. Her Aunt Tyesha had invited Deza for a sleepover at her house in Brooklyn the night before the tour started, to enjoy a last night with family. But Deza couldn't resist the lure of a big hotel, and room service, and a night in the club. Tyesha was less than a decade older than her, but more like an older sister. She should've listened. Now she felt untethered.

"Do you think maybe you could say something after the show tonight to the other artists?" Claire asked. "Explain to them that you were having a bad morning? Something?"

"I don't know," Deza said, careful to hold her head still as she spoke. "I'll think about it. I'm not a very good liar."

Claire's jaw was tight. She nodded, and both she and the roadie walked off the bus.

Deza pulled out her notebook and scribbled the line that had bubbled up in her head:

I gotta trust/if I just/get on this bus . . .

But then the rhyme fizzled. She stared at the blank page for a while, then gave up. She'd been blocked since they started calling her a prophet.

She spent the next forty-five minutes attempting to take the world's best Instagram photo of herself on the bus. She moved slowly because of the headache, but she put on eyeliner and lipstick. She debated the false eyelashes and decided against them. In the past, she would have taken a shot of herself lounging on top of the table in a low-cut tank and booty shorts. But what were urban prophets supposed to look like on Instagram? Male artists just leaned back and didn't smile. But she was somehow supposed to look sexy and deep at the same time. She ended up taking the photo in leggings. She sat cross-legged on the bed. Sort of like she might be someone who meditated. She certainly wasn't.

She finished posting and waited impatiently as she only racked up a couple hundred likes in the first few minutes.

Claire came back onto the bus with a midsized, wheeling suitcase.

"So, it looks like we're just about ready to go," she said. "Let me introduce you to your new DJ."

Claire leaned down into the stairwell. "We're ready to get going," she said to someone just outside the door. "You can bring your equipment onto the bus. There's plenty of room. We'll get it all stowed properly later."

Deza was surprised to see that it was a guy. He had broad shoulders that rippled a bit as he held two crates of records that covered his face. The roadie came up behind him with a pair of turntables. Bringing up the rear was the driver.

Records and turntables? How old was this guy? Like fifty?

Then the DJ set down the vinyl crates on the couch in the lounge. And that was when she saw the Puerto Rico tattoo.

Deza's mouth had already fallen open by the time she saw the brown eyes, the full lips, the sprinkling of freckles. It was Damián from the club the night before.

Damián was equally speechless. He turned to Claire. "You want me to DJ for *Deza*?" he asked.

"We can talk about it on the road," Claire said. She gestured to the driver, and he closed the door after the roadie exited. Putting the bus in gear, the driver pulled away from the curb.

Deza and Damián stared at each other suspiciously. Deza's headache flamed behind her eyes.

The "Face To The Sky Tour" was underway.

Chapter 3

Chicago

As a kid, Deza would never have had to fight so much if she hadn't had a younger sister. First of all because Deza was pretty. Pretty girls in the hood always have a level of power. But Deza was the right kind of pretty. She wasn't light-skinned—the type of pretty that attracts colorstruck attention on the one hand, and resentment about colorism on the other. Not a dark chocolate that would have attracted Black self-hatred and taunts for being too black. She was a delicate milk chocolate.

As a baby, she had liked everyone. She babbled and cooed all day long. Her aunt was still alive then—her great-aunt Lucille, and she took care of Deza a lot of the time. Not that her mother was working. Unless you count riding along with your drug dealer husband so he doesn't cheat on you to be work. Her mother would have said it was.

Her mother, Jenisse, was fifteen and at least a decade younger than Zeus when he knocked her up with her first son. He was lukewarm about her having the baby. Deza was their third child, nearly a decade younger than her older brothers.

When Deza was around five, everything seemed to happen in a short span: her brothers got locked up in juvie, her aunt died, and she came to live with her mama and the new baby, Amaru. That was when things got bad.

Sometimes, they would stay with their grandmother—Aunt Lou's sister—but by the time Amaru was two, their grandmother's health was failing. Starting then, Deza was in charge of her younger sister. Their mom wasn't around. Their brothers were caught up in the criminal justice system. The two daughters were left to fend for themselves. At eight, it was Deza's job to get herself and her little sister to school. She dropped Amaru off at the Head Start on the way to second grade.

"Deza, is that your little brother?" a knot of her classmates asked.

"I'm a girl!" Amaru shouted.

It was a little hard to tell. With Amaru's short hair and her dark shirt over jeans. She had a little crew at preschool that was both boys and girls who liked to play rough. In the open-minded environment of preschool, the kids her age seemed to accept that she had a short haircut and her favorite color was blue, but she was a girl and could run faster than all of them. Older kids were the problem.

When Amaru started elementary school, Deza was in fifth grade. Two fifth grade boys cornered Amaru behind the dodge ball wall and pulled down her pants, to see if she was "really a girl."

Amaru went crying to the office but wouldn't say what happened. She only asked for Deza. When the older sister was called from her social studies lesson, she came down to the office and comforted Amaru.

"I'll take care of it," she whispered into her sister's short Afro. "Don't you worry."

The next morning, she filled a drawstring canvas bag with quarters from a big jar her mother had on her dresser. She caught up with the boys on the way to school and swung it at their heads.

"That's for messing with my sister," she said. "And if you ever fuck with her again, I'll get my older brothers on you, or maybe even my daddy."

Zeus and his boys were known in the neighborhood. But Deza knew her dad was unlikely to intervene. He had pulled his sons into his work but hadn't had much use for daughters. But these boys who targeted Amaru had older brothers, cousins, uncles, and maybe even dads. She needed to offer them some vague threat that retaliation would be a bad idea.

Still, kids continued to hassle her sister. Deza fought regularly with anyone who put a hand on Amaru. By the end of elementary school, everyone knew you didn't mess with Amaru the tomboy, because her big sister was crazy and she would kick your ass.

And in middle school, just as Amaru's drama calmed down, Deza's friends turned on her. In eighth grade, they spread some rumor that got another girl on a mission to kick her ass. Every week it was something else. She got pulled into the principal's office regularly for fighting. By then, her aunt Tyesha was in college. She was the one they would call, because they could never reach Deza's mom, Jenisse.

Chapter 4

@NashonnaStan
I WANT MY FUCKING MONEY BACK! I bought front
row tickets for Nashonna. Not Deza. Seriously? My
cousin is named Shaquana. Only white people think it's
so rare. The box office said my seats are for the Face
To The Sky *Tour* not Nashonna, so my tix are nonre-
fundable? Fuck that!

@Deza4Everr
What did you pay for your tickets? I'll buy them from
you!

@LadyRockFangirl3
I'll pay double!!

@LuvvieLuvLuv
I don't have the money, but have you seen Deza in concert? She really shuts it down. You might wanna keep
those tickets.

@NashonnaStan
Nah. I didn't work a month of overtime so I can be up

close to anyone but Nashonna. But y'all got me curious. Tickets to the first person who will PayFriend me the full refund price plus a pair of tickets in the cheap seats. I'll see if this girl is all she's cracked up to be.

@LadyRockFangirl3
Good call. You want to see Deza. Plus those other acts? I am the biggest fan of Anasuya Blackwell. #SingerSongwriters!

@LuvvieLuvLuv
also, it's a small price to pay to see Nashonna in next summer's blockbuster action movie! #Strut! #BigGirlsOnTheBigScreen

Emcee Kweens Weekly Update

Some people say all Black people look alike. Some find us to be interchangeable. Which might explain why Paperclip Records spent a whole year hyping up their Face To The Sky tour with Nashonna as headliner, then replaced her with Deza. Nashonna only asked to get out of a couple of dates to film the new movie *Strut!*

"Face To The Sky" is a reference to the final line of the song "Facing the Sky" on Nashonna's new album. So, basically, Nashonna's being replaced on a tour that was named after her work. But they're counting on the average fan not to know that.

The two artists could not be more different. Nashonna, the former sex worker, came to prominence with her song "What the Stripper Had to Say." She's raunchy and rebellious. Deza, on the other hand, is more of a lyrical badass. She comes out of Chicago, and she's always had a drill hip hop sound, but a little more positive. Likely thanks to her lineage as part of Chicago's Black community organizing. For Deza, critics coined the term *Drillternative*. Overall, Deza's debut album with Paperclip is on the hot girl bandwagon, but since the murder of Shaqana Miller, Deza has been reinvented as some sort of oracle. Maybe an overreach. She could own a lane as just a good rap artist. And for the record, I like both Deza and Nashonna and won't get into the "which girl rapper is the best?" trap. Remember, Paperclip announced this tour as what looked like an obvious PR move, after those two young women died backstage at the Dymond Lyfe concert last year. Even though no criminal charges were pressed, and the civil suit was settled with the family (in exchange for a gag order). And after the NYT article, "Paperclip Records: Where Women Go to Die," where they talked about how many female hip hop artists they had signed and never supported. Then it came out that Nashonna was trying to get out of her contract.

Suddenly, they had a huge tour brewing. And the artists are on social media saying what a "great surprise" it was to get invited. Surprise, as in *they-hadn't-actually-planned-that-shit*, it was just damage control. So of course, they're just gonna swap out the headliner if it's at all inconvenient, because it was never about showing respect to women in hip hop anyway.

Chapter 5

Outside Scarsdale, NY

Damián sat back on the bus and watched the city recede. Tall brick buildings, then lower brick buildings, then houses, then trees. He had been so excited to get the call that would take his career to the next level. He was ready to get out of NYC. He had recently moved out from living with his girlfriend, Lisette. They had been together for about five years and had lived together the last three. She was a couple years older. After her thirtieth birthday, it was like a switch went off in her head. She had been hinting for a while that she wanted to get married and start a family. He wanted those things, too. But not yet. New York City was expensive. He worked at an after-school program near their apartment in Washington Heights, which paid enough to cover his half of the rent. And he had the inconsistent income from DJ gigs. It cost a lot to raise a family. He wasn't ready to give up his DJ career to get a "real" job. Not just yet. Like when he was almost picked to be one of the big New Year's Eve DJs for a huge party in Brooklyn. That could have been a game changer. And he was this close to being picked as an opening DJ for Nashonna. So many close calls. He couldn't quit yet.

But after her thirtieth, Lisette was fed up. A full-time position became available at the Brooklyn site of the program where he worked. He didn't even tell her about it, but somehow, she found out.

The two of them sat around the apartment eating Chinese takeout. "Hey, Papi," she asked. "Did you see that posting for a full-time hip hop educator? That's totally you. You should apply." She smiled and bit into an egg roll.

"I can't see it," he said. "They would want me to be in Brooklyn from eight AM to three PM. Last time I worked a day job, I got fired. I was just too tired from DJing at night. Maybe if it was noon to eight. But I can't work that early."

"You could take a nap," she said.

"It's all the way in Brooklyn," he said. "By the time I got home on the train, I'd just be getting ready to go back out for an evening set."

She nodded. "Maybe you could swing it if you just DJ'd on weekends."

"I'd love that," he said. "But I'm the weeknight guy trying to move up to be the weekend guy at the gigs that really pay. I've put in years at these places. When these Friday and Saturday DJs move out, I'll move up. Eventually I'll be able to make a better living at this."

"Look, Papi," she said. "Will you just apply? You could maybe talk to them about flexible hours or something. Could you just fill out the application?" She made a slightly pouty face. "For me?"

She wasn't going to let it drop unless he agreed, so he did.

The next day he did apply. He did a half-assed job, and didn't think any more about it. But Damián was well-liked. The kids loved him, and he was reliable and easy to work with. His supervisor put in a good word for him.

When he got the call for an interview, they told him it was really just a formality. The job was his if he wanted it. He scheduled the interview and acted excited, but inside he felt panicked.

That night, he told Lisette about the interview. "I don't know," he said. "If they won't let me come in late, I don't think I can do it."

"Chacho," she said. "You act like I'm asking you to take a job at Walmart. This is hip hop education with kids of color. Two of the things you really love."

How could he explain this to her? His dream wasn't teaching hip hop to young people, it was being part of it. He wanted to branch out into making beats, producing music. Not just talking about the art, but actually being on the creative end.

"Just go to the interview and ask, okay?" she pressed.

Reluctantly, he agreed.

The next day, he put on a jacket and a button-down shirt and practiced in the mirror, "It's an honor to be offered a job like this, but I can't come in till noon."

He got his chance to say the line, and the interviewer looked thoughtful. "Noon would be too late," she said. "Do you DJ every night of the week?"

"No," Damián said. "Usually just weekends and a couple of weeknights. But it's not always consistent."

"I'm sure we can work something out," she said. "You could come in at ten a couple days a week—I'll try for eleven, but I can't promise. And you could do some after-school stuff on days you come in late. Why don't you email me your DJ schedule for next month so I can get a sense of what it looks like and I'll see what I can do on my end?"

He found himself agreeing, shaking her hand, and walking out without declining the job.

When he got home, Lisette was waiting with a home-cooked meal and an eager smile on her face.

"How did it go?"

"I don't think I can take the job," he said. "They wouldn't let me come in late."

"They wouldn't be flexible at all?" Lisette asked.

Then it all came out, that they were willing to be flexible, but he still didn't want it.

"What do you think this is, Damián?" she asked. "I work full time. I wake up early when I don't fucking feel like it. I'm not doing my dream career. But this is the real fucking world. People don't always live their fucking fantasies. *Puñeta*, we can still have a good life if you would just grow the hell up."

"Lisette, I've put in a decade on this career and I'm finally getting close to being able to do it full-time and make a living. Why are you trying to—to fucking sabotage me before I get there?"

"You know why?" she asked. "Because you're living your dream on my back. I work full time. Plus, I cook and keep the apartment clean. Plus, I hustle harder for you than you do for yourself. Sabotage you? I get you half your DJ gigs. I definitely got you that after-school gig that worked so well with your DJ schedule."

"I didn't realize I was such a burden," he said.

"I didn't say that," Lisette said. "I'm just saying it's not fair that I'm the one doing all the compromising and most of the work."

"Sounds pretty burdensome to me," he said. "You know what? I can just lift that burden off your shoulders, no problem." He stood up.

"Come on, Damián," she said. "Don't be dramatic. What are you gonna do? Move back in with your parents?"

It was the contempt with which she said it that pushed him over the edge.

"Yeah," he said. "I'd rather be living in my old bedroom and doing what I love than being with someone who doesn't fucking support my dreams."

"Support your dreams?" she asked, outraged. "I've been fucking financing your dreams for years now. Because I thought we were building a life. Building toward a family. But you'll never be ready to have kids because you're not done being one. So maybe you belong at Mommy and Daddy's."

He packed up and moved out that night.

But living back with his parents way up in the Bronx was quite a demotion. Without her, he wasn't quite adulting. He loved his parents, and redecorated his tiny room, but he certainly couldn't bring girls home. He couldn't even hang with his boys at the house like he had when he was living with Lisette. From the single bed of his childhood, he had to reflect on the fact that Lisette really was the one who had hustled to make their life happen—had gotten the great apartment and connected him with the people who had hired him in the after-school program. She was always promoting him, telling people he was a DJ.

The commute to the after-school program in Washington Heights was a hassle, and then he had to come back home to get his DJ equipment before he went back downtown for the evening. He spent half his life on the subway. He cut back to one day a week in the after-school job. DJing was the only good thing, and even that was different now. When they split, he realized that most of the friends who came to his gigs were really her friends. It was awkward to see them now.

The ultimate irony was about the Face To The Sky tour. It was through one of her connections that he had gotten the gig. A friend of Lisette's from college who worked at Paperclip Records. She and Lisette must not be that close, or she would have known they'd split and wouldn't have hooked him up. So on the one hand, he had Lisette to thank for this big break. But on the other hand, he would've had to bail on the full-time job if he'd taken it.

But this gig was next level. They even sent a car for him, and the driver helped him bring all his DJ equipment down from the third floor and load it into the trunk. He could get used to this.

They hit traffic on the way into Manhattan, but he kicked back and didn't worry about it. It was the label's car. Their driver. He wasn't late. He was operating on a new level now.

He closed his eyes to get a little sleep before he had to get on the bus.

Chapter 6

Outside Norwalk, CT

"Claire," Deza said. "You need to get this guy off my bus. He's like an underage dinosaur up here with all these crates of vinyl. What the fuck—1987 called and wants its DJ back. Besides, this tour was supposed to be all women. How am I up here sharing a bus and a bathroom with a guy I don't know? And you saw how unhappy he was when he found out who he was DJing for."

Claire set the clipboard down in her lap. "There's plenty of room," she said. "And we only ended up with a man because it was a last-minute substitution. Because you ran everyone else off your bus. They refuse to come back, so there's no more room on that second bus. Now you're stuck with this guy. And if you wanna call the label and argue about getting a third bus so you can have one to yourself, be my guest."

"What if I could find a female DJ?" Deza asked.

Claire shrugged. "Maybe," she said. "He's not under contract yet. We haven't even had time to set up the paperwork."

"I could get on the phone right now," Deza said.

"The label won't pay her way to catch up with the tour," Claire said. "Or the price to fly him home."

"I would cover all that," Deza said.

"Make your calls," Claire said. "But you only have today. The label is gonna want signed paperwork on this guy before tonight's show."

"Thank you," Deza said. "I'm on it."

Deza called every female DJ she knew in New York. And all of them in Chicago. They asked how much it paid. How long it lasted. Did it include health insurance? Half of them couldn't come because they had kids. A few were taking care of older relatives who were sick or disabled. Or they worked full-time on top of DJing. They couldn't give up stable jobs with benefits for a short-term gig.

One of them got excited and called the places she DJ'd for to see if she could take a couple months' leave. But the manager said she'd need to give up her spot. The girl called back, nearly in tears.

"These fucking club promoters don't care," she railed. "All the work I did to promote his shit. For years. And he would just replace me? But I need this gig. I can't go out on tour with nothing to come back to. Not in this economy."

Deza called Woof to see if he knew anyone, but everyone he suggested was already on her list. She called Coco Peila, a hip hop artist in the Bay Area who was always talking about putting other women on.

"Y'all already bout to hit the West Coast?" Coco asked. "I thought that tour just started."

"I can't find a woman DJ anywhere between here and Chicago," Deza said. "Not one who can up and leave at a moment's notice."

"Yeah, sis," Coco said. "These men got wives and girl-friends who will hold it down for them. See them off in a cheerleading uniform. Take care of the kids and pay the rent while they're gone. Most women artists ain't got it like that."

"So I'm learning," Deza said.

"You're lucky you're on a tour that's all women," Coco said. "These tours with dudes are brutal. I mean, I'm grateful to be out here doing my music. But even with some of these so-called conscious dudes. Sexism is sexism."

"Yeah," Deza said, looking around at the empty bus. "It's great to be on an all-female tour."

After she hung up with Coco, she remembered how it had been after she and Royal broke up. Just before she left Chicago. Rapping with a crew of girls. Everyone else had fallen off for different reasons. Kayla went to college. Jayonda and Ellasee both got pregnant. And Aisha's parents were strict. No way they were letting their daughter out in clubs at night by herself. Even though she was over eighteen. "My house, my rules," her father had said.

Deza didn't have that problem. Her parents didn't bother to supervise her life. From the beginning, late nights in clubs had been easy to pull off.

There was always the sexual harassment. But Royal had swooped in and nobody messed with her. She was Royal's girl. He was twenty-six and she was seventeen going on eighteen. But he treated her well and they made a huge name for themselves in Chicago.

After they broke up, she was vulnerable to all the sexual harassment again. She might have made it big sooner, but she never knew when some producer wanted her to come record in his home studio if she should go or not. Her aunt coached her that unless a few of her girls could go with her, she should pass on those opportunities. Deza was signed now, and she was Thug Woofer's protégée. But that didn't keep men in the business from treating her like some sort of groupie, hitting on her at shows and industry functions. She looked around at the empty bus again. She should have been glad to be on a tour with all women. If only she hadn't fucked it up.

She scrolled through Instagram. Photos of Vienna and Anasuya on the other bus. Candids of their band members playing in the living room area. That could have been her.

Or if she were a man, she would probably have a wife or girlfriend traveling with her. Like Coco said. At the very least a different groupie on every leg of the journey, stroking her ego. Now she had nothing.

Picking up her notebook, she felt that churn in her stomach. That thought that she wasn't enough. But looking around at the empty bus, the dismay bubbled up, and she finally found some words:

> *I feel like a cliché/young female and brown*
> *I'm on the come-up/but I'm feeling let down*
> *Like all the artists say/predictably*
> *Fame ain't all that it's cracked up to be*
> *Rolling down the highway/feeling alone*
> *From stadium to stadium/never at home*
> *I got a double mattress I sleep on at night*
> *but the other side of the bed is always packing*
> *   light*
> *it's been a minute since I was loved to the limit*
> *and only my vibrator is in it to win it*
> *I'm a cynic about men and love these days*
> *But am I truly jaded or only afraid?*
> *Of feeling heartbreak again*
> *So I make love to my pen*
> *And have rhymes and bars as my only*
> *   boyfriend.*

The moment she finished the rhyme, she knew she'd never record it. It was more of the old stuff. Love. Romance. She needed something next level. But what? Fuck it. At least she was writing again.

* * *

Damián hadn't expected his big break to be so awkward. The night before, he was feeling like such a big man because he had danced with Deza. Flirted with Deza. But now that they were together on a tour bus and she was ignoring him, he wasn't sure. Had they flirted? Maybe it was all on his side? He had hit on her when he thought he was feeling a vibe, but was it all in his head? He'd had a couple of drinks. And he even slid into her DMs after he realized it was her. Liquid courage had him too hype. But now it just seemed sort of desperate. Ugh. He really hoped he hadn't been that guy.

He had a moment of showing what was definitely unwanted attention when he tried to strike up a conversation with Claire, the rep from the record label. She glanced up quickly from her laptop and shut down any conversation. She was working.

He wasn't hitting on her; he just wanted someone to talk to. But maybe he needed to be working, too. He pulled out his own laptop and started to develop his DJ set list for the evening.

They hadn't told him a lot about the tour. Just the names of the cities and that it was called "Face To The Sky." And how much it paid. Maybe he could get an apartment when he got back to the city. Provided that he could get some source of income going. And maybe—if this tour raised his profile— he could get some new gigs. Deza was obviously a diva who demanded a bus to herself and was upset that she had to share with a latecomer. Or one of those head-case artists who are like pathologically shy and can't talk to anyone offstage.

Damián was an introvert. Most DJs were, but that didn't mean he enjoyed five hours of total silence in a bus. He was looking forward to meeting other artists and finding someone he could talk to.

Finally, the bus pulled into the stadium venue in

Providence. The stage entrance was just a pair of double doors in the back of a grimy white wall with several painted-over graffiti tags.

Inside, he was escorted to a green room where the other artists sat around eating and drinking. He noticed right away that they were all women. Even down to the crew.

He recognized some of the artists. Anasuya Blackwell with the locs and the natural fabrics. The skinny white girl in the neon dress looked familiar, but he couldn't place her.

Claire from the label stood in the doorway. "Hey, everyone," she said. "This is Damián, Deza's new DJ."

"Just for tonight, right?" one woman from Vienna's band asked.

"Nope," Claire said. "As soon as he signs his paperwork, he'll be joining us for the rest of the tour."

The groan that went up from the room was not quite a wail of disappointment, but definitely more than a murmur.

Damián wanted to shrink down into the carpet. Or, at the very least, walk back out the door.

"Come on, Damián," Claire said. "Eat up. We won't have another proper meal till after the show."

He followed her to the buffet and put together a plate of cold cut sandwiches. Meanwhile Claire was making two plates to go. Probably one for her and one for Deza.

As he made himself a turkey sandwich on rye bread, he could feel the eyes on the back of his head. Suddenly, he missed the quiet bus where nobody spoke to him, but nobody threw him shade, either.

When Claire swept out of the room with her takeout, she didn't invite him back to the bus. He picked a folding chair in the corner and sat down to eat. He was hungry. It was after three in the afternoon and he'd had nothing but an energy bar for breakfast.

After an awkward meal, Damián got his wish for some

alone time. He was the only person in the men's dressing room. But that was just for a half hour, because then he was helping set up his DJ equipment on stage and checking the sound. Soon Deza was on stage, and he was doing a run through of her set. He was glad he got all the cues right and she didn't have any reason to complain.

Then he was in the big, empty men's dressing room again, waiting for the show to start.

The Providence arena was half-full, and the crowd was lukewarm. It was the tour's only New England show. Anasuya's set was great. She had that sort of India.Arie vibe. Vienna's set didn't move Damián much. It had a lot of electronic beats and high-pitched synth. But she had a lot of energy and the crowd seemed to love her.

In contrast to both of them, Deza seemed to be phoning it in. The crowd clapped between songs. Some of them danced. Only when she closed with "Almost Home," the song the press was calling "The Black Lives Matter anthem," did Deza seem to come alive. Or maybe it was the fact that the somber mood of the song fit the low energy of the audience.

As Deza rapped about Shaqana, her energy was grieving, reverent. But then she fired up at the end to a place of anger:

> *The time to stan for reform is done*
> *Gotta make a plan so we can defund*

Maybe Deza drew her energy from a small knot of Black teens who had clustered at the front of the arena. About a dozen of them stood with fists in the air, cheering and riled up. They were a lone spot of energy in the cavernous stadium, as everyone else clapped half-heartedly and then gathered their things to go home.

Deza didn't seem to want to debrief. She just went directly

to her dressing room, and from there straight to her compartment on the bus.

That night, he was lurking on her Instagram again, looking at everything she posted. He followed her, but she didn't follow back.

Damián didn't see Deza again until sound check at their next gig, in DC.

Chapter 7

Washington, DC

Damián opened the DC show with a great set. He had a few go-go remixes with some of the latest hits and the crowd loved it. Including a couple go-go/Latin mash-ups that had Deza wanting to dance backstage.

After his opening set, Anasuya went on.

The singer-songwriter was coming back into the dressing room area as Deza was headed toward the backstage.

"Nice set," Deza said to Anasuya. This DJ couldn't be the only artist on the tour who was talking to her.

Anasuya gave Deza a quiet nod of thanks.

Deza was getting her body mic adjusted. Mostly she held the mic, traditional emcee style, but there was one dance number she did that required that she go hands-free.

The emcee had just introduced Vienna and the crowd was cheering.

Behind Deza, Claire was complimenting Damián. "Great opener," the tour manager said. "The go-go was a nice touch. I see why Paperclip sent you."

"Thanks," he said, and turned to Deza. "I made an instrumental go-go remix of 'Deza Daze Ya.'" It was one of her hottest songs. "Just in case you wanted to rap to it."

"That would be great," Claire said. Although he hadn't asked Claire, only Deza.

To be honest, Deza was scared. Other than Providence, she had only done one stadium show before. And that was just as a guest. Plus it was with Thug Woofer, and he had spent the five minutes before she went on hyping her up like crazy. So the audience was not only ready to hear her, but ready to like her. Now it felt like the audience was only ready to judge her. For not being Nashonna, for not being able to predict the future like a party trick. Sometimes, when she got nervous, she could be off her game. She liked to be able to trust that she could go on autopilot if she got overwhelmed.

"I don't know," she said. "It might throw me off."

"You could at least try it," Claire said.

"Yeah," he said. "You could listen on my phone. Just check it out."

"Go to the dressing room where you can hear," Claire said. "I'll have them turn off the stage sound and come get you when it's time."

Five minutes later, they were in Deza's dressing room listening to the track. Deza sat in front of the lighted mirror on her makeup chair, and Damián pulled up an armchair. The sound was tinny on his phone, but the energy and dance potential was unmistakable.

Deza closed her eyes. Listened for her intro in the new version. She botched it the first couple times. She hated messing up in front of this new guy. But she sensed that his intuition was right. It was the first major city of the tour, and the first Chocolate City. She needed it to be something people would be talking about. She wanted these fans to love her. Or if they already did, to love her even more.

She took a deep breath and asked Damián to restart the track.

After they'd rehearsed a few times, she sat down in the tall chair at the lighted mirror.

"So what's the verdict?" Damián asked.

"I don't know," Deza said. "Last-minute changes make me edgy."

Damián smiled. "It could be edgy in a good way," he said. "It's a great song. And the lyrics would work great with the go-go beat. It gives a new life to a song that your fans already love. But I'm not you. I can't tell you what you need out there tonight."

She nodded. "Lemme think about it. I'll let you know before we go on." She watched as Damián headed back to his dressing room.

Deza knew what she needed tonight. She needed a win. She needed all the people in this stadium to be on their feet screaming for her by the end of the night. She needed the other women on the tour to respect her. Or at least accept that she was the one who all these people had come to see.

When Claire came by, she told her to tell Damián yes.

He had been right. The crowd ate it up, were all on their feet dancing, were filling the aisles. So when she closed with the song "Almost Home," the fans were screaming for an encore.

"We didn't plan nothing else, y'all," she said and walked over to Damián.

"Do you have another go-go remix?" she asked him off mic.

He grinned and murmured the opening line to one of her early songs. Then he raised an eyebrow. Like asking her if she wanted to do it.

Deza was stunned. How did he even know that song? It wasn't on the album.

She nodded. This was her old anthem. The song she could rap in her sleep. Her DJ ex had four different drill remixes and she had rapped to each one of them.

She told Damián yes and strutted out on stage with the opening lyric:

Black girl Black girl, so much to say
So many obstacles get in the way
But we ain't scared of this big, bad world
We gon be there for you, badass Black girl

He had made a go-go remix. Even without a rehearsal, she rapped it all perfectly, without missing a single word.

After the set, she came off the stage, drenched in sweat, the crowd's applause thundering in her ears.

"That was fantastic," Claire said. "Both of you. Good work."

Deza and Damián walked together toward the dressing rooms.

Vienna and her band were loading out. They walked past without speaking.

"Thank you," Deza said to Damián.

"For what?" he asked.

"Pushing me to try something new," she said. "And I have to say I'm surprised. You're so old-school with your turntables and your stone-age technology mixer. I didn't expect you'd be the one pushing me into the future."

"First of all, those turntables are practically new," he said. "And second of all, I can feel the difference. I got Serato. I can use that kind of setup when I have to. But it doesn't sound the same. The vinyl responds differently to the touch of my hands."

"But you did the go-go remix on your computer, right?" she asked.

"Yeah, but only because we were on the road," he said. "If I'd been in my home studio, I would have used vinyl. I missed the hiss at the beginning of the song."

"Okay then, Old School," she said. "Let's keep trying new shit. If we've got twenty-eight more cities, we need to keep it interesting."

"Sounds good to me," he said. "Can I ask you something?"

"Sure," she said.

"What's—" he began, his eyes glancing from her to Vienna and back. "What's with the bad vibe around here?"

Deza just shook her head. She wasn't willing to risk pissing off the only person still speaking to her by explaining how she'd fucked up.

Later that night, she found him on Instagram. He was already following her. She followed him back.

Chapter 8

Chicago

"*Tomorrow gonna be a new day/gonna take all the fear and pain away*," Deza's ten-year-old voice was shaky and strained as she rapped the lyrics to a song their mother played sometimes, a Chicago femcee one album wonder named LustraSkill. Deza crooned it like a lullaby to her sister Amaru, who lay in her lap shivering and crying.

Their family had moved into a new house. It was much bigger than the old one, but it was laid out differently. In the old one, Deza and Amaru shared a bedroom that used to be a sunporch on the side of the house. Their parents' bedroom was two rooms and a hallway away. So any noise that went on was much harder to hear. Like, for instance, if they were screaming at each other or banging on a wall. If a kid was a reasonably sound sleeper, they might sleep through most of those fights. They might do so for years. But in the new house, their parents' bedroom was right next to theirs.

"*Sun gon rise again/problems gonna get cut down to size again.*"

It wasn't the ass-shaking hit on the album that Deza's mother Jenisse liked, but Jenisse had the whole album in her music library. "Sun gon rise" was the song that Deza loved. Later, as a rap artist herself, she would recognize the cliché. The collection of bland platitudes. But as a ten-year-old, it felt like a lifeline. The only adult voice she could access anymore to soothe her.

"*Hold your head up/Even when the hard times don't let up.*"

Her aunt died when she was in kindergarten. Her aunt who had soothed her when she was scared.

When her parents fought, she had called Auntie Lou.

"*Deep down inside you always knew this/stay strong, you can get through this.*"

In the year before she died, Auntie Lou had taught her how to dial the phone for the nights she spent with her parents. She made it like a game. A four-and-a-half-year-old can learn a pattern on a keypad. She showed her how to press the buttons in the right order on the landline. She clapped and kissed her when she got it right.

Which is how Auntie Lou's phone had rung after midnight a few weeks later.

"Hello?" Deza didn't understand about caller ID. She thought Lou was just magical and knew it was her calling.

"Deza? Is everything okay, baby?"

Deza couldn't speak. Her parents' yelling voices had woken her up. And the crash of a glass splintering against a wall.

At the time, it was just noise. Angry voices. Terrifying sounds. Later, she would learn to decode it. Zeus would cheat and Jenisse would go berserk, scream, break things. She would land a couple of blows on him, but he was so much bigger and stronger. He allowed it as his penance.

But to four-year-old Deza, everything was a jumble of sound coming from the kitchen. Zeus had threatened to leave. "I ain't gonna stand here and listen to this shit." Zeus had grabbed a coat and headed toward the front door. Toward the bedroom that Deza slept in by herself before her baby sister was born. Their fight had migrated into her orbit and she overheard through the kitchen wall in the near dark, with only a fairy princess night-light. The winged blond girl smiling vapidly at her from atop a little pink mushroom.

The light was a comfort, but the fairy was no help. What did she know about parents who fought and yelled?

"Take deep breaths, baby," Auntie Lou directed. "I'm right here with you. We gonna stay on the phone all night if we have to."

Auntie Lou would sing to her. It didn't drown out the sound from the bedroom next door, but it buffered her from it.

Deza would wake up in the morning with the phone next to her face. Auntie Lou was no longer on the other end. But the sun was up, and the night-light had gone off. The winged blond girl still smiling, useless from her pink mushroom perch.

Chapter 9

The next day, the *Washington Post* arts section had a front-page article, "Deza Slays Ya."

Claire had brought the paper, along with breakfast, onto the bus. Deza read the article and handed it to Damián.

He was disappointed that they hadn't mentioned him by name. But glad that things had warmed up on the bus considerably. The three of them had a sort of camaraderie.

"I have more good news," Claire said. "After last night, there's a sportswear company in DC that wants to do an endorsement deal with you. Maybe have that go-go remix playing in the background of the ad."

"Are you kidding me?" Deza said.

"Rock.it," Claire said. Deza knew the brand. They did urban athletic wear and had a logo of a rocket blasting off. "You'd be the first woman they ever had as a celeb endorser."

Deza wasn't surprised. The clothes seemed to be designed for men. Deza had tried them on a few times, but they were cut too narrow in the ass.

"Hell yeah," Deza said. "Tell them to set up the meeting."

Maybe Deza could get them to vary the proportions of their women's styles a little bit more.

Claire went off to arrange it.

"Are you sure about that?" Damián asked.

"About what?"

"Rock.it," he said. "Don't they also have an endorsement deal with Murda Lockk?"

Deza's eyebrows went up. Murda Lockk was a notorious pair of rappers from Atlanta, also with the Paperclip label. Between the pair of them, they had dodged allegations of murder, domestic violence, and sexual assault. Whether or not they had done it, they certainly bragged about that type of thing in their music. Ugh.

Deza put Murda Lockk and Rock.it into an internet search engine.

The sportswear company explained that they were not interested in censoring artists. They had gone as far as including a clause in their contract that the company was not responsible for anything the artists said as part of their "freedom of speech."

"I don't know," Deza said. "In this business, I can't be all bothered about who else is on the bill where I play. This is par for the course. This tour is the first time I've been in an all-girls set."

"So was the previous DJ a woman?"

Deza nodded.

"I kind of fucked up the vibe?" Damián asked.

"It wasn't you," Deza said. "It was—" she broke off. "Don't worry about it. Besides, this is turning out to be a good news day."

"I don't mean to fuck up the vibe even more," he said. "But can I give you a little bad news about Rock.it?"

Deza rolled her eyes. "What could be worse than Murda Lockk?"

"Rock.it is under fire for using sweatshop labor in Indonesia," he said. "I heard a few activists say that some of the conditions fit the definition of slavery."

Deza let out her breath and slumped back in the seat. Every silver lining seemed to have a big ass rain cloud attached.

When Claire came and gave her the phone, Deza had a cheerful conversation with the head of the clothing company. She didn't ask about Murda Lockk or sweatshop labor. But she also didn't commit to doing it. She said she'd love to see what they had in mind. Send the contract to her manager.

She kept her eyes averted from Damián. She didn't want to be judged. Slavery was a pretty heavy allegation. But she didn't want to turn down the deal of a lifetime based on some hearsay from a DJ she had just met. Even if he was really handsome. And especially hot after he just woke up, with those big eyes looking slightly disoriented.

The old Deza wouldn't have hesitated. Sportswear deal. Big money. Blam. But her new identity included being some urban prophet who was supposed to be so "woke." Maybe Damián was right. Maybe she should turn it down.

Chapter 10

Miami

By the time the tour stopped in Miami, Deza and Damián had gotten into a solid professional rhythm. They would talk through the song order on the bus, then do a strong forty-minute set. They had encore numbers ready but didn't get to use them in Virginia.

The stank attitude of Vienna and her band had faded into the background. Anasuya would always greet them, but didn't chitchat. The tour had settled into a sort of middle school vibe.

It was great working with Damián. Royal had bossed her around. Other DJs had been more passive. Damián was a nice middle ground. He seemed to actually respect her art. He was impressed by the prophet thing but didn't seem to be looking for her to be anything but herself. Also, he knew some of her old music and encouraged her to resurrect certain tracks for the shows. He made suggestions but didn't boss. He followed her lead but had his own ideas. And they were usually good. In Miami, Damián reached out to a DJ friend who was working on a Latin trap remix of one of Deza's songs.

"DJ Wanderer hasn't gotten back to me," Damián said after the sound check. "Too bad. It would have been great."

Deza had started her set when there was a bunch of distracting movement offstage to the left. Just past Damián, a young Latino man was waving both his hands. A security guard was preparing to pull the young man off the stage. Damián made eye contact with the guy and motioned for the guard to stand down.

Deza finished the song and the crowd was cheering. In that moment, Damián came up to Deza and identified the young man as DJ Wanderer. "Is it okay if he comes up?"

Is it okay? She appreciated how he asked. Not entitled. Not scraping, but respectful. It was her show and he knew it. And didn't seem to feel ashamed to not be the alpha.

She nodded and stepped back.

"Now, I'm not the only DJ in the house tonight," Damián said. "Because right here to my left, we got one of Miami's own."

"DJ Wanderer," Deza said, stretching out her arm to him. The crowd screamed for their local guy. The security guard stepped back and let Wanderer make his way to the DJ stand.

The two men embraced. "So Wanderer," Damián said. "I heard you been deep in the studio working on something. *Verdad?*"

"Yes, yes!" DJ Wanderer said. "I been working night and day on this. Deep in the basement, where I don't got cell service. But I finished it and I got it ready."

"Y'all wanna hear what DJ Wanderer cooked up for you in the basement?"

The crowd roared that they did.

"But most of all, Miss Deza, do you wanna hear what DJ Wanderer got for you?"

She smiled. "I would be honored to see what Miami's own got for me," she said.

"No, Mami," he said. "The honor is mine."

And he plugged a USB drive into Damián's setup.

The opening beats were simultaneously foreign and familiar to Deza. A certain banging Latin sound that—if it were pared down a bit more—would be something her auntie would have had her dancing to in a West African dance class. But then the horns came in, and the hook and the familiar melody from the second single from her album. It was Latin meets some old-school Fela Kuti meets Deza's own melodic style of rap. She knew just where to come in, and the timing was good.

He had stuck to the original bar structure. So when the song went to the break, she knew just how long she had to dance before she needed to get back on the mic. The beat was infectious. Everyone in the audience caught it, too. The fans were dancing, hip-shaking. A pair was partner dancing in the aisle, salsa style, until security shut that down.

The audience ate it up.

When the number ended, Deza was flushed, sweating. "The mix master of Miami, DJ Wanderer, everybody!"

He bowed and gave thanks to both her and Damián before he walked back off the stage.

After the set, DJ Wanderer came and embraced her and Damián.

"Mix master of Miami?" he said. "I gotta get that tattooed somewhere."

Damián made a proper introduction between the DJ and Deza. His real name was Juan.

"Was that okay?" Damián asked. "That I asked him to come up? I didn't want to put you on the spot, but I felt like we had talked about it before, right?"

"Yeah," she said. "You did right."

"Great job," Claire said.

"Fabulous set," Anasuya said. It was the first thing other than "hey" or "hello" that she had said since they left New York.

Usually, Deza and Damián debriefed a little more after a show, but he was speaking in a fast, excited Spanish with DJ Wanderer.

Deza drifted back to her dressing room. She hoped she

QUEEN OF URBAN PROPHECY / 59

might catch Anasuya again, but the singer-songwriter had disappeared into the women's dressing room.

The two women who came out were Vienna's backup singers. Neither of them said a word.

Deza lingered outside her big headliner dressing room, alone again, noticing she really missed hanging out with Damián after the show.

"I didn't know if the new DJ was gonna work out," Claire said. The tour manager had come up behind Deza.

"I didn't either," Deza said. "But so far, he's been nothing but upside."

Now that they had been on the bus for a few days, Damián had seen Deza first thing in the morning, as well as perfectly done up to go on stage. To be honest, he couldn't really tell the difference. Not that he couldn't see that sometimes she had fake eyelashes and sometimes she didn't. Or didn't notice the bright blue shades of eye shadow. But the thing that made her eyes so mesmerizing had nothing to do with the cosmetics. The allure of her lips didn't depend on a bold red or a deep burgundy. It was about *her*. He loved being around her. At night, their compartments were far diagonally across from each other on the bus. He would wonder if she was sleeping or writing or scrolling through her phone like he was. He wanted to knock on her door and just . . . talk. They were all business, but he wanted to ask her some personal questions, too. He wasn't sure about where to start.

This morning, it wasn't Deza's face that greeted him, it was Claire's. She tapped on his door around noon and let him know that Deza had invited him to join her interview.

Damián blinked twice. He had been up late drinking with DJ Wanderer while the stagehands loaded the bus. He wasn't totally hungover, but definitely a bit bleary-eyed. Claire let him know Deza and the reporter were in the lounge area.

Damián nodded and grabbed his toothbrush. It wouldn't

do to go all dragon on the reporter. In the small lavatory, he also realized his hair looked crazy. His curly Afro was flat on one side. He was definitely off his game. If he'd had any idea he would be speaking with a reporter, he wouldn't have had those last two tequila shots. Or would have invested in more hydration and aspirin before he went to sleep.

Too late now. He slugged back a bottle of water and went to meet his doom.

The reporter was a buttoned-up white guy. Someone Damián couldn't quite picture dancing.

"So the two of you have been doing a sort of local remix series with Deza's hits," the reporter said. "Was that the intention from the beginning on this tour?"

Damián looked at Deza, because he had no idea what to say. They had stumbled into all of it, but he didn't think he was supposed to just say that.

"To be honest," she said, "when I first started on this tour, I wasn't sure how to approach it. I'm a debut artist and usually someone would be a lot further along before they headlined a tour like this. But Nashonna got that movie offer, and she turned a one-eighty for Hollywood. Nobody blames her."

"And the timing," the reported added. "With the death of Shaqana Miller."

"That, too," Deza said. "I'm glad we're playing Oklahoma City. I look forward to connecting with the community there."

"But back to your collaboration," the reporter asked. "Had you worked together before?"

Deza had a flashback of dancing with Damián.

"I was familiar with Damián's work as a club DJ," Deza said. "When things didn't work out with my previous DJ, the label called Damián and I signed off. But I didn't realize he had such skill as a remix DJ. Not only him, but his connections with other DJs have been amazing. Did you catch the set with DJ Wanderer last night in Miami?"

"I didn't see it live," he said. "But it was those videos on Instagram that got me calling my editor late at night and getting the green light to come talk to you. Damián, how would you describe what you're doing, musically?"

"I guess," Damián said, "I'm sort of code switching with how I mix the music, based on location."

"But what inspired you to do it that way?"

"I don't know," Damián said. "I speak English. I speak Spanish. And Spanglish. And different types, too. I spoke standard English in school. I spoke hood English with Black American kids when I was coming up." He turned his wrist so that the reporter could see the Puerto Rican tattoo on his forearm. "I don't know where you're from, but I'm from the Bronx. Puro Boogie Down. Yeah, I'm Latino, but I'm also Black. Obviously. It was important to me to be able to have language to speak to all my people."

"So you would say this was a result of your growing up in the Bronx?"

"Not really," Damián said. "Hip hop was born in the Bronx, but it's bigger than the Bronx. To me, it's about language. Music is a language. And now hip hop is a language unto itself. It just made sense to me to speak to people in their local dialect. My parents raised me to be respectful when you go to someone's house. It's about showing respect when you come to a community by speaking to them in their language." His eyes got bright as he talked about it. "When I got the call to join the tour, I looked at the map of all the cities where we were going. I started to look up some of the local musical styles, past and present. That's how I got the go-go remix for DC. I knew better than to waste my time with the Latin remix for Miami, because DJ Wanderer could do it better and faster than me."

"So what do the two of you have cooked up for New Orleans?" the reporter asked. "Something bluesy?"

Deza smiled. "My grandmama used to go to blues clubs in

Chicago, and I heard rumors she danced sometimes, but this generation needs something with a much harder beat to dance to. I don't know what we'll do yet."

"Don't put it past me, to mix something blues into it, though," Damián said.

Deza laughed. "That's so real," she said. "Like that go-go remix. I was listening to it later—you know—after the show. Before the show, I had been listening as a rapper. Making sure I knew where my bars fit in the song. But afterward, I was listening like a music lover. You put crazy stuff in that mix. Did you really sample Barack Obama?"

"Yeah," he said. "It was the DC remix. I had to sample the one Black president."

The three of them talked a little longer, then the reporter thanked them for their time.

The moment he stepped off the bus, Damián turned to Deza.

"Did I do okay?" he asked.

"You were great," she said. "Claire gave me a little more of a heads-up because she knew I would want to get my face together. It took me a while to get to sleep last night. I was so high from the show."

"Claire gave me no time to get my face together," he said. "She almost let me walk into the interview with my Afro flat on one side."

Deza shrugged. "You're the DJ," she said. "And a dude. You could get away with it onstage if you wanted."

"I'll pass," he said. "My ma taught me to go out the house looking a certain way."

"I'm so glad you're on the tour," she said, and leaned forward to give him a big hug.

Damián gave her a quick squeeze, but then took a step back. "You can't be hugging a brother so early in the morning before he's had a chance to shower. My ma also taught me to go out the house smelling a certain way." He laughed.

"But I can't tell you how glad I am to be on this tour with you, Deza. It's like I'm living the dream."

"Same," she said.

"And I caught what you said back there," Damián said. "That you were familiar with my work as a club DJ. More like danced and flirted with me at the club."

"Excuse me?" Deza asked playfully. "Don't you have a shower to take or something?"

"Yes I do." Damián laughed. And with that, he headed off to the bathroom.

When Deza hugged him, it had just been an impulsive gesture. An explosion of nerves from the interview. But when their bodies contacted, she felt something. The same thing she had felt on the dance floor. But not just that. Her body was lonely. She didn't have contact with anyone here, except the few fans that came backstage and asked for hugs. His body was a mix of hard and soft that she could sink into. She'd like to wake up to see his Afro flat on one side.

And now he'd acknowledged that they'd flirted. Well, it wasn't like they hadn't both been there.

But it was probably best that he had pulled back before anything got too heated between them. She shouldn't mix business with pleasure, especially after she was about to be linked to Damián in the press, *Rolling Stone* no less.

"She's not a professional," still rang in Deza's ears from when the previous DJ said it. Nothing looked less professional than fucking the only man on the tour. She needed to keep it all business with Damián.

She set about the business of tightening up some of the tracks in the back of her hair that were coming loose. She could play them off for the reporter, but not during the dance numbers on stage.

Chapter 11

Atlanta

The Atlanta show went off without a hitch. Damián played the popular trap remix for Deza's top two songs. The audience loved it, but it wasn't new to them. Deza had been doing trap remixes for a while. Damián came off the stage and fist-bumped her.

"Nice job," she said. "We really do make a good team."

His smile was so inviting. She wanted to hug him but kept herself back. *Damn, he could get it, though,* she thought to herself.

Instead, she said, "Now we just need to do it again in twenty more cities and each time act like it's totally fresh."

Damián laughed and Deza disappeared into her dressing room to escape that infectious smile.

The big surprise was on the bus the next day. Damián got a call from Lisette. He debated whether or not to pick it up. But maybe he'd gotten some mail that was urgent. Or worse yet, maybe someone had died. He didn't want to be the asshole ex who didn't even pick up.

"Lisette," he said. "Is everything okay?"

"Hey, Papi," she said.

Papi? He wasn't expecting Papi.

"I just wanted to call you," she said. "To check in. To apologize, really. I saw you in the *Rolling Stone* article."

It was out? He hadn't seen it yet.

"That article was everything I could see about you when we first met," she went on. "You have this big vision in music. I'm just sorry that I didn't believe in you enough. Sometimes . . . it just sort of seemed like even though you had the talent, you didn't have the hustle. I should have trusted in you more. I'm really sorry."

Damián blinked. Wow. She was sorry? "I'm sorry, too," he said. "I didn't ask you if it was cool for you to carry all the responsibilities in our relationship. I should have asked. And made a plan, you know, like a deadline. If I didn't get X by Y date, I would get a day job."

"Yeah, but that should have been a last resort," she said. "I shouldn't have pushed you."

"In some ways you're right that I didn't hustle enough," he confessed. On this tour, watching these artists on their grind all day, he realized how lax he had been. "Sometimes, I didn't quite know how to get to the next level, and I didn't want to ask anyone for help. I just sort of waited to get discovered. And you had so many good ideas. After a while I just sort of shut down to them, because I didn't want to seem like . . . like I couldn't do it on my own. I wasn't—wasn't really an adult about it. You were always the grown-up one. I didn't realize how lucky I was to have you in my corner. You were the one making our life work. I didn't see it and it wasn't fair. I'm really sorry."

He could hear Lisette getting emotional.

"Oh Damián," she said. "It means so much to hear you say that. I've just missed you so much, but I felt like I couldn't— I shouldn't call because . . . because nothing had really changed.

But now it seems like everything has changed. We could both get what we wanted. And I can admit to myself that I really miss you."

"I miss you, too," he said. And he realized he did. The road was exciting sometimes, but also boring a lot of the time. And lonely.

"Living with my parents really showed me all the ways I was still acting like a kid," he said. "And without you holding it down, I had to live like a kid. I love my folks, but it definitely was a rude awakening."

"When you come back to New York," she said. "How about you move back in?"

The "yes!" was on the tip of his tongue when he remembered that hug with Deza. Not just the hug, the chemistry they had in the club, and still had every night on stage. He had just been written up in *Rolling Stone*. Just because his ex could suddenly see his potential didn't mean that it was going to be all good when he got back to the City. Besides, even if things didn't work out with Deza, who knew what types of opportunities would come his way? He didn't want to be tied down right when he was starting to fly.

"I'm trying to be more of an adult these days," Damián said. "I would love to just say 'yes!' but I need to think it through. The two of us need to talk it through. What are the expectations? I had to give up my gigs in New York. I don't know what my life will look like when I get back. Or if I'll get opportunities out of town. I don't want to make any promises I can't keep."

He could visualize her doing that smile and head shake thing she did. "No, Damián," she said. "I can feel it. This is the breakthrough we've been waiting for. Whatever the new thing is, we can make it work. I can come visit you on tour."

"I'm not ready for that yet," Damián said. "I'm the rookie here. Still getting my bearings. Let's sit down and talk when I get back to New York."

"What?" she said. "I thought you missed me."

"I do," he said. "I really do. But I've finally got a shot at something big here. I don't want to be distracted. I want to stay focused. And having you around would definitely jeopardize that."

She said a few flirty things. And he flirted back. But he meant what he said. He wanted to stay focused on his work.

And then there was Deza, too. He definitely wasn't trying to have a girlfriend on the tour. He needed to see what was on the other end of that hug.

Deza was fucking furious. The *Rolling Stone* article painted a picture of Deza as a sexy girl with no substance, who was way out of her league. He rehashed her early innovation in what they called "Drillternative" hip hop out of Chicago. Her music had that Drill sound, but with a slightly faster tempo and more optimistic and positive lyrics. Still, the writer attributed the innovation to Royal. As far as the writer was concerned, the Shaqana coincidence had been a fluke. He called Deza's work "otherwise unremarkable." And Damián, the slightly older, more seasoned artist, was responsible for her success in DC and Miami. Yes, Damián brought a lot to the table, but how was the reporter gonna dismiss her as eye candy? She couldn't tell which was worse, Black people's prophecy hype she could never live up to? Or white boys telling her to stay in her lane?

Deza leaped up off the couch and stormed across the bus. She banged on the door of Damián's compartment.

The door swung open and Damián was grinning.

"I was just gonna come find you," he said. "A friend called and told me the *Rolling Stone* article was up."

"You've read it?" she asked.

"Not yet," he said. "I was gonna suggest we read it together."

"Well, you're in for a treat," she said flatly.

"Did he dis us?" Damián asked.

"No," Deza said. "Definitely did not dis *us*. You'll see." She stormed off.

This was what he didn't like about Deza. What the hell was wrong with her? She ran hot and cold. She was like, *I'm gonna say something mysterious. Figure me out.* He didn't have time for that shit. He was sort of regretting he hadn't responded more strongly to Lisette. She was someone who knew how to fucking communicate. Who said what the fuck she meant. Whatever. His ass was in *Rolling Stone*, and he was gonna go read all about it.

At first Damián was so excited to see his name in print that he couldn't take the whole article in. "Rising star DJ," the guy wrote. "Expansive talent." The first read-through was like hearing everything he'd ever wanted to hear about himself. From his parents, who didn't really appreciate his DJ-ing, to Lisette, who lost faith after a couple years.

He thought about his uncle, who had mentored him as a DJ. If only he were alive to see this. "This one's for you, Tío," he said. He could feel himself getting emotional about it, so he went and reread the article.

As he did, he had a dawning sense of horror. The reporter totally dismissed Deza. He didn't see them as a team, he saw Damián and his focus on local hip hop styles as sort of rescuing her from mediocrity. And the shit about Black Lives Matter was kind of offensive. Like it was a gimmick to sell music.

He leaped up off the bed and went knocking on Deza's door.

"It's not a good time," she said.

"I just want you to know that article was some bullshit," Damián said. "How did that dude get off dissing your talent like that? And it was mad racist. I'm about to say something on social media. I'll tag you."

"Whatever," Deza said.

Damián returned to his bunk and took a screenshot of his name in the article. He posted it on Instagram with the caption, "This breakthrough is bittersweet. I been wanting to see my name in print like this for years. But not at someone else's expense. Deza is an incredibly talented performer. She inspires me as an artist. *Rolling Stone* has never given women in hip hop their due. I thought them writing about Deza was a step in the right direction, but it turns out it's just a backhanded way to put her down? This is some bullshit. I hope all my fans go out and buy her record right now. Or better yet, come to her concert and see for yourself how good she is. Back in the 80s, Chuck D and Public Enemy talked about Prophets of Rage. Deza has been expressing the rage and hope of Black women for a while now. Heads need to stop watching her like a jack-in-the-box that might pop out some sort of prophecy at any moment. Listen to what she says in every rhyme. It's more complicated than people make it out to be. Heads need to just listen."

Chapter 12

In some ways, the tour became more and more like middle school. Deza and Vienna didn't like each other. Vienna's band took her side, and Anasuya tried to be neutral.

It was also like middle school in that Deza and Damián seemed to have crushes on each other, but it stayed at the crush stage. Like if you were a nerdy kid in sixth grade.

At the shows, Deza stayed in her dressing room when she was backstage. Invited friends in or near each city to come to the show. She hung with her own people, her own clique. She passed the other artists on her way to and from the stage like middle school hallways. Sometimes, her friends would be big fans of one of the other artists, and the two of them would engage in the fiction that they were all cool. The friend would take selfies with both of them, everyone smiling.

Which is why the folks who came to see her weren't really friends. Not anyone she could tell what was actually going on. More like a tour guide, welcoming them to this amazing celebrity world. Deza could play the gracious host who was kind enough to invite them along. The other artists just wanted to keep the fans happy. If some of them were Deza's friends? All good.

None of them threw shade on social media. Except the DJ

who had walked off the bus. But she had signed a nondisclosure, so she couldn't be explicit about what had happened. She just alluded to "drama" and a "toxic environment" that led "all the way to the top." She concluded, "You know how women can be."

@BadBeyotch971
Thats what I'm talmbout yall.
#FaceToTheSkyTour=Shade behind your back tour. You can't expect a group of women to get along. I been saying from jump, Deza ain't a prophet. She's a basic chick with an expensive weave. I coulda prophesied some backstabbing bitches & drama.

@Deza4Everr
No way, sis. "All the way to the top" means the record label. Why you always blame the women, tho? These record execs have NO RESPECT for Black women. Think they own us. Rappers laboring in these streets like cotton fields. They might pay us now, but still treat us like property.

@BadBeyotch971
You kumbaya bitches always wanna blame the white man, but don't wanna acknowledge that black women be backstabbing drama factories sometimes. Admit it.

@Deza4Everr
Yes, I'll admit that we have a lot of internalized sexism (+racism) & we act it out on each other. LIKE ASSUMING IT'S DEZA'S FAULT. Get the facts before you sling the mud, tho.

The tour dates were wonky in the Southeast, and their bus crisscrossed back and forth to the coast. The day they stopped in Charlotte, NC, Deza did an appearance in a video shoot for her girl Rapsody. It was a relief to get away from the drama of the tour, and great to spend an afternoon with another Black female rapper. Even though it was an insanely long day, she came back to the venue refreshed.

But it wasn't until South Carolina, when her aunt surprised her, that Deza finally connected with someone she was really close to.

Thug Woofer and Tyesha had showed up unannounced.

Deza shrieked and hugged them. "You're gonna make me spoil my makeup!" Deza wailed as she began to cry at the sight of her aunt.

"Lemme give you two the room," Woof said.

"Don't go far," Deza said. "You better be willing to go onstage for a minute."

"I thought this show was all ladies," he said. "I ain't tryna ruin the vibe."

"We got a male DJ," Deza said. "You won't be the only one."

Deza poured her heart out to Tyesha in the dressing room. She did spoil her makeup and had to do her face again. She was just finishing up when it was time for her to go on stage.

But instead of the high voice of the AM radio DJ introducing her, she heard thunderous applause.

"What's good, Cackalacky?" Woof's voice boomed through the speakers.

Thug Woofer was a South Carolina rapper who had made it to the top. He was their own.

"I know some a y'all read in the gossip papers that I recently got engaged," he said. Many of the women in the audience booed heartily. Backstage, Tyesha laughed.

"Sorry, ladies," he said. "When you meet the one, she's the one. But before she was even my girlfriend, she gave me a demo by her niece. I get a lot of demos. But just like Tyesha Couvillier is the one and only for me as my woman, her niece was the one for me as a protégée. I'd been looking for a young woman I could mentor and support to do big things in hip hop. Somebody who was a voice for our times. Who came from the hood, but also had a vision of the world we wanted to see. That emcee is Deza."

The crowd cheered again.

"Deza didn't really need me," he said. "She would have blown up anyway. We live in a world of male rappers constantly disrespecting women—and I've been guilty of that in the past—but in addition to changing my ways, I wanted to lift up a Black female voice. Deza is the voice we need to hear. Right. Now. And her album has been an important voice for Black Lives. So please give this young lady a warm South Carolina welcome as she comes to the stage. Your girl from the South Side of Chicago, Deza!"

Woof made such a difference. For the first time on this stadium tour, Deza stepped onto the stage feeling like she didn't have to earn something. She sat on the edge of the stage and rapped one of the songs about heartbreak. Like she was just telling one of her best friends about it. One of the girls in the front row was crying, and her friend had an arm over her, comforting her. Deza rapped in a softer voice than usual:

> *Time to pick yourself up off the bathroom floor*
> *Keep it moving, girl, there's better in store.*

The crying girl raised her hand like she was testifying. Like she was ready for the better that was in store to get there.

After the rapping part was done, Deza encouraged the crying girl to come up. Deza wasn't the greatest singer, but she reached out and sang the hook to her:

> *Message from my future self*
> *Listen to me and no one else*

After the song ended, the girl began screaming as if she were in church.

"Yes!!" she shrieked. "She blessed me! Deza blessed me!"

But Deza felt like the big game changer was having Woof there, South Carolina's own, so publicly giving her his blessing.

Chapter 13

Brooklyn

The first time Deza met Thug Woofer, she was decidedly not looking her best. She was in her late teens. Her parents had just had a huge blowout of a fight at the Brooklyn hotel where they were all staying. Deza had called Tyesha, and she had come to swoop Deza and Amaru. Now she was driving them to her apartment.

Deza had always thought of that as the night that everything changed. Tyesha had taken them in before, but as a college student in a dorm. For the first time, something more was possible.

When they arrived at the brownstone where Tyesha lived, they had to circle the block looking for a parking space.

After her father had stormed out of the hotel, her mother had turned her fury toward Deza. In the back of Tyesha's car, Deza was still furious and wounded from the encounter.

And then her sister Amaru said the magic words that erased every bit of pain and fury from Deza's mind: "Auntie Ty, is that Thug Woofer on your front stoop?"

Deza looked up, and it was.

"Oh my God," Deza said. "I look totally fucking crazy." She pulled down the passenger vanity mirror and wiped under her eyes. She smoothed her hair.

"I need lipstick!" she yelled.

"Don't look at me," Amaru said.

"Auntie Ty, you got some for me?"

Tyesha shook her head. "I ran out with just my wallet to come get you."

Tyesha found a tiny parking space and deftly maneuvered the car into it.

"Thug Woofer," Deza said. "I'm meeting Thug motherfucking Woofer. I need to look like I'm ready to be a star."

"Deza," Amaru said. "You're a rapper, not a model."

"You so damn butch, you don't understand," Deza said.

"Lipstick or not," Tyesha said. "Here he comes. Put your head up and believe in yourself."

Tyesha stepped out of the car. "Hey, Woof," she said. "What are you doing here?"

"I was worried about you," he said.

Something had happened at Tyesha's job. Whatever. Deza checked that she didn't have anything in her teeth.

She and Amaru stepped out of the car while Thug Woofer gave their aunt a hug.

Tyesha took Woof by the hand and introduced him.

"I'm looking forward to hearing your demo," Woof said.

Deza was uncharacteristically tongue-tied. She just nodded and smiled.

Tyesha led them all up the stairs and opened the door of the brownstone.

"The girls were just coming to sleep over," she told Woof.

"I'm sorry to interrupt," Woof said.

"Interrupt my auntie all you want," Deza said. "In fact, we don't need a babysitter or anything, Auntie Ty. Like if you and your company wanted to go out or something. We can make ourselves at home."

"Are you sure?" Tyesha asked. "Amaru, you're okay?"

"I got six-thirty practice," she said. "I'm going to sleep in the next fifteen minutes." She was pulling off her loose jeans to reveal a long pair of cotton hoop shorts that hung to her knees.

"And I'm gonna stay up and binge-watch the latest season of Femcee Battle."

Deza draped a jacket over Tyesha's shoulders. "And you shouldn't be out without your coat. Here. Have fun." She closed the door behind them.

"Dang," Amaru said. "You practically pimped her out to him."

"Go brush your teeth," Deza said. "You need to be asleep in fourteen minutes."

Chapter 14

New Orleans

Two days later, Deza visited the Hurricane Katrina Memorial. She stayed largely dry-eyed, but found herself stumbling through sound check.

They were doing a bounce remix of "Deza Daze Ya."

"Shoutout to Big Freedia!" Damián shouted from the DJ stand.

That was Deza's cue to come in, but she was late. Above her head, the jumbotron monitor showed a glamorous photo of the Queen of Bounce. Big Freedia, the gender-bending diva, with a bone-straight black weave and a tiara.

"I'm sorry," Deza said after missing the cue. "Lemme try that again."

"Somebody get Deza some water!" Claire called from off-stage. "Deza, do you need to take five?"

Deza shook her head. "No, I'm fine."

An assistant came over with a glass of room-temperature water, and Deza drank it.

Damián took off his big headphones and walked over to her. The band of the headphones had made a dip in his Afro.

"Seriously," he said. "You okay? Did somebody on the tour say something crazy to you?"

Deza gave a chuckle. "Nothing like that," she said. "I went to the Hurricane Katrina Memorial."

His eyebrows rose. "Let's talk after sound check," he said. She nodded and finished her water.

After sound check, the two of them walked back to her dressing room. The caterers had set out Chinese food. The two of them fixed plates for themselves on the way.

"I don't know," Deza said. "One of the few times I saw my mama cry was about Hurricane Katrina when I was little."

"I know what you mean." Damián nodded. "Hurricane Maria hit right around my birthday. I was out drinking that night. I woke up the next day to find the homeland had been trashed. My moms was crying hard. My dad was trying not to cry, but he couldn't hold it in."

"When I was in the museum, I just felt so helpless," she said. "It's so big. These natural disasters—"

He cut her off. "There's nothing natural about this shit," he said. "Katrina, Maria, Harvey, they're all part of the climate crisis. And the way the US responds? Who's considered disposable? That's all man-made. Made right here in the USA."

"This is why I want to do that endorsement deal," Deza said. "If I had big money, I could really do something about stuff like that."

"By exploiting sweatshop labor?" he asked.

"I'm not saying I'm gonna take that deal," she said. "But I just wish I had the funds to make a difference."

"You already have what you need to make a difference," Damián said. "Tonight, you're gonna be on stage talking to ten thousand people. Right now, your platform is where you can have an impact."

"But I don't have a song about hurricanes or New Orleans," she said. "And the show starts in a couple hours."

"We don't have a song *yet*," he said.

"What?" she said. "We're supposed to come up with a whole new song in two hours? It takes me a month to come up with a good hook."

"No," Damián said. "We can remix a song and maybe even change the lyrics to the hook a little."

"Which song?"

"'Much Too Much.'" Damián picked a song from deep in the album. It hadn't been released as a single, and they hadn't really planned to. But the moment he said it, her eyes flew open. The hook was *I come pounding like a hurricane*.

What if she changed it? What if they adapted it?

"'They come pound you like a hurricane/four hundred years later, my people still in chains/These storms make our condition plain . . .'"

"Yes, Mami," Damián said. "That's what I'm talking about."

The two of them gathered the equipment they needed. Damián's dressing room was bigger, so they set up shop there. He worked with his headphones and laptop while Deza paced around the room with a pen and notebook.

"'In Puerto Rico we grew sugar cane/Louisiana we grew the same/Stripped us naked when the storms came/Can't let the flood put out the freedom flame.'"

This time, when Deza took the stage, she wasn't nervous. She had been overwhelmed with emotion since the museum. She ignored the advice of her vocal coach. She let it all out. The rage. The grief.

They closed the set with that song.

Damián had mixed in snippets of Mos Def's "Dollar Day," particularly the "Katrina clap" sample. He had also mixed in a West Coast Puerto Rican emcee Deza had never heard of, Rico Pabon. The track started with a list of devastations to the island of Puerto Rico, and then Pabon said, "'and I ain't even talking about the hurricane.'"

Line by line, Damián's track was in conversation with Deza's rap. They built a clear picture of colonial brutality against Puerto Rico, of racist violence against Black communities in the US. The music pounded like a hurricane, and Deza howled like the wind.

It brought the house down. A freelance reporter was in the audience, and she would later write for *The Atlantic*:

> around me, members of the audience were screaming and crying. This pop music concert had suddenly become a sort of public healing. Touching wounds the audience hadn't realized they had, or thought they had already healed under the scars. But Deza's vocals and the DJs track tore open the wounds, cleansed them. The beats reset the broken bones. By the end of the concert, it felt less like a rap show and more like a revival. The dance as critical release of all the pent-up pain.

Anasuya came to congratulate them. "Deza, that was amazing," she said, tears in her eyes. "I—" She shook her head and just hugged Deza. Anasuya was the first of many of the artists from the other bus who came to congratulate and appreciate her. But not all of them. Vienna strode past to the women's dressing room without bothering to even look Deza's way.

But it couldn't bring down Deza's high. She had four wins under her belt: DC, Miami, South Carolina, and now New Orleans. She wasn't a prophet, she could never be. But now that people had some higher expectations of her, she felt like there was an occasion to rise to—she could use her lyrical skills for more than just trying to get put on. She could use her power for healing. To lift people up.

After the concert, rhymes began to pour out of her. She grabbed some paper and a pen from Claire and rushed to her dressing room to write them down before they slipped out of her mind. She vowed to start carrying her battered notebook around again. Just like when she was an aspiring rapper.

Black girl, Black girl, so much to say.

Chapter 15

That night, all the artists but Vienna walked to the buses together. For the first time, the good night wasn't awkward. Standing out in the parking lot, they smiled and even hugged one another in the humid night. Then the bulk of them went onto one bus, and just Deza and Damián climbed onto the other.

"You tired?" Deza asked.

"Are you kidding me?" Damián said. "We'll practically be in California by the time I fall asleep."

"We're not going West next," Deza said. "I think we're going Midwest."

Damián nodded. "Hood public schools," he said. "I don't really know my geography."

She nodded. "Where in New York are you from?" They had skipped the basics of introduction. When they first met, it was all dance and flirting. Since they had met again on the bus, it was all business. But the concert had blown everyone open. Claire was asleep in her compartment. The driver was focused on the road. Deza needed to connect. To talk to someone. To be human—not a robot who rapped and danced and woke up the next day to do it all again.

"South Bronx," he said.

"I stayed with my aunt in Brooklyn for a while," she said.

"I know," he said.

"What do you mean, you know?"

"I saw you rap when you were in New York," he said. "I used to go to that hip hop open mic Yolanda Gutiérrez does in Brooklyn. You were a regular for a minute there. I even subbed for her as a DJ a couple times when she was out of town."

"Get the fuck outta here," she said.

"Yeah," Damián said. "You can even go way back in my Instagram timeline. I posted a picture of you and said 'this emcee is gonna be huge. Look out for her.'"

"But you didn't recognize me in the club?"

"With those big-ass shades that covered your face?" Damián said.

"Yeah," she said. "I know it was corny."

"But I was right about you," Damián said. "The way you brought it tonight . . . It was just . . . so fucking powerful."

Deza began to choke up. "I just feel like it's not enough," she said. "The shit people have gone through . . . with the hurricanes . . . everything. The shit people are going through now. The disasters still coming down the pike. I just wish I could do . . . more, you know? What good is all this fame and whatever if I can't make a difference to my people. To all our people?"

"Nah, Deza," Damián said. "You got it all twisted. They make us think that celebrities are like superheroes. And they're not. They're just people who have a little more money and a little bigger platform than regular folks. You can't put that kind of pressure on yourself."

"Putting it on myself?" she asked. "They're calling me a prophet. I don't know how I'm supposed to live up to that."

"Don't live up to it," Damián said. "Just live. Look for your chance to make a contribution, and do it. Things don't change in the real world because one caped crusader makes it happen. It takes movements of millions of people to change things. Look at the Movement for Black Lives. Look at the climate movement. Look at #MeToo. Sure, celebrities have a role to play, but the weight isn't all on your shoulders."

"Yeah, but—" she said. "But the pressure is real. And it comes from different directions. Sometimes I just think of all the people I left behind. Kids where I grew up in Chicago. Girls I used to rap with. I'm traveling around on a bus doing what we dreamed of. And they're back home living the lives we tried to get away from."

"That sounds like survivor's guilt," he said. "I know how you feel. We all have people we love who didn't make it out."

Deza rolled her eyes. "My aunt talks about that shit, too."

Tyesha had moved to New York, gotten her master's degree, and was the executive director of a clinic in Manhattan. She owned her apartment in Brooklyn outright. Sure, she was also engaged to Thug Woofer, but if that didn't work out, she would still be just fine. So unlike Deza's grandmother, who still lived in the projects. Or Deza's mom—Tyesha's sister—whose life revolved around her man—a philandering drug dealer.

"It's just par for the course," Damián said. "I work with kids in this rough high school. Even just DJing in the city, I was living their dream. I don't know what kind of lives they're gonna have, given where this country and this world is headed. Correction, kids I used to work with. I quit my job to take this gig. Just ghosted on them, like so many of their dads. I definitely felt guilty. I didn't even get a chance to say goodbye."

Deza shook her head. "Damián, you're really talented," she said. "Music is your thing. You should be doing this full time. Not just on this tour, but permanently."

"I just feel selfish sometimes," he said.

"You have a gift," she said. "You know how to dig deep into regional hip hop styles. Like that *Rolling Stone* journalist said. And the samples you put in. Did you grow up in a record store or something?"

Damián shook his head and laughed. "My uncle was a DJ," he said. "And I just loved music that much. While other kids were playing video games, I was listening to music, all different kinds. He had a great collection of hip hop that went back to the seventies. And I would always ask him where each artist was from. And eventually, I could hear some of the regional differences."

"I can tell from the way you mix," she said.

They talked about music until late into the night. So many times the chemistry rose between them and it seemed like they might lean in, might kiss, but at each moment, one of them held back, and the conversation continued. Platonic. Businesslike.

The next day, she got a DM on Instagram from a Black climate activist with a huge following.

She walked out into the lounge and found Damián sitting eating some cereal.

"I just got a DM," she said. "You ever heard of this girl Jenna Devin?"

"Jenna Devin DM'd you?" he asked. "She's huge!"

"Really?" Deza asked, scrolling through the photos on Jenna's IG. A mix of pristine wildlife landscapes, climate action protests, and West Coast residents walking around in heavy masks with unnaturally gloomy lighting due to the smoky air.

"What does she want?"

"A meeting, I guess," Deza said.

Damián's face lit up. "That's amazing," he said.

"But why does she want to meet with me?" Deza said. "I'm not an activist."

"We just did a huge concert about hurricanes," Damián said. "I think that qualifies as activism."

"Will you come to the meeting?" she asked. "I just—" She

shook her head. "I just don't want to look stupid. I don't know anything about this stuff."

"She's not gonna quiz you," Damián said. "She probably just wants to get you on board with a project or something. Take the meeting. Of course I'll sit in. But I don't know that much more than you do."

"Yeah you do," she said. "I'd never even heard of this chick."

Jenna Devin had chopped off the long dreadlocks from her profile photo. The dark brown face looking into the computer had a septum piercing and no makeup. She was drinking from a mug that said "Sunrise Movement."

"Deza, thank you so much for making time in your busy schedule," Jenna said. "I'll get right to the point. You're doing amazing work around climate justice, and we want you to be one of our climate ambassadors in hip hop."

"What does that entail?" Deza asked. "I mean, I'm so new to all this. I can barely remember to recycle."

Jenna laughed. "It's not about recycling anymore, sis. It's about big policy changes. We need to be demanding a Green New Deal that's free of fossil fuels. We need to be transitioning every industry to renewable energy. Just like the Movement for Black Lives is talking about defunding police, we're talking about defunding fossil fuels and making green jobs with livable wages for everyone."

"I mean," Deza said, "that sounds great. But what would I do as an ambassador?"

"First of all, you'd just keep doing what you're already doing," Jenna said. "Finding opportunities to talk about this stuff. Like you did in New Orleans. Second of all, we're pushing the entertainment industry to go green. Fewer flights. Renewable fuels on the road."

"Cool," Deza said. "But I don't make those decisions."

"But you could," Jenna said. "As the headliner, you could

make a demand. The record label won't care, as long as it doesn't cost them any more money. You would just need to commit to using renewable fuels. We'd ask you to post about it on social media. We're trying to get the hip hop audience to start thinking of climate as their issue."

"Is there a catch?" Deza asked. "Cause otherwise you're just saying keep doing what I'm doing, ask the record company for something that won't cost any money, and some new angles for social justice content to post. I don't see a downside."

"No catch," Jenna said. "What's good for the planet is usually good for the people."

"What are the renewable fuels, though?" Damián asked. "We're just driving regular buses."

"We looked at photos of your buses online," Jenna said. "They're all diesel. So we can transition without any problem. We can give your tour manager a list of all the biodiesel fueling places along your route, and we have a network of activists who can bring additional recycled biodiesel fuel to each of the tour stops."

"But what's your long-term campaign?" Damián asked.

"To get the entertainment industry to move toward total sustainability," Jenna said. "No more flights. Ground transpo only. Solar electric buses."

"They're not gonna like that," Damián said. "That would definitely cut into their profit margin."

"It's not just for the sustainability of the planet," Jenna said. "It's also for the sustainability of the artists. They need to pay better wages and not force artists to fly every day and play every night. They pick a handful of artists and make them the super-hot thing, then exploit them till they burn out and move on to the next crop of fresh meat. Their business model is based on burning through people as much as fossil fuels."

Deza blinked. That was exactly what it felt like. She was

only gonna be hot for a minute, so she had to burn as brightly as she could while it lasted. But what if they were just trying to burn her out?

"Sounds good," Deza said.

"Fantastic," Jenna said. "I'll send a follow-up email. But there's one thing I want to put on your radar: Make sure to check the oil filters and change them the minute they get dirty or your fuel lines will clog up and you'll feel the downside."

"I can do that," Damián said. "What do you say, Deza? Are we in?"

Deza nodded. "Looks like the Face To The Sky Tour is going green."

At their next tour stop, an Asian guy in an old Mercedes drove up with several large cans of gas. Deza and Damián were doing an Instagram Live post about it when the bus driver came out and got off the bus. He glanced over at them and shook his head.

"Not everyone is quite as excited about this as we are," Damián said.

The bus driver walked off to smoke a cigarette as the Asian guy showed Damián how to change the oil filter.

"Check it every time you fill up," he said, and left them several clean filters.

Post show hangouts became Deza and Damián's thing. They would check the oil filter on the bus, then debrief after the show. That was how it went in Little Rock. Topeka. Sharing their favorite music with each other.

Then they had an off night in Omaha. The concert was poorly attended. The energy was low. The crowd not particularly responsive.

Part of the problem was the weather. There had been freakish, heavy rain, and people were worried about flooding. Not that there were actual advisories, but so many people had been traumatized in recent floods that they were scared to drive all the way out to the concert for fear of getting caught if things took an unexpected turn.

"Why'd they even book this tour in Nebraska?" Damián asked.

Deza shrugged. "Nashonna's mother was from here," she said. "It made sense when she was the headliner."

Damián shook his head. "Man," he said. "Just when I get to feeling like this is gonna work out to be my new life, something like this show happens and I see how precarious it all is. How hit-and-miss."

"What do you mean?" Deza said. "This is definitely your new life."

"But it's different for you," he said. "You're signed to the label. This is your full-time job. And for the foreseeable."

"Which is all the more reason to keep doing what you're doing," Deza said. "You gotta believe in your gift of music."

"I feel like we're up here every night giving each other the same pep talk," he said. "What the hell?"

"Then we gotta promise," Deza said. "That we'll never give up on doing our music and doing it for the people. For real. Pinkie promise."

"You wanna pinkie promise?" he asked.

"Yeah," Deza said. "I used to do that with my little sister."

"Okay," he said. "How does it work?"

"I promise to put my music first," Deza said. "And to ignore the voices of the haters, both inside and out."

She stuck out her pinkie. They twined little fingers and he repeated the phrase.

"I promise to put my music first," Damián said. "And to ignore the voices of the haters."

"Both inside and out," Deza prompted.

"Both inside and out."

The two of them held on, fingers intertwined.

"Okay," Damián said. "I needed this pep talk. Cause I been at this a long time. I don't—up till now, I never been able to make a living. So I sort of coasted. Let other people pay most of the bills."

"Living with your family isn't anything to be ashamed of," she said. "I was living with my aunt in Brooklyn when I got signed."

"Not just family," he said. "My ex. I realize now that I let her support me . . . I mean, I was contributing, too. I just. I don't know. I just . . . the way I came up. If you don't have money, you're not really a man."

"That's ridiculous," Deza said. "Hood logic."

"I know," he said. "But I was raised up in that. And it's not just about the money. It's about not being able to provide for your family. Not being able to protect your family. I mean, in these times, you gotta have so many resources to be able to survive and pivot if shit goes down where it is you're living. My folks got a rent-controlled apartment. What would they do if it burned down? Or got trashed in a hurricane. Or a tornado. This climate shit is crazy. Anything can happen."

"Did you . . . did you have family in Puerto Rico?" Deza asked. "During Hurricane Maria?"

Damián nodded. "Most of them are in the US now," he said. "Except my uncle." He shook his head. "He didn't make it."

Deza put a hand on his shoulder. "I'm so sorry."

He nodded. "That was the thing," he said. "He was just visiting PR, you know? He lived in New York. When we finally realized how bad it was gonna be, we tried to get him outta there. He had sickle cell. We knew he wasn't strong. But we didn't have the money."

"It shouldn't be on individual families," she said.

"Yeah, but it was," Damián said. "And we couldn't come

through. My parents had just put all their money into a house to retire to in PR. We lost the house . . ." He trailed off and shook his head.

"It was my dad's brother. My pops has been depressed ever since. He goes to work and just drinks when he comes home. What's the point? He's worked all his life to lose all his savings. To end up in a small apartment in the Bronx? That wasn't his dream. It's been hard to watch him . . . every day. Just like a ghost."

Deza nodded. She had lost her great-aunt. She knew what it was like.

"My uncle was the original DJ," Damián said. "Half of this record collection is what I inherited from him. The old-school shit. He was the one who taught me how to be a vinyl snob. I don't know if it was because he was scared of the new technology or if he really believed it. But he was right. I can hear the difference. And I feel like the vinyl is his legacy, you know? Part of how I pay tribute and keep a part of him alive."

Damián looked almost like he was about to cry. Deza leaned over to hug him and found herself surprised by the feel of his body. Maybe it was the pinkie promise. Such a girl move. But his body was definitely male. The broadness of his shoulders. The stubble that scratched her cheek. She wasn't sure who initiated the kiss. But they both felt it, the moment their bodies noticed each other. Beyond the emotion of the moment. Just the two of them. Like it had been at the club. Their bodies were having a separate conversation.

Keep it businesslike, a voice urged.

But they had moved beyond that. Her hands were tangling in that delicious Afro. He was wrapping his arms around her waist.

Fuck businesslike, Deza thought to herself as they backed into her sleeping compartment.

Clothes were coming off now. Hers. His.

She unbuckled his belt, but then faltered.

"Do you have a condom?" she asked.

Damián blinked. Lisette had been on the pill. He hadn't thought about birth control for half a decade. He shook his head.

Deza faltered. That was what freaked her out so much. *She thought about doing it anyway.*

And then the businesslike voice in her head was screaming: *Stop stop stop stop!*

She dropped Damián's belt buckle like it was on fire. It clanked against the bed frame.

"You need to go," she panted, and pushed him out the door.

"Deza," he said. "Wait, we don't have to—are you okay?"

"I'm sorry. I just need to be alone right now," she said, closing the compartment door and locking it behind her.

Had she lost her goddamn mind? She was considering fucking with Damián *without a condom*? It would be bad enough if she was still in Brooklyn or Chicago. But she was Deza now. The #1 female rapper in the nation couldn't just roll into the Planned Parenthood in Memphis or St. Louis and ask for an abortion. She couldn't miss tour dates. She couldn't be recognized. Did they even still have abortion clinics in this part of the country? What the hell was she thinking?

Even though they had done some incredible collaboration, she couldn't help but feel that having Damián on the tour had been a terrible mistake.

Book 2

Chapter 16

Chicago

Y ears after Auntie Lou died, and Deza was the one comforting Amaru, she had realized something about her parents, something about fighting and sex. In seventh grade, one of her friends at school had shown her something on a phone screen. Two naked people tangled up, and the woman was making sort of screamy sounds. Deza recognized those breathy squeals from the latter parts of her parents' fighting.

"Ugh," Deza shrieked. "Don't nobody want to see that!" She pushed the phone back toward her friend. It fell and the screen cracked. That was the first fissure in her middle school friend group. Her friend demanded that Deza pay for the phone and Deza felt like her actions were justified.

The next time her parents fought, Deza gripped Amaru tight and tried to rap the same old song, but it didn't work. The platitudes fell flat. She saw the flashback of the tangled bodies on the screen. Not only did Deza's own voice fail to drown out the yelling, but the words—stale to begin with— were too well known by then. A path she could walk blindfolded. She needed something to occupy her mind.

She began to write new words.

"Mama and daddy fighting through the wall/yelling and cussing like a waterfall

But you and me we gotta hang on tight/even if it lasts till the morning light

Cause we're sisters/resisters/when their words blow in like a twister

A cyclone or tornado of noise/the peaceful night it always destroys

But I got you/you're never alone/we got each other in this mess called home

They might have been the ones to make you and me/but we two sisters are the real family."

By eighth grade, Deza was functionally numb to the drama of her parents. Amaru would still wake up crying through it, but Deza would rap to her. Deza eventually learned to recognize the yells from the moans, the screams of climax from the screams of rage.

By the time her mother was screaming, "Fuck me!" instead of "Fuck you!" Deza would be exhausted. She didn't really understand but could tell by the tone and the cadence that things would soon be settling down.

But that first night when Deza wrote her own lyrics, Amaru curled against Deza and let the words lull her. Their parents had moved to the other side of their bedroom, and the noise had dulled a bit. Amaru was cried out and fell asleep. But Deza was awake for another hour, continuing to rap to herself, her sister's smaller body breathing against her side. Not protective like Aunt Lou, but still reassuring that she wasn't alone.

Chapter 17

Outside Iowa City

Damián couldn't believe he had fucked this up so badly. He should have been prepared. He went on tour as a DJ and didn't bring a fucking condom? He had fantasized about getting laid. If not Deza, then one of the other artists. Or maybe even one of the fans. How could he have been so stupid?

But if he didn't have his game tight as fuck, he shouldn't have stepped to Deza at all. He shouldn't have tried to take advantage of her to make it sexual. He felt like a creep. He did consent workshops with the kids at work. You were supposed to ask, "Can I kiss you, Deza?"

But underneath it all, he felt like a punk, because he knew he had been in his feelings, and that was part of why he tried to make a move on her. In the moment, anything seemed better than falling apart. Kissing her. Having sex. The bus catching on fire.

But now they were on the bus together with dozens of dates to go and nothing but awkwardness between them. Was this how he planned to handle his big break? Juvenile behavior and sabotage? *Way to go, Damián.* Way to fucking go.

* * *

Deza just wanted to sleep. She didn't want to think. Didn't want to lie awake beating herself up for being so stupid. So she took a sleeping pill. The next stop would be Chicago. She spent the next half hour sending emails to all her Chicago folks. It was too late to text everyone but her mother, who never had her phone on at night. Her mother had confirmed that she got tickets to the show. But Deza needed to remind her. Jenisse was likely to "forget." Then, Deza contacted more than thirty of her people before she crashed into a chemical doze.

Deza was completely disoriented when Claire rapped on her door the next morning at nine.

"You have a Zoom interview in five minutes," Claire said.

Deza blinked. Her eyes were gummy, and her throat was dry. "Make it a phone interview," she croaked from the bed.

It was the first of a dozen interviews. A few were big local outlets in Chicago, but the rest were national. By noon, Deza had gotten her face on and was doing video interviews. There was an in-person taping that afternoon. She would have to change up her hair later.

She was able to compartmentalize. During the interviews, she would focus, and managed to do well. But it was hard. The sleep med hangover had her a little foggy. Like there was a half-second delay in her brain. She should have been fresh and sharp for these conversations. She would have been if she hadn't practically fucked Damián last night. After each interview, she would take a moment to berate herself.

In between a national newspaper and taping a happy birthday shoutout to a late show host, she ran to the bathroom. Damián was just coming out and they nearly collided.

"Sorry!" he said.

"My bad," she said, eyes cast down.

"Deza—" he began.

"I only got a second between interviews," she said, and

slipped past him into the toilet. When she came back out, she was grateful that he was gone, his compartment door shut.

The Atlantic article on the New Orleans concert had just come out. And Deza's concert made the front page of the *Chicago Sun-Times* arts section.

"Apparently Chicago is very excited for your return," Claire said.

Deza wished she was excited. She just felt regret. This could have—should have been a victorious return. Instead, she felt like a lonely loser. Who had practically fucked her DJ, the only man nearby. She had always pictured herself with someone more . . . powerful. Like Lauren London and Nipsey Hussle . . . may he rest in power.

Deza and Damián didn't cross paths until sound check.

He nodded at her from the DJ booth and she nodded back. Neat. Civil. Professional.

Part of the way through sound check, he approached her. "Listen, I'm really sorry about last night," he said. "I sort of lost my head."

"Don't worry about it," she said coolly.

He walked back to the DJ setup and began to spin one of the Chicago remixes of "Deza Daze Ya."

"I know that mix," Deza said. "I hate it."

Damián had played Royal's mix. Royal, her ex. She still couldn't stand to hear any of those mixes, because they were all she rapped to when they were together. When she was signed to the label, she had to fight to have all new tracks to the songs. Paperclip wanted to get those mixes. But Deza refused. She needed to have her life at the label completely separate from him. They had worked hard to find a DJ who could mimic Royal's Drillternative sound.

And speak of the devil.

When they got out of sound check, Royal was waiting

backstage. He was even more handsome than she remembered. He had his hair all slicked down. He always called it "the Royal Wave." He looked like a romance novel cover with his pouty face and two-dozen long-stemmed roses for Deza.

Her chest was a cement mixer. Churning rock into a new shape. Her hurt and rage at him had calcified. But it had begun as a way to protect her from how much she had loved him. The memories flooded back. She had poured concrete over her heart, had never really let go of those old feelings for him.

"Is there somewhere we can talk?" he asked. That deep voice. People always said he should rap, but he liked to stay behind the scenes.

Deza looked around at Damián and the other artists, watching the two of them like it was some reality TV show.

"My dressing room," she said.

She walked down the hallway with her head held high. Royal trailing behind her with the giant bouquet.

Once inside, she closed the door behind him, but didn't ask him to sit.

"Daze, baby," he began. "I am so sorry. I know I blew it. I texted you like a million times."

"I changed my number," she said coldly.

"I emailed, too," he said. "I tried to DM, but I was—"

"Blocked," Deza finished his sentence.

"I deserve this," he said. "I know I do. I just wanted to be able to apologize to you—face to face. On foenem, Deza, I am so sorry. And I understand if you can't give us another chance. But I wonder, could I just spin one song with you tonight? Just one? For old times' sake?"

"I don't think so, Royal," she said.

"Please," he said. "Just think about it."

He set the flowers down on a side table and walked out.

Deza exhaled. Now that he was gone, she slumped down into a chair.

Had that really just happened? Royal had *apologized*? And she had survived it. The thing she dreaded most every time she had come back to Chicago. Seeing him. It had happened. She didn't have to worry if she was gonna see him. In theory, it cleared the way for her to get on with her business. But the churning hadn't stopped.

She took a swig of water. She needed to get her head in the game. She had a show to do.

Fifteen minutes later, she had begun to do her makeup when Claire came in.

"Everyone at the label loves the idea," Claire said.

"What idea?" Deza asked.

"Royal doing a guest spot," Claire said.

"I didn't agree to that," Deza said. "Did he say I agreed?"

"No, no," Claire soothed. "He said you were thinking about it."

"I didn't say I would think about it," Deza said. "I told him no. He asked me to think about it and left before I could tell him no again."

"I know it's tough," Claire said. "But I think it's a good idea."

"For the fans?" Deza asked. "For the hometown reunion vibe? We don't need it."

"Not just that," Claire said. "The energy out there is going to be so strong tonight. It's your hometown. You will inevitably crush it with your performance. It'll also undercut that dick at *Rolling Stone* who acted like Damián is the source of your power. It'll be good to show him and the world that you are a solo act. You are the star, and the DJs are interchangeable."

Deza nodded. She could see that. Also, it was good to show that she could still work with Royal. She wasn't scared of him. She was gracious. Throwing him a bone on her national tour.

* * *

Damián didn't like the slick guy who showed up with flowers for Deza. Fortunately, by the way she looked at him, Deza didn't seem to like him, either.

"Who is that?" he asked Anasuya.

"You don't know?" she replied, surprised. "That's Royal. Her ex."

Damián mentally smacked himself on the head. Had he really played her ex's remix? No wonder she didn't want to hear it.

So Damián was surprised when Claire introduced him a while later. The two men shook hands, sizing each other up in the way men did. Royal was a little taller and slimmer. They were about evenly matched in terms of weight. Damián thought he could take Royal if he needed to. But mostly because Royal was a pretty boy. He'd be trying to protect the face.

Claire had been right about the show. The energy was through the roof. Deza's fans felt like they were the insiders. Some had known her in high school. Many of them had seen her perform before she moved to New York. Before she was famous. They felt more deeply invested in her. She was their girl.

Sasha Go Hard was the local opener and a crowd favorite. And the energy stayed up through Anasuya and Vienna's sets.

Deza's set with Damián went great. But the crowd really went crazy when Deza invited Royal to the stage. She smiled at him, but no teeth. Nothing sexy.

"I always knew we would be up here on this stage one day," Royal said. "I came to my first big concert here when I was in middle school."

"Tell them who you came to see," Deza said.

Royal cringed. "Do I have to?"

"You brought it up," Deza said.

"So I wasn't as woke as I am now," he said. "I came to see Car Willis."

A round of boos went through the audience. Car Willis was serving a sentence for statutory rape. He had been Chicago's notorious bad boy R&B singer who had—allegedly—groomed and sexually exploited dozens if not hundreds of underage girls. There had even been a documentary about him.

"What can I say?" Royal asked sheepishly. "I was young and I didn't know better. I was raised on music that disrespected women, and I thought it was okay. But it wasn't. I did my own share of disrespectful things." He looked straight at Deza. "If I had it to do over again, I would never, ever be so wrong. But I can't change the past. I can just move forward. The only throwback tonight will be this track that Deza, with her incredible lyrical skill and star power, has turned into a monster hit." He turned to the audience. "Chicago, are you ready to dance!?"

And then he began to spin the track. The crowd went crazy.

Deza fell into the rhythm like something familiar. When Damián spun, he was silent, but Royal would jump in. He was a hype man on stage. Supporting her with the words, not just the music. If only he had been as loyal outside the spotlight.

He even started up the banter they used to do. "Tell me, Deza, what does a badass Black girl need in this world?"

He started slow, tentative. Not assuming she would want to play along. But she did.

After the song ended, the crowd was cheering and stomping. For Deza. For Royal. For both of them.

"Thank you so much," he said. "That's my time."

But the crowd yelled that they wanted one more.

Royal looked at Deza. She looked at the crowd. They definitely wanted Royal to spin another one.

"We didn't have anything else planned," she said.

"Don't worry, baby," he said. "I got something else."

From the opening notes, she knew the track. It was a love song she had written in her late teens.

Darren Thomas. He had broken her heart. Then come back six months later asking for a second chance. She had turned him down flat and written this song. She still remembered the lyrics.

When the song opened, she came in right on cue:

> *I keep it moving/I don't backtrack*
> *You want it easy/you betta step back*
> *You had your chance/for the fairy-tale romance*
> *You know you blew it/now you can't get a*
>   *second glance.*

Deza grinned as she fell into the nostalgia. But was surprised when Royal began to rap the guy's part from the DJ stand:

> *I got nothing but regrets that I failed to see*
> *All I had with a badass like you next to me*
> *I promise to do better second time around*
> *If you just give me a chance, I'll never let you*
>   *down.*

Deza was supposed to cut him off, her line coming in fast and furious:

> *DOWN goes another brother begging for me*
> *DOWN goes your plea for mediocrity*
> *If you was DOWN from the first I wouldn't be*
>   *rapping this verse*
> *Won't even bother letting your ass down gently.*

But she missed the entrance spot in the track, and then it moved to the hook and the rhythm changed. She couldn't really rap that part after the fact. So his plea for her to take him back just hung in the air.

Royal. She had been heartbroken over him for so long. Yes, she had changed her phone number, but she had read every single one of his emails, begging her for a second chance. She'd had to read them on the phone with her aunt or she was afraid she'd open the door for them to reconcile. How much could he really have changed after two weeks? After a month? Two months? But now it had been two years. Two years, two dozen roses. Him begging her for a second chance in front of all these people. She knew why he had never been a rapper. He had stuttered as a kid. Was terrified to stutter on stage. He had faced that for her? To beg her to take him back on the biggest stage in Chicago. She hadn't wanted to consider it. But maybe . . .

Suddenly, Damián came into her mind. The moment with him, when they had almost had sex. Royal was the last time. She hadn't intentionally been saving herself for him, but all the men she met were in the business, and both her aunt, Woof, and Coco all said not to fuck any other men in the business after things had gone so badly with Royal. She hadn't wanted to go on dating apps because she was increasingly recognizable. Nobody wanted to have some fool talking about their Bumble date on social media. She never met any men IRL who weren't somehow in the music business.

She looked over at Royal. His eyes were sincere. He was so fucking handsome. And she remembered how he knew how to please her in bed. Perhaps it was those memories that softened her most. The recollection that she could let it all go with him after she had owned the stage. She needed some-place to exhale. Not worry about anything. Not have to be in charge. She craved it. Royal always knew how to take care of her.

The song ended, and Royal's voice brought her out of the memories. "I just want to thank Deza for giving me a second chance to spin for you tonight with that encore," he said. "I remember coming up here, hoping Deza would give me that second chance."

She knew he wasn't talking about DJing. It was corny, but sweet, too. She smiled and hugged him, then continued with her set.

The two men passed each other as Royal walked offstage and Damián walked on. Deza had always thought of Damián as light-skinned, but he was actually a pecan brown compared to Royal's more creamy skin. Damián wore his hair in an Afro, and Royal's was always coiffed, waved, tamed.

Of course, she ended her set with "Almost Home." There had been another police shooting the week before in Southern Illinois. Deza had the whole audience take a moment of silence for the young man who had been killed before she started her final song.

The crowd screamed for more. Deza looked at Damián, and he spun "Black Girl." It was different in Chicago, because these were her old fans. Many of them had bought her mixtape. They knew these lyrics. Black women chanting along from the audience:

"We gon be there for you badass Black girl!"

After Deza came off the stage, she was mobbed by friends and acquaintances in the green room.

After she'd held court in the backstage area, she went back to her dressing room to find that Royal was still waiting right outside her door.

"Deza," he said. "It was so good to see you. Girl, you look soooo good. I was wondering. I mean after the concert. Can we talk?"

"The bus leaves really soon," she said. "I gotta—"

Her phone rang, and it was her mother. Good. She couldn't understand why her mother hadn't come to the green room with all the other folks. But Jenisse was funny. Maybe she

wanted a private audience with Deza. Maybe she was sum-
moning her to the VIP. Well, Deza would come to her mother.
After all, Jenisse had finally come to one of Deza's shows.
The box office confirmed that the VIP badges had checked in
before the concert, but in all the drama, she hadn't had a
chance to catch up with her mother yet.

"Hold on, Royal," she said. "I've gotta take this. I'll come
back out to say goodbye.

"Hey, Mama," she said, stepping into her dressing room
and closing the door.

"Sorry I couldn't make it," Jenisse said. "Your father had
to work, and I didn't want to go alone."

"What?" Deza said. "But you checked in." Her voice was
too damn high. She was scratching the edge of a whine.

"No, baby," Jenisse said. "I gave those tickets to one of
the neighbor girls."

"Why didn't you come with her?" Deza asked.

"What would I have looked like with some young girl at a
rap show?"

"You could have brought anyone, Mama. Grandmama?
One of your friends?"

"Your grandmama way too saved to go to a hip hop
show," Jenisse scoffed.

"You could have brought anyone."

"Next time," Jenisse said.

"Mama, I been performing for ten years and you've never
made it to a single show," Deza said, her voice tight, almost
choked. "I thought this would be different because it was the
biggest theater in Chicago. But if this can't get you to come
out, then I guess nothing will."

"Don't talk to your mama like that," Jenisse said.

Deza felt her rage flare. "Then I won't talk to you at all,"
she said, and hung up.

It was supposed to make her feel better. She was grown
now. She didn't have to put up with this shit from her mother.

But it didn't. She felt like a girl at a school talent show with neither of her parents in the audience.

Someone knocked on the door. "The bus is ready, Deza," Claire called.

"Gimme a minute," Deza called back

She could feel the tears boiling behind her eyes. But she couldn't spoil her makeup. She took deep breaths. She just needed to get to the compartment on the bus, then she could fall apart.

But when she came out of the dressing room, Royal was still standing there. He had the roses. The hopeful smile on his handsome-as-fuck face. The walk to the bus felt like miles. Her feet hurt in the high heels. In the bus she'd have to face Damián, the site of her latest fuck-up. Royal looked like an oasis in the desert.

"Baby girl," he murmured in her ear. "Let me take you home with me."

Deza couldn't quite bring herself to speak, but she nodded, and they left together.

Chapter 18

Chicago

A little before Deza's eleventh birthday, Zeus moved out for a while. At first, Deza was grateful for the reprieve. But soon Jenisse's rage found a new target. Everything, apparently, was wrong with Deza. From the way she looked to the way she spoke. Her grades weren't good enough, but she was a mouthy know-it-all. She was never fast enough to respond to Jenisse, but she was somehow also underfoot too much and Jenisse couldn't get any space.

Jenisse was "too stressed." Everything was on her "last nerve." She started going out. Sometimes she left groceries, sometimes she didn't. The girls got breakfasts and lunches at school. None of Zeus's income was legal and they were poor on the books.

Now Deza often had to cook dinner for herself and her sister as well. On weekends, they scrounged through the house and took pennies to the corner store. She learned about a food pantry at her school and got a bag of groceries. When she looked through it, she found big sacks of beans and rice. Deza looked at them with a knit brow, tears filling her eyes.

"Do you know how to cook these?" the woman handing out the bags asked her.

Deza shook her head.

"Wait here," the woman said.

When there was a lull in the line, the woman wrote the instructions on the paper bag with a Sharpie marker.

Deza cooked rice and beans every week after that. She went to the food pantry twice a month. She and Amaru never went hungry, and they used the spare change they could get from Jenisse for treats at the corner store.

Jenisse went out drinking and partying every night. She would eventually come home and crash.

She was generally a ghost to them, except for the rare times she would be at home and awake at the same time as the girls. Then she would fly into a rage.

"What the fuck is wrong with you, Deza?" she would demand. "How come this house is such a goddamn mess?"

The first time, Deza listened to the content of her mother's rant like it was actual information. "Girl, look at this frunchroom," Jenisse said. She told Deza she was "nasty" for living like this. When Jenisse was her age, she had known how to step up when her mama needed a break, how to take care of her younger sister. That Deza was "useless" and "a disgrace." That first time Deza took it all in. She could fix this. She would do better. It wasn't fair, but her mama was obviously hurting with Zeus gone.

That week, Deza cleaned the whole house. She spent her carefully scrounged money on some pine-scented cleaner from the dollar store. Jenisse needed her to step up? She would.

She and Amaru scrubbed both the kitchen and the bathroom. They picked up all their stuff. They did laundry. They even folded it.

On Sunday, she called her grandmother and asked if they

could go to church with her. Of course, she said yes. They took two buses to meet her.

"Why we gotta do all this?" Amaru complained. "I wanted to play with my friends."

"We need to be grateful," Deza instructed her. "The Lord will help us with that."

When they got home, Jenisse was just waking up.

"Hey, Mama," Deza said.

Jenisse nodded in a bleary-eyed acknowledgment and got up to pee. Deza waited for Jenisse to say something about the sparkling bathroom. She said nothing and went back to bed.

That evening, Jenisse got up and took a shower. From the smell of perfume in the bathroom, she was obviously getting ready to go out again.

Deza had been saving this next surprise for something special. She wanted to double it up with the clean house.

"Hey, Mama," she said when Jenisse got out of the shower. "I got all As and Bs on my report card."

She waved the white paper in front of her mother like a flag of surrender.

Jenisse snatched the paper out of her daughter's hand, looked at it, and crumpled it up.

"What?" Jenisse said. "You think this makes you all that now? You shoulda *been* getting good grades. When I wasn't much older than you, I had a job to help pay the bills. School is your only job. You so spoiled. I didn't have none of those fancy clothes. Got teased for wearing gym shoes from the secondhand store."

When Jenisse called her spoiled, something about the word landed with the full force of her mother's disgust. Not just that Deza was a brat, but actually rotten and decaying. And that was when the words began to spool in Deza's head, weaving a net, a shield, a counternarrative to the toxic rain of Jenisse's words.

Spoiled, decaying, that's what she's saying
But she's wrong: I'm fresh! I got it going on
Nothing I've gotten is because I'm rotten
I'm cooking and cleaning and she's not even
  seeing
She doesn't even treat me like a human being
Fuck her and her blindness
Cuz you can't deny this
I'm the one with the future that's glowing with
  brightness
She's the one whose man left cause she's pitiful
  and spineless.

The unspoken burn did two things: It cemented the armor against Jenisse's tirade. And it also cemented her sense of herself. In many ways, it was her mother who forged Deza into an emcee. Jenisse was her first rap battle adversary.

From then on, Deza began to freestyle in her head.

Chapter 19

Outside Rockford, IL

Damián sat on the bus berating himself. The flat Midwestern landscape stretched out beyond the bus windows.

He had seen it all unfold in front of his eyes. The DJ showing up with flowers. The DJ asking to spin *one* song, but then slipping in another one. Him using the song to beg to get Deza back. Damián could see she was not on board at first, but then she started wavering. Fuck! Why hadn't he handled his business right last night? If he had, he could have been the reason she said no to this slick-haired, fake ass motherfucker. Damián knew why men brought two dozen roses. Because they had fucked up and done some shady shit. Damián had brought Lisette two dozen roses early in their relationship when he had smoked some weed with a friend and was kind of trying to talk to this other girl. He and Lisette weren't exclusive yet, but had already started having sex. He'd stood Lisette up, and when he saw her again, he came with two dozen roses. But unlike this clown, Damián had come through. Locked it down and didn't stray after that. This dick undoubtedly had a frequent flyer card at some Chicago florist.

After the set, Damián saw the two of them standing closer

and closer together. Deza touching his arm, his shoulder, poking him playfully in the chest.

Damián's own chest was a dull ache. His stomach a churning ball of heat. But there was nothing he could do. He had blown his chance. He had to listen to the laughter and the hum of cozy conversation.

Stay cool, he willed himself. *You just need to hold out till it's time to get on the bus.* He would figure out how to get her back. Once they got on the bus, he would do whatever it took to build their connection back up. *Deza, I messed up the other night. Tell me what you need from me to make it right? I have mad respect for you as a performer, and I'm really attracted to you as a woman. You can call the shots. How do you want this to go?* Yeah, he wanted to be her man. But he knew the only way to make that possible now was to put the ball in her court. No pressure. She obviously had pressure enough.

The apology ran in his head. He wanted it to be smooth when it came out of his mouth:

Deza, I messed up last night.

Deza, I messed up last night. Tell me what you need from me to make it right?

The rhyme was unintentional. Should he keep it? Toss it. He didn't want to seem fake. Or worse, like he was imitating the other DJ.

Deza, I messed up last night on the bus. Tell me what you need from me to make it right?

Deza, I messed up . . .

"Hey, Damián," Claire called. "Time to hit the road."

"What?" Damián said. "Deza's not out yet."

"She's spending the night in Chicago," Claire said. "She'll fly to meet us in Minneapolis."

Damián's breath stopped for a moment. Across the parking lot, he saw a couple getting into a big SUV. He couldn't see for sure if it was Deza and Royal. But somewhere inside, he knew.

He got on the bus, his heart heavy and his stomach sick.

Deza woke up the next morning in Chicago feeling sleepy but satiated. She expected to cry with Royal, but she hadn't. They had stayed up half the night making love, but also catching up. He had been following her career and showed genuine joy at her success.

"You're going all the way, baby," he said. "I always knew you could, and you would."

She told him about the Rock.it endorsement deal, and he encouraged her to take it. "No question, Daze," he said. "It's the chance of a lifetime. You can't think small. You gotta know the sky is the limit for you."

It was only seven thirty in Chicago, but business was open in New York. Royal held her hand as she called her management and told them she would take the endorsement deal. This was how she had always wanted it to be: the two of them as a power couple. Jay-Z had cheated on Beyoncé and she had forgiven him. This could be her own *Lemonade*.

Royal brought out a diamond necklace with a D pendant. "Will you be my woman again?" he asked. "Just you and me. Nobody else. Like it shoulda always been?"

She cried and said yes. They took dozens of selfies to post over the next few weeks till they could see each other again. #PowerCouple

She would rejoin the tour in Minneapolis in a long-distance relationship.

At a rest stop in Madison, Wisconsin, a few of the other artists came off the second bus to smoke.

Anasuya came out and saw Damián, who didn't usually smoke, had bummed one from Vienna's drummer.

"You taking up the habit?" she asked.

"Can't sleep," he said.

"Stimulants aren't gonna help," she said. "But I'm hoping to have a little more space tonight. Okay by you if we join your bus?"

Damián shrugged. "I'm just along for the ride."

Anasuya and one of the band members took the third compartment on Deza's bus.

At breakfast the next day, Damian and Anasuya sat next to each other at a diner in St. Paul.

"You get any sleep?" she asked.

Damián shook his head. "I dozed a little. You?"

"Slept great with all that room," she said. "I think the militants on our bus are ready for a peace treaty. I never had anything against Deza, myself, but she did cuss out that other DJ, and I promised to be in solidarity with any other artist who was being mistreated by someone higher up. Of course, I was thinking more like sexual harassment from a label exec than a meltdown of a new headliner, but solidarity is solidarity. Want a French fry?"

The two of them sat together on the bus. Anasuya praised his remixes. She had seen him spin once in New York. She liked his work. He liked her style. She was a singer-song-writer type. He suggested that they could collaborate sometime if she wanted a bigger sound than just girl and guitar. She didn't like to work with DJs live, but maybe they could work on some remixes.

"So you always have insomnia?" she asked. "I've never seen you at the late-night smoke stops before."

He shook his head. "It was a rough night for me," he said.

"Something happen in Chicago?" she asked.

"I just—" he started. "I think I'm falling for Deza."

Her mouth opened into an O.

He hadn't meant to blurt it out. But there it was. True. And incredibly painful.

"And she stayed in Chicago," Anasuya said, nodding, reading between the lines. "I figured she stayed with her family. But maybe it was that DJ guy? Royal?"

Damián could only nod.

"Ugh," Anasuya said. "Tough break. Especially since the two of you are stuck on a bus for the next several weeks."

"Tell me about it," Damián said.

"Well, on the bright side," Anasuya said. "We're all on your bus now. We can be a little bit of a buffer."

Damián nodded. "I'll take any buffer I can get."

Deza rolled into Minneapolis just in time for the sound check. She felt jubilant. But things were chilly between her and Damián. Now he was the one who was all business. When he suggested a few Prince sample remixes for her set, he might have been a vacuum salesman showing her some samples at a suburban home in the 1950s. Cool. Professional. Not hitting on the housewife.

When she did her set, you could see that her diehard fans liked it, but there was nowhere near the energy and response of their previous shows. It was almost as bad as the flop in Omaha.

But she didn't need to be firing on all cylinders at once. She had an endorsement deal that they would be announcing soon. And she had her man back. Royal. She could still feel the taste of his kisses and the memory of a tingle between her legs.

As they waited for the buses to be loaded up, she called him.

Damián was standing around waiting to get on the bus. Claire was inside giving a no-more-drama-on-this-tour pep talk to the artists who wanted to switch buses, now that Deza would be on as well.

Damián was standing awkwardly outside, smoking a borrowed cigarette, when Deza's phone rang. He could tell by her voice that it must be the DJ. Royal. What kind of fucking pretentious name was that?

It was excruciating to hear Deza's voice get soft, coy. He wanted that for himself. He wanted her to be talking sweet to *him* on the bus. Yes, Anasuya was right. Thank goodness there were other people now. If it were just the two of them, it would be unbearable.

"I miss you already," he managed to overhear a complete sentence. Just the one he didn't want to hear.

"Okay, baby," Deza cooed. "I'll talk to you tomorrow."

Tomorrow would be better. He would be able to get on the bus right after their set. He would carry his AirPods at all times. He was on Clubhouse now, and would just stay plugged in to that social network, and lurk in all his favorite rooms. This would give him the technology, the willingness, and the resolve to always tune her out when she was on the phone with old boy. He would have to. Otherwise, he would never make it.

Wait, Deza thought. *Why are all these artists waiting outside my bus?*

"So Deza," Claire began. "Now that you're off the phone, I have news. These artists will be joining your bus. They all agree that they want a little more space and no drama. I assured them that you wanted the same. Can you confirm that?"

"Absolutely," Deza said. "My bus is your bus. No drama whatsoever."

"Great," Claire said. "Let's head on out to St. Louis."

Damián and Anasuya were sitting in the lounge as the bus sped through Iowa. He was sharing some beat ideas for her album.

"This is amazing," Anasuya said. "I might even reconsider my no-DJ-stuff in the live show."

"See?" Damián said.

"I said I *might*," she said.

Then Deza walked by, talking on her phone. Her laugh had the unmistakable flirtation of a woman in love. She opened the fridge and took out a spring water, then walked back to her compartment.

After she walked out, Damián deflated.

"I'm sorry," Anasuya said. "But bruh, you gotta let that go."

"We made out," he said. "The night before Chicago."

"Ohhh . . . So you know she does like you," Anasuya said. "Yeah, that makes it harder."

"We almost did more," he said. "If only I'd brought a condom, maybe she would be with me, instead."

"Oh shit," Anasuya said.

"I shouldn't have told you that," Damián said. "She deserves her privacy."

"I'm not gonna tell anyone," Anasuya said. "But seriously, my dude, you gotta let it go."

Chapter 20

Oklahoma City

The morning of their Oklahoma City show, a clip went viral on social media. A local radio station had a contest for listeners to call in to win tickets to the concert. One young woman listener sent a video via social media.

In it, the girl was sitting cross-legged on her bed.

"My name is Brandi. I been calling and calling the radio station," she said. "But I can't get through. And I need these tickets. My dad got shot by that same racist cop that killed Shaqana. But he survived. He just in a wheelchair now. But I really need to go to this show, you know. I already listened to Deza, but now, since she knew some kinda way about Shaqana, I feel like we're all connected. And I gotta be there. I gotta bring my dad." Tears began to stream down her face and her voice choked up. "I remember the night he got shot." She wiped saltwater from under her eyes with perfectly manicured nails. "We was calling and calling the police station. Calling and calling the hospital. We even called the morgue. We didn't know if he was locked up or dead or what. Now I'm just calling and calling the radio station. We need these tickets. We can't afford em since my dad's disability barely pays the rent. Please Donna-in-the-Morning. We need these tickets."

The furor over Deza-as-prophet had died down nation-ally, but now that she was so close to where Shaqana had been killed, it all rose up again.

Donna-in-the-Morning offered VIP tickets to the family.

"Claire," Deza, approached the tour manager a little be-fore noon. "I want the Movement for Black Lives at this show tonight."

Claire blinked at her. "Sure," she said. "But . . . I don't re-ally have those contacts."

Deza looked at Claire's pale face, her blond ponytail. She felt stupid. "Of course you don't personally," Deza began. "But I thought . . . I mean, the label had me make that video for M4BL back before the tour."

"Do you remember who you spoke with?" Claire asked.

"I'll look back through my emails," Deza said.

"Great," Claire said. "Get me the names ASAP and I'll set them up with VIP tickets for tonight's show."

Deza dug through her emails and found the right one. She called the publicist and asked to be put in touch with M4BL.

"I can give you the contact I had for their national cam-paign," the publicist said, and shared the email.

Deza sent it and proceeded to fix her hair for the show.

An hour later, she hadn't heard back. She called her aunt.

"Hey, boo," Tyesha said. "How's it going?"

"I—" Deza began

"Actually," Tyesha said. "You'll have to just give me the headlines, because I'm about to go into a marathon meeting."

"I'll make it quick," Deza said. "I need a contact for the Movement for Black Lives in Oklahoma City."

The other end of the line was quiet for a second.

"Wow," Tyesha said. "Okay."

"I have an email for one of the national coordinators, but he's not getting back to me. And the concert is tonight."

"Yeah," Tyesha said. "The leadership of the Movement for Black Lives is pretty decentralized. Lemme see what I can do. I'll text you something within the hour. Love you, boo. Gotta go."

"Love you, too."

After Deza hung up the phone, she set it faceup on the bed. She wanted to see the text the second it came in. She should have set this up days ago. Maybe even before the tour began. It just made her feel more like a fraud. Did she even know anyone in Black Lives Matter—The Movement for Black Lives? She had read their demands before she did the TV shows. Which only reminded her of the awful CNN interview. Then she felt worse.

Fifteen minutes later, Tyesha sent a text with the name and number of a friend of hers in Chicago.

Deza called and a woman's voice answered.

"Hello?" then away from the phone, "Marchand! Get down from there!" Then into the phone. "Sorry. My son tryna break his neck. Who's this?"

"I—I got your number from Tyesha Couvillier," Deza stammered. "I needed a contact number for the Movement for Black Lives in Oklahoma. She said maybe you could help me."

"I probably can," the woman said. "But who is this?"

"Deza Starling."

"Shut the front door!" the woman said. "Girl, we been talking about you. I was gonna reach out to Tyesha to see about getting you to do a benefit concert later this year. Do I reach out to you directly or to your management?"

"Reach out to me," Deza said. She gave the woman her info.

The woman gave her the IG handles of a couple of folks in the area who might be able to help.

"I remember seeing you a few times in Chicago," the woman said. "Sis, you been doing us proud. I couldn't get to that show you just had in Chicago. These kids. But back in the day, me and your aunt used to be out in these streets. I knew your great-aunt, too. You come from a long line of activists."

"I just—" Deza stammered. She wanted to talk to Tyesha, but she couldn't. If this stranger went way back with her family, she decided to take the leap. "I'm new to all this. I feel like I don't really know how to do it."

"Do what, baby?"

"Just . . . you know . . . activism stuff," Deza said. "Like there's a right way to do it and I don't really know. Like I don't have enough information. Or facts. Or statistics or whatever."

"Oh, no, sugar, you are doing a great job."

Deza could feel her body relax under the woman's praise. "Are you sure?" she asked.

"Yes, baby," the confidence in her voice continued to soothe Deza. "You got this. Just do you."

Deza thanked her and hung up. Next, she DM'd all three Oklahoma activists on Instagram and hustled off to sound check.

I know this is a little random. But this is Deza Starling.

She said where she had gotten their info and asked if they would be willing to come to the show. To speak to the audience.

An hour later, she completed sound check and fished her phone out of her purse. She had a text.

Yes! We'll be there. Thank you!

They went back and forth with details, including planning an after-party on Clubhouse. The organizer gave her two names: Crystal, she/her, and Jean, they/them.

Deza stared at the screen. Had she really set this up? She gave the two names to Claire.

"I think it's great that you're doing this," Damián said to her. "I was thinking, I got this really stripped-down version of 'Almost Home' I been working on. It's like just the beat and a synth sound. Like just a hint, you know?"

"Let's hear it," Deza said.

He played it for her in the dressing room. It was perfect.

It was nearly the end of the show. The crowd was responsive, and Deza was sweating. But she hadn't fully connected with the audience yet.

"Before we do our last number," Deza said. "We wanna invite some friends up here. First up is Brandi, a young woman who was determined to get to this concert. And her father, Terrell."

Brandi came out on the stage, pushing Terrell in a wheelchair.

Deza hugged them both and handed him the mic.

"Five years ago, I was working construction," Terrell said. "I had a job in Shelton, and had stayed late. It was dark, and one of the areas of the construction site wasn't well lit, so I had a flashlight to keep from tripping over anything on my way. I had just finished up and was walking to my car. I still had the flashlight in my hand, but it was turned off.

"On my way to the car, I got stopped by the police. He yelled, 'Drop your weapon.'

"I guess I didn't drop it fast enough, because the officer shot me. I was lucky to survive. We tried to get the district attorney to press charges, but they wouldn't. Then when we sued, they threw out the case."

The audience booed loudly.

"Well, as some of you already know, that white police officer is the same one that shot Shaqana Miller."

The booing got louder. "Defund the Police," someone yelled when the noise died down.

"I don't know how to tell you what it's been like," Terrell continued. "Doctors say I'm never gonna walk again. I can't work. Can't feed my family. Which is why I appreciate these young people. Up here making sure what happened to me won't happen anymore. Black Lives Matter!"

The audience exploded into applause.

Deza offered the mic to the young woman, but she shook her head.

"Thank you both," Deza said. "Now, don't go anywhere. I wanna invite two activists from the Movement for Black Lives. Crystal came all the way from Tulsa. And Jean came all the way from Dallas. Show them some Oklahoma City love."

Jean took the mic. "Thank you, Deza," they said. "Thank you for choosing to shine your light on this epidemic of police violence in our nation. And it's not just the killing and harming of Black bodies by the police. It's the economic violence, the cultural violence, the entire structure of the society that is designed to promote Black death and exploitation. But we have become the biggest movement in US history by fighting back against all of that. We had three main demands and the first one we already achieved. We defeated our white nationalist president. Our next two demands are defunding the police and investing in our communities. Because we won't stop our movement until we transform the United States into a place where Black people don't just survive but we thrive. And that means *all* Black people. Women, men, trans, nonbinary and queer folks, poor folks, folks with disabilities. No one is expendable. No one left behind. Our ancestors have been fighting since we got here, and we won't stop till everybody is free!"

The applause was so loud that Deza felt the sound vibrate inside her chest.

"If you wanna defend Black lives, if you wanna join our movement, text DEFEND to the number above and it'll go to the Movement for Black lives."

From the stage, Deza could see the glow of phones coming out.

Underneath all the speeches, Damián had been playing a stripped-down track of "Almost Home."

Deza thanked her guests and they exited the stage.

"A while back," Deza said. "I wrote a song about a girl. Like me. Who lived in the hood. Who was coming back from school. Who got shot and killed by a police officer."

She glanced over at Damián. He was still playing the spare track.

Their eyes met and he nodded slightly.

"I coulda named her anything," Deza said. "I considered many different names. Because it could be any of us getting killed. Like they said, that Black person could be male, female, trans, nonbinary, younger, older. Black folks from all walks of life are in danger from the police in this country."

Thump! Damián scratched in a bass note to punctuate her statement.

"I hadn't yet been signed to Paperclip Records. I didn't know it would end up on an album that would have national reach. And I certainly had no idea that I would be standing on a stage in Oklahoma City talking to an audience that had been through something so similar to what I rapped about. People want to call me a prophet? I want to call the system racist. People want to say this is special? That's the whole point. How not special it is. How the killing and brutalizing of Black people is so ordinary it doesn't even always make the news." She gave Damián a sideward glance. "And the Movement for Black Lives is here to say *we are not gonna take that anymore*!"

With an old-school DJ scratch, Damián started the full background track to "Almost Home." The audience was on their feet. Screaming. Testifying. Wailing. It was even more intense than New Orleans.

Deza herself started to cry in the middle of the song. She had to start a verse over. She was so grateful that at least her eye makeup was waterproof.

Damián knew how to restart the track in the right place, and she picked it back up and finished the song.

At the end, Damián spoke, too—through his samples. He scratched in Malcolm X saying, "We see America through the eyes of someone who has been the victim of Americanism." It was from Malcolm's speech, "The Ballot or the Bullet." And then, as the song faded and it got quieter, the listener realized that it had been playing softly throughout the song the whole time.

The audience was thundering for more, but Deza shook her head and rushed off stage. No encore. She sat in her dressing room and sobbed by herself.

At eight the next morning, she still hadn't talked to Royal. He hadn't called back before they played Oklahoma City, just sent her a shoutout on Instagram, and privately DM'd her a heart. But he didn't actually call until during her concert set. And he knew when she'd be onstage, because he had sent out the info on his Instagram. He left a voice mail.

She blinked as the memory came to her. That was the same thing he used to pull when they were together. He would always say, "I called you," but he had timed it when he knew he would only have to leave a message.

Did this mean he was back to cheating? *No, girl, don't go off the deep end about this.*

She had tried him again, after the show. His Instagram said "active now," but he didn't pick up.

She had gotten a message from her manager that she had made the Freshman issue of *XXL*. She would be one of the debut artists on the cover. Of course, this was huge. Really one of the best things that could happen for a rapper's first album. But she couldn't manage to feel excited about it. Her man ghosted when she needed him and she was about to walk into the house of a woman whose daughter's death she had low-key predicted. What good did a magazine cover do her right now?

She looked at her phone for the last time before stepping

out of the taxi in front of the light blue, single-story house in Shelton, Oklahoma.

After the show, the two activists had given her the address and encouraged her to visit. Deza looked down at the paper: 2643 Lincoln Avenue.

She had made all the arrangements. A hotel. A taxi. A plane ticket to catch up with the bus. If she could do it to spend the night with Royal, who wasn't even fucking calling her back right now, she could certainly do it for this family.

Deza stepped out of the cab. They had arranged that he would wait. Shelton was not a taxi town. It was an hour and a half from here to the airport. The timing was tight.

Deza's heels were unsteady on the brick walkway. In her tour wardrobe, she only had tall heels, sneakers, and house slippers. She wanted to look respectful toward this grieving family. Sneakers wouldn't do.

On either side of the brick walkway was what had until recently been a well-tended garden. Pink rosebushes on either side, and other flowers Deza couldn't name.

Weeds had started moving in. From her dim memory, she recalled gardening with her great-aunt at the urban center. From the size of these weeds, Deza could tell that this garden had been well tended until a few months ago.

Deza made her way up the walkway and knocked on the blue door.

She might as well have worn the sneakers.

The woman who answered the door was the opposite of put together. So far from the carefully coiffed mother Deza had seen in video clips.

The woman wore her hair back in a stiff ponytail. Her ends were straightened, but her roots were kinky, with a sprinkle of gray at the temples. She had on a T-shirt. A robe tied at the waist. No bra. House slippers.

She was maybe in her early thirties, but grief had hardened her pecan brown face. She wore no makeup and had a few lines on her cheek from a pillowcase.

"I'm sorry," she answered the door with an apology. "I overslept my alarm." She pulled the robe closed at the neck.

"It's fine," Deza said. "Thank you for making time to see me."

She introduced herself as Monique, and invited Deza in. Deza declined her offer of tea, but Monique went ahead and made some for herself.

Deza sat at the cluttered table. The house was as disheveled as its occupant. There were empty cardboard boxes all over the small living room furniture. In the kitchen, the sink was full of dishes.

"The girls from Black Lives Matter told me that the concert was really good," Monique said as she poured hot water from the kettle. "I thought about going, but I just . . . I'm not really one for crowds these days." She brought her tea to the table.

"Understandable," Deza said.

Monique sat down and moved the pile of newspapers and unopened mail aside.

Underneath it was a photo album. "Shaqana" was written across the cover in glittering letters.

"She made it herself," Monique said as she put sugar into her mug.

As Monique sipped her tea, the two women looked at photos. The first in the album was of a young Monique with a heavy, pregnant belly, eating cake. "My nineteenth birthday," she explained.

And then baby Shaqana. Toddler Shaqana. Preschool Shaqana.

She was a good student. She ran track. She loved to bake. She was crafty. They went to church sometimes. Monique's own mother was a little overboard with it.

Deza laughed and talked about her grandmother, who was super-saved, too.

"When it happened, though," Monique said. "I wondered if Mama had been right. If I shoulda been in the church more or been praying more or something."

"No," Deza said. "We can't blame ourselves for these killer cops. Besides, I know your mother must have prayed every day for your daughter."

Monique suddenly laughed. "Cover her, Lord," Monique began.

Deza joined in, emphatically, just as her grandmother had always said it: ". . . with the blood of Jesus."

Monique laughed and then, in a twist of tone, the laughter turned to tears. "But it wasn't Jesus's blood. It was my baby's blood." She lay her head on top of the pile of mail and newspapers and sobbed.

Deza scooted over and put her hand on Monique's back.

"On God, I don't know what the hell to do with myself," Monique said. "These nice white people gave me a paid leave of absence from work. I used to be always busy with Shaqana. And now I got nothing to do with myself all day. My friends all working and got they own kids. They come see about me on the weekends. What the fuck am I supposed to do?"

The wave of tears slowly ebbed away.

The two of them sat in the silent house. The only sound was the nearly inaudible swish of Deza's hand against the fabric of the robe as she patted Monique's back.

"Let's go weed your flower bed," Deza blurted out.

"What?" Monique asked, wiping her face on a napkin.

"I mean—you—you got a beautiful garden," Deza stammered. "It's a shame to see those flowers get overrun by weeds. Come on." Deza stood up. "I got a few minutes before I gotta catch this plane. Let's do it."

"I'm not dressed," Monique said. "I should at least put on a bra."

Deza shrugged. "Just get a sweatshirt."

Monique put on a zip hoodie from a hook near the door, and the two women walked out into the cool morning.

Deza took off her high heels and knelt in the dirt, her indigo jeggings getting grass-stained at the knees.

"Oh my lord," Monique said. "I hadn't really looked at this garden. These weeds going crazy."

"Last time I did this I didn't have these stupid nails," Deza said. She had trouble getting a strong grip, because she couldn't make a tight enough fist to pull the bigger weeds.

"You just get the little ones," Monique said. "I'll get the big ones."

Monique gritted her teeth and pulled hard on some crabgrass, and it ripped up along a strand of roots.

Five minutes later, the two of them had a sizable pile of uprooted greenery.

Deza sat back on the grass, adding stains to the butt of her jeggings as well.

"I'm sure you've gotta go," Monique said as the two of them brushed off their hands. "Thank you so much for coming by. And thank you for your song."

"I just—" Deza waved away the appreciation. "I feel so strange about it, Monique. People wanna act like it's more than what it was—just a coincidence. Really what matters is how sorry I am for your loss. And that our people need to keep fighting to make sure that it doesn't happen anymore."

"Yeah, but I thank you," Monique said. "Because of you, everybody is gonna know my baby's name. She won't be forgotten."

The two women stood and hugged each other. Both getting a little dirt on the other's back.

"Where you headed next?" Monique asked.

"Santa Fe," Deza said. She brushed her hands on the thighs of her jeggings. She was hoping to save the shirt from getting dirty. "You going back in?" Deza asked Monique.

"No way," Monique said. "I'm fixing to get my gardening stuff. I got gloves up in here somewhere. And tools. These weeds bout to go."

Deza smiled and hugged her again.

She walked back to the taxi with her high-heeled sandals in her gritty hand.

On the plane, she had three missed calls from Royal. She couldn't quite bring herself to call him back. He had missed so much of it. The concert. Last night, when she had been so anxious about the visit to see Shaqana's grieving mother. Deza had been filled with nervous questions: What should she say? What if the woman broke down? And then Monique had broken down. And it had been okay. Better than okay.

As she waited on the plane for takeoff, she tried her aunt. It rang to voice mail, and Deza hung up. Just then she got a text from Tyesha: **Meetings all day. Everything ok?**

Deza texted back: **I'm good. Love you.**

She scrolled through Instagram. A photo on social media had gone viral, showing Deza and Monique kneeling in dirt. Deza's sparkling gold sandals lying on the bricks in the foreground.

Who had taken it? She hadn't noticed anyone.

Yet the photo had nailed it. Something about letting the glamor go for what really mattered. She found herself longing to talk to Damián. He would get it. He had been at the concert.

She realized she couldn't call him. She didn't even have his number. But then the announcement came that it was time to turn off phones for their short flight from Oklahoma City to Santa Fe.

* * *

When Deza got to the venue in Santa Fe, the bus wasn't there yet. She walked alone into the stadium, and texted Claire, who responded ten minutes later.

Bus broke down a couple hours outside town.

Deza was scrolling on her phone when a young white woman walked in and asked where she could find Deza's bus.

When folks from the venue told her there was a delay, the girl asked where to leave the gas.

That was when Deza recalled her promise to check the filter with every delivery of biodiesel gas. She hadn't done it since before Chicago. Damn. She texted Claire:

What's wrong with the bus?

Some problem with the fuel line. Fixed now. Be there soon.

When the bus finally pulled in, Deza and Damián both rushed to apologize.

"I can't believe I forgot to check like we promised," Damián said.

"Nah," Deza said. "I'm the headliner. I shoulda been responsible."

"Well, the mechanic said that biodiesel is cleaner than regular diesel," Damián explained. "It sort of cleans all the deposits out of the gas tank and they get caught in the fuel line."

"Sounds nasty," Deza said.

"It should be clear now," Damián said. "But I'll still check after every show."

"Thank you," Deza said. She had originally wanted to suggest that maybe they could do it together—like they had before Chicago—but now it felt awkward.

"See you at sound check," she said, and boarded the bus to change clothes.

Deza came out of her compartment later that afternoon and heard Damián and Anasuya laughing together in the lounge. Comparing favorite '80s and '90s songs they'd always wanted to sample.

"Ma, I woulda had you pegged for Arrested Development," Damián said.

"That's the obvious choice," Anasuya said. "But what about slowing down some of those rumpshaker-type tracks from the early '90s?"

"Slowed down?" Damián said. "Okay . . . I'm trying to imagine . . ."

"Like 'Tootsee Roll,'" Anasuya suggested. "But like at half tempo."

Damián leaned back in his chair and laughed.

Were they flirting? Internally Deza sucked her teeth. See? It was nothing special. Damián had just been hitting on the only sister on the bus. The minute there were more, he was going after the next one. Just like a dog.

She opened her compartment door and the two of them turned to her.

"Hey," Damián said.

"Welcome back," Anasuya added as Deza came out and got a bottle of water.

"How did it go?" Damián asked.

"Good," Deza said. "I just need a minute to myself."

"Of course," Anasuya said. "See you at sound check."

Deza closed the door behind her. She was so glad she hadn't hooked up with Damián. But she was also starting to question her choice with Royal.

It really started with Deza, but Damián realized it was bigger than her. He noticed how much he loved collaborating with women artists, because they didn't let their egos get in the way, like the men did. In particular, with Anasuya it was even better in some ways, because she had a man, and there was no question of romantic confusion. The two of them would work together in the lounge for hours, making beats for the album. The entire bus was alive with music, Anasuya singing to the tracks and playing her guitar. It was a joy.

Yet the work wasn't as intense as it was with Deza, and he still missed her so much. She was right there, of course. Every hour of every day. In the same vehicle. In the same building. On the same stage. He didn't miss *her*. He missed what it had been like when they had a more intense connection, when it seemed like there had been potential for more. So much more. It was different than with Anasuya because he didn't just make the beats for her, the two of them performed together on stage. It was an intimate conversation between the two of them, with only a stadium full of people watching. Not just the sexual attraction, but the creative chemistry. And every time Deza walked by on the bus, or even backstage, or when they went out there together, he felt a pang for all that could have been. But he saw the Instagram lovefest between her and her man. Royal seemed to have it cuffed up.

Chapter 21

Phoenix

The day after their concert in Santa Fe, Claire asked Deza to join her for lunch. They didn't often stop for midday meals, usually got takeout, but this time Claire wanted a sit-down with just Deza.

Uh-oh. Deza had the feeling she was in trouble. Like when she would get called into the principal's office. But for what? She tried to flip through any possible things she had done. And her mind went back to the spot where it kept returning—especially since Royal had stopped calling as much—to that kiss with Damián. Had Damián said something? She was sort of like his supervisor. Was that kiss technically sexual harassment? Ugh. How had she become that girl? The one female that some asshole could bring up to say "See? Sexual harassment goes both ways!" Still, Damián didn't seem like he would snitch about it. And if it wasn't that, what else could it be?

Deza stepped off the bus, still startled by the dry air in the Southwest. She would be sure to drink extra water.

Claire gave everyone an hour for lunch in downtown Phoenix. For their meal, she picked a café that served sandwiches and salads.

The place was well-lit and cheerful. If she hadn't been so nervous, Deza would have really enjoyed the change from cavernous amphitheaters that were bare and dark until the bright, man-made lights bore down on her.

She looked out at the low-slung buildings of a western town. The drive through the Southwest had been stunning, with its hills and deserts and huge outcroppings of rock.

"I used to visit when my aunt lived here," Claire said. "This was our spot. She lives in Salt Lake City now."

"Cool," Deza said. "It's nice to have things that are familiar when you're on the road."

Deza still felt like a child sitting in a plastic chair in the principal's office. Claire wasn't that much older than her, but she was white and represented the label. Deza felt a pull to make small talk—to chat like they were friends. But she was trying to be a professional. She wanted to ask about Claire's salad. Wanted to say, "I hope you're not on a diet, girl. Cause you look good just how you are." Claire was the type of thick that Black people liked but white people thought was too fat. Deza resisted the urge toward girl talk. She took a breath and sat up straighter.

"So Claire," she said. "What's up?"

Claire smiled. She looked a little relieved to have Deza ask. But only a little.

Deza's fries came. And in the small bowl she had requested, she mixed the three condiments she had also asked for: ketchup, Tabasco, and barbeque sauce.

"So I want to start by saying that I've been very impressed by how much you've grown on the tour," she began. "We had a very tough start and the DJ substitution. I have to be honest, I was worried. But you've really stepped up. The tour has been doing much better than I thought."

Deza used a pair of fries to stir the sauce. "But?" Deza asked. "I know you didn't call me all the way here to have the 'Wow, you've grown' speech."

Deza dipped the fries and ate them.

"Hang on," Claire said. "Lemme finish the good part: Also the stuff you've been doing with Black Lives Matter. And the climate stuff. It's really powerful. I'm—I'm proud to be part of this."

"Okay," Deza said. "But?" She ate several fries.

Claire nodded. "Yes. There is a but. But the tour hasn't done as well as the label hoped."

Deza's eyes flew open wide. "You're canceling the tour?" she asked.

"No, not canceling," Claire said.

Deza finished chewing and swallowed hard. "I'm fired?" Deza said. "You're kicking me off the tour?"

Claire shook her head. "Deza, no," she said. "Can I finish my sentence?"

Deza took a breath. "Yeah," she said. "Sorry."

"The label thinks that they put a little too much pressure on you when they had you headline and replace Nashonna. Your album, and especially your single, are doing so well, but you haven't been around long enough to have those multi-album, die-hard fans. There was an initial big spike in ticket sales when they announced you, but it hasn't continued."

"But the venues are seventy-five percent full," Deza said. "You showed me the stats."

"That was before, when we were in the East and Southeast. Our numbers in the middle of the country are sagging."

"Well, of course they are," Deza said. "It's hip hop. It's not gonna be as big in Salt Lake City as it is in DC."

"We've accounted for that," Claire said. "And it's not just the ticket sales. It's also the fact that in order to get that seventy-five percent, they've been pouring money into promotion. At least fifteen percent of the seats have been promo giveaways."

"Is the tour losing money?" Deza asked.

"Definitely not," Claire said. "They just want to maximize their return. And the label has been pleased with your performance. But in hindsight, they think they were . . . they maybe jumped the gun . . . that they gambled on the notoriety of the . . . that the coincidence of . . ."

"Shaqana," Deza said.

Claire nodded. It was as if she couldn't quite say the name herself. "They think they may have capitalized on the moment but didn't think it through."

"So if I'm not fired, what are they gonna do?" Deza asked.

Claire took a breath. "They believe that the tour could be more profitable with another headliner. Especially in the middle of the country."

Deza drew back. "They're not gonna promote Vienna over me, are they?"

Claire burst out laughing. "Vienna? Hardly."

"Well then, who're they gonna put up there?" Anasuya was a great singer but had more of a coffeehouse vibe. Like really good coffeehouse, but not stadium-filling material.

"The label wants to bring in an artist from outside the tour," she said. "Someone who's guaranteed to fill the stadiums."

Deza went through the mental rolodex in her mind of who it could be. There weren't that many women artists who could fill a stadium. "I thought Beyoncé was busy with her new movie," Deza said sarcastically. Beyoncé wasn't on their label anyway. The only other big female acts on the label were Nashonna and Vienna.

"Actually," Claire said. "They want a male act."

Deza blinked. Men? "How are they gonna work on our buses?" she blurted out.

"They'll have their own bus," Claire said.

Deza shook her head. "But I thought that this was supposed to be a tour spotlighting women," she said.

"It'll still be mostly female artists, with all the same acts,"

Claire said. "We'll just trim everyone's time a little and cut the local opening act to make room for a stronger headliner that can sell out all the venues."

"And who's the headliner?" Deza asked.

"They've decided . . ." Claire began. As she spoke the words, her face was strained. As if she knew Deza wasn't going to like it. As if she didn't like it, herself. "They're going with Murda Lockk."

"Murda Lockk??" Deza asked. "Are you serious?"

"Dead serious," Claire said.

"Aren't they the whole reason they needed to do this tour in the first place?" Deza asked. "Didn't a pair of teenage girls die backstage at one of their shows?"

"No," Claire said. "That was a different group on the Paperclip label, Dymond Lyfe."

"Oh," Deza said. "Right. So many misogynist artists to choose from."

"Murda Lockk definitely wasn't their first choice," she said. "Nicasio Louis was the number one pick, especially since Anasuya is on the tour. We thought being with his girlfriend would be a big draw. But his next album won't be ready in time for our West Coast dates. They tried to see if they could push production, but the artist put his foot down. He was right. It would have been an inferior product."

Deza tried not to get distracted by the news about Anasuya. Nicasio was her man? Then she and Damián were just friends? *Focus, Deza.* "Okay, but they gotta find someone better than Murda Lockk," Deza said.

Claire opened her mouth, then closed it.

The waitress came and served Claire's salad and Deza's sandwich.

When the waitress was gone, Deza turned to Claire. "What were you about to say?" Deza asked. "Go ahead and say it."

"Between you and me, I agree with you," Claire said.

"And the last thing I need is to babysit artists like that. I . . . actually I threatened to quit. And I demanded a raise. And I demanded the same for all the artists, because those boys are gonna be a royal pain in our ass. And they said yes. For them, it's all about the money. They are gonna make so much damn money off this tour with those guys headlining. Even in the flyover states. They're huge in Salt Lake City."

"But they have so many different male artists to choose from," Deza said, feeling desperate. "What about Thug Woofer?"

"He doesn't want to tour right now," Claire said. "I tried for him. Nicasio. We couldn't make it work. It's Murda Lockk, and they're signing the deal today. It's my job to inform all the artists. I wanted to tell you first, privately, because you're losing your headline spot. It's a courtesy, Deza. They already made the decision."

Deza wanted to cry. She felt humiliated.

Professional. *Keep it professional, Daze.* "Claire, I really appreciate you letting me know," she said. "I need a minute."

She stood up and left her elaborately concocted mild sauce and the fries cooling on the plate. The sandwich was untouched.

Deza was back on the bus, fuming and flipping through Instagram when Claire walked onto the bus. Deza had called Royal when she first got back. She needed his support. Where the hell was he? They had only managed to talk a few days in the last week. He said he was just busy in the studio. But was that really it?

Every day, he said something romantic on Instagram. But was that about her or about self-promotion? She also saw his number of followers grow every day. Hers stayed pretty stable. In other words, he was the one obviously benefitting from the relationship. She watched Damián and Anasuya hanging out. If Nicasio was her man, that explained the times she'd seen Anasuya standing in the corner on her phone. That must be rough. She didn't even have her own compartment.

Deza tried her aunt, Woof, Coco, even her little sister. No one was picking up. She just felt like she needed to check in with someone before Claire announced to everyone that she was being bumped as headliner.

Claire walked over to her with a white paper bag. "I got your lunch to go," she said.

"Thanks," Deza said. She realized she had been a little hasty, walking away from perfectly good food. The snacks on the bus were okay, but they were just snacks.

"I'm gonna make an announcement in a minute," Claire said.

"Can you wait till sound check?" Deza asked, a little desperate.

"Okay," Claire said. "But no later. They may announce later today, and I don't want anyone on the tour to hear it somewhere else first."

"Okay," Deza said. "Fair enough."

She had two hours till sound check.

For the first half hour she ate lunch in her compartment and scrolled through Instagram while waiting for the phone to ring. None of her folks were calling her back?

When she went out to the bathroom, Damián was sitting in the lounge with his headphones on, working on his laptop.

From the rhythmic dipping of his Afro, she could tell it was a fast beat. She stood behind him and watched. She liked the look of him, even from behind. The curls at the edge of his hairline, the fine swirl of hair at the nape of his neck that disappeared down into the back of his T-shirt. He was the perfect combination of hard and soft. She could imagine how that fine down covered the muscles in his back and shoulders.

He turned suddenly.

"Everything okay?" he asked. "Did you want to say something?"

"I—" Deza stammered. "I don't—"

"I mean," Damián began. "I can see in the reflection on the screen that you've been standing there for a minute. Like you had something to say."

"Actually," Deza said. "I—I do."

She slid into the plastic chair across from him. She would have preferred to talk to Royal. Or Tyesha. Someone who would baby her a little. Let her pout about it. But Damián was her work partner. He was going to be affected by this. Like Claire wanted the artists to hear it from her, Deza should probably be the one to tell Damián.

She looked around. The communal areas of the bus were empty right now, but people were always coming in and out of compartments. To get water, snacks, to use the restroom.

She would have preferred to discuss it privately, but going to either of their compartments would send the wrong message.

Deza leaned forward and kept her voice low. "They're replacing me as headliner," she murmured to him. "Claire's gonna tell Anasuya, Vienna n nem at sound check."

"What?" he asked. "That's bullshit. You're killing it out there."

She hadn't expected him to be so immediately supportive. "They want to fill all the venues," she said.

"What kind of fucking double standard is that?" Damián asked. "When their boy band Sandcastle went out last year, they didn't sell out all the venues like they predicted. They didn't change a damn thing on that tour."

"Yeah," Deza said. "But they couldn't have replaced them with anyone bigger. That's what they're gonna do here. I stay on the tour. We both do. But they're bumping me down to second place. They have a bigger headliner."

"Who?"

"Murda Lockk."

"*Canto de cabrón*," Damián yelled. "Are you serious?"

Suddenly, Deza laughed. "That's exactly what I said when Claire told me. I mean the English part."

"It's the only reasonable response," Damián said. He didn't laugh, but he smiled a little.

"I'm really sorry, Deza," he said. Impulsively, he put his hand on hers.

Deza felt the buzz of excitement from the connection, but when she looked in his face, she saw concern. It wasn't a romantic gesture.

"We'll get through this," she said.

"The fans might get ugly when they realize that you're a much better rapper," Damián said. And now he did laugh.

Deza squeezed his hand and let go. Which was good timing, because Vienna came out to the lounge then.

"Claire's gonna announce at sound check," Deza said. "See you then."

She walked back to her compartment and checked her phone. Tyesha, Woof, and Coco had all sent texts explaining why they couldn't pick up. **Is it an emergency?** Tyesha asked. **I can cancel my appointment.**

Nothing serious Deza texted back.

Royal hadn't responded at all, but he had posted another selfie of them on Insta.

When Claire called the meeting, the entire group of artists was assembled on the stage. Deza's stomach was tense and sour. Damián reached over and squeezed her hand again. She squeezed back. He was turning out to be a good friend. Anasuya was standing with her folks. They all turned to look at Claire.

"So, I have some news," Claire said. "Ultimately, I think it will turn out to be a good thing, but it will require some adjustment."

"Is the tour canceled?" Anasuya asked.

"No," Claire began. "But the label was concerned about—"

"Oh God," Vienna said. "Just rip off the Band-Aid."

"I just want to preface this with—"

"Just rip it off already," Vienna insisted.

Claire took a deep breath. "They are adding a new headliner. Not instead of Deza. In addition to."

"Who?" Vienna asked.

"Murda Lockk," Claire said.

There was a moment of stunned silence. A truck groaned by on the street. The wind chimes tinkled on the front of a nearby store.

"Put the Band-Aid back on," Damián said in a high voice. He was going for levity, but it just fell flat.

Deza squeezed his hand again. She appreciated him trying.

"Too soon?" he asked.

"This is your fault," Vienna said, suddenly turning on Deza.

"My fault?" Deza asked. "How you figure?"

"If you hadn't gone all ghetto on your DJ, we would have been an all-female tour," Vienna said. "It was the guy DJ that opened the door a crack. Now the floodgates are open."

"That's not fair, Vienna," Anasuya said. "The label is gonna do what the label is gonna do."

"Seriously, Claire?" Vienna said. "You mean to tell me that the label would have been just as ready to put a testosterone hyperdrive opening act on a tour that was all female?"

"You're both right," Claire said. "If there hadn't been any men on the tour, they would have been less likely to add male headliners. But more likely to just cancel dates."

That shut Vienna up.

"So," Claire said. "They'll be joining us in Salt Lake City. If anyone wants to jump ship, let me know now, and we'll start the paperwork. But I did manage to get us all a ten percent raise. Because these boys are gonna be . . . more work for everyone. Anyone want out?"

Claire looked around at the group. Nobody moved.

"Okay then," she said.

"Which bus are they gonna be on?" Anasuya asked. She looked a little nauseous.

"Oh God," Claire said. "They'll have their own bus. The label owes you that much."

"Thank God for the little things," Damián murmured to Deza.

Chapter 22

Chicago

Sometimes, Deza and Amaru would sleep at Tyesha's dorm when their mom ghosted, chasing after their dad. Maybe that was when Deza's greater love of hip hop really started, beyond just her own rhymes. It was Deza's searches through Tyesha's eclectic collection of hip hop that introduced her to Missy Elliott, OutKast, Lauryn Hill, Eve, Bone Thugs-N-Harmony, and Lil' Kim. In Deza's teenage world, Drake and Nikki Minaj were always center stage, but Tyesha's collection gave Deza some history and context.

One time, when Deza was in middle school, Tyesha took her and Amaru to a college party. It was like a magical place. The lights were low, and the music was loud, the rhythm hypnotic. Deza had grown up with hip hop as the soundscape to her life. Her mama played it in the house. Her dad played it in the car. On the street, it blasted from people's windows. Or from speakers when they sat on their porches in the summertime.

But this was the first time that she was in the intimate dance space of it. Where it wasn't diluted with the open air of a sidewalk or even a car. The room was the small com-

mon room of a dorm, but the crush of bodies left less
room for the music, it was somehow concentrated. And it
was the music, the puppet master in the room, making
everyone dance on the same beat. It was a mass hypnosis.
A tent revival. That voice. That voice that seemed to come
from everywhere in the room, with the six speakers and
the subwoofer pulsing below. But it was when the DJ put
on Nicki Minaj's "Super Bass" that something changed. All
the previous voices had been male. Men bossing everyone
around, especially the women. But suddenly, there was a
woman pulling the strings. A female voice telling everyone
what to do. Could women really have that much power?
As she watched the college girls shaking and twerking on
the dance floor, swinging their hair and laughing, watched
the college boys swarm to them, transfixed, Deza wanted
to pull those strings, wanted to hold that sway, wanted to
be that voice.

Amaru didn't like to freestyle, but Aunt Tyesha did. They
would go on for hours when they had sleepovers at
Tyesha's dorm.

"I'm a sexy bitch—" Deza began one day, and Tyesha interrupted.

"Girl," her aunt said, "what you know about being a sexy
bitch?"

Deza cocked her head to the side. "Auntie Ty," she said,
sucking her teeth. "Grown men been calling me sexy since
I was eleven. And that's the nice shit they say."

Tyesha rolled her eyes. "Girl, I know," she said. "Creepy
ass dudes. Same shit happened to me when I was your age.
But that's what they tryna say about you." Tyesha put a
hand on Deza's shoulder. "What you tryna say about yourself? You all about that sexy bitch life? In hip hop—if some
shit is fake, people feel it. Don't just copy other female rap-

pers out there. What you tryna say? You oughtta rap about what you know,"

Tyesha had started the rhyme:

> *Black girl, Black girl, so much to say . . .*

The two of them sat on the sidelines of the college basketball court while Amaru practiced.

Deza picked up the rhyme where Tyesha left off:

> *Black girl, Black girl, so much to say*
> *So many obstacles get in the way*
> *But we ain't scared of this big, bad world*
> *We gon be there for you, badass Black girl*

Amaru drove toward the basket and did a layup. First on the right side of the basket, then the other. Then she did both sides again, shooting with her left hand. She didn't run straight, but in an irregular pattern, as if she were imagining opponents trying to block and guard her. The ball hit the backboard and went into the net every time.

> *Bitches tryna hate*
> *Tryna bring me down*
> *Smiling in my face and spreading rumors*
>   *all around*

Deza went on for a while about "jealous bitches" who were gonna get what they deserved.

"You got girls giving you a hard time at school?" Tyesha asked after she was done.

"Yeah," Deza said. "But I was also thinking about my mama."

Tyesha raised her eyebrows.

"Why does she have to be such a complete bitch to me all the time?" Deza asked Tyesha quietly.

It was no secret that her mother and her aunt did not get along. Besides, Tyesha was a young aunt, closer in age to Deza than her mother, and the kind of adult you could talk to.

"It's not about you," Tyesha had said. "Jenisse doesn't think about other people. She's not really mother material."

"Who you tellin?" Deza said. "I think she had us as accessories. No way to get Zeus as a baby daddy without any babies."

Tyesha sighed. "Your mama loves you in her own way. Lord knows our own mama didn't really provide much of a model."

"At least the only man Grandmama is always chasing after is Jesus," Deza said. "She can always find him at the same church, and he keeps daylight hours."

"Real talk, girl," Tyesha said.

"With Jenisse," Deza said. "It's like I'm the mama and she's the teenager."

"Well, if you're the mama," Tyesha said, "and you call on me when you need help, what does that make me?"

"My own personal Jesus," Deza said.

The two of them laughed. But the next year, Tyesha transferred to Columbia in New York City.

Chapter 23

Salt Lake City

It made sense that the tour was deep into the western part of the US when Murda Lockk came on the scene. It was like an old gunslinger movie, where the bad guys come into town and walk slowly down the main street. Deza and her crew came walking down the street from the other direction.

In reality, it wasn't a street. Instead the two groups walked toward each other across a stadium stage. On one side was Deza, Damián, Anasuya, and Vienna's whole band. Although Murda Lockk was officially two rappers and a DJ, there were just as many people on their side of the stage.

"Who are all those guys?" Anasuya asked Deza in a murmur.

Deza murmured back, "The entourage."

The two rappers were brothers: Lil Trey and Nasty Axe. The DJ was Swampman. Deza recognized those three. The hangers on were a typical half-dozen guys in designer clothes and gaudy jewelry making noise with no purpose.

"Hey, ladies," Lil Trey said, giving the women a nod and a grin.

"It's been a brick since we had girls on the tour," said Nasty Axe. "I like it." He said the last part with a bit of a leer, even though Deza noticed that all of the women had dressed far more modestly than usual.

As had Claire. She stepped forward and shook hands with the three male artists. "Welcome, Trey, Axis, and Sawyer," she said, calling them by their government names. "And welcome to all your people. It's good to have friends and family on the road."

"But we ready to make some new friends," Trey said. "No cap."

"And I'm sure you will," Claire said. "Your fans are already getting very excited for the tour. So here's what I need to let you know, especially since you have so many friends joining you. Your crew is restricted to your dressing room and they have special passes. Everything you could possibly want is back there: food, drinks, restrooms. You are welcome to invite guests backstage, but everyone needs to be at least eighteen. Twenty-one if you have any alcohol." She gestured to a security guard. "Rafael here will be carding people."

"Seriously?" Trey asked. "What if some of my friends didn't bring ID?"

"Then your friends can wave to you from the audience," Claire said.

"This is bullshit," Axis said.

"It's in the contract you both signed," Claire said. "You gotta read the fine print."

"Don't worry about the backstage," one of the guys in the crew said. "That's why we got the bus."

"Okay," Trey said. "Rafael won't be babysitting us on the bus, will he?"

"Nah," Rafael said. "I'm with the venue, not the tour. We not tryna get sued."

"So there you have it," Claire said. "Follow the rules, and nobody gets sued. Let's go ahead and start sound check."

* * *

That night, after the show, Damián trooped out the back-stage door to the bus. Deza appeared to have caught Royal on the phone after the show. She was talking to him with that bright smile and that glowing face she had after she performed. It was one of her faces he liked the most. He found it irresistible. Her charisma. Before The Great Mistake, he had been the one she came to with that face. Not anymore.

He trooped onto the bus and checked the fuel filter with his phone light. It looked clean, so he boarded the bus and went to his compartment. The door stuck sometimes, and you had to push hard. When the door swung open, Anasuya was sitting on the bed.

"What the fuck, Damián?" she asked.

"What are you doing in my spot?" he asked.

"Claire said she was moving me here," Anasuya said. "She said you already knew."

"What?" he asked. He turned and strode down the aisle to find Claire.

The blonde was outside, supervising the loading of equipment onto the bus.

"What's up, Claire?" Damián asked. "How come Anasuya's in my spot?"

"You've been moved, Damián," Claire said.

"To where?" he asked.

"To the guys' bus," she said. "Now that we have one."

"Since when?" he asked.

"Since we amended the tour," she said.

"Yeah, but you weren't gonna tell me?" he asked.

"It was all in the amended contract you signed," she said. "I saw it myself. You initialed that you understood that you would need to move. And that you were going to get your personal items out before showtime. Which you didn't. And I had to do it myself. Which I did not particularly appreciate."

Damián had a vague memory of an email that day. And an online portal where he checked boxes and put initials. Just like when an app said they had changed their terms of service. Nobody actually read that shit. He was on tour with Deza. It was the opportunity of his life. Of course he was going to sign the new contract. But he probably should have read it.

"I'm really sorry," Damián said. "In the future I'll be more professional. I'll go apologize to Anasuya."

Damián walked over to the Murda Lockk bus like a man heading to his own execution. The bus itself was shrink-wrapped in brightly colored graphics and lots of gold paint. The driver was outside, smoking a cigarette.

"Hey, man," Damián said. "I'm the DJ with one of the other acts. The label says I'm joining the guys' bus."

"Yeah," the driver said. "They gave you the back compartment, by the bathroom."

Damián nodded and climbed on board. He stepped into a cloud of marijuana smoke. Damián had smoked a bunch in high school, but he rarely did it now that he was DJing more seriously. He liked the high feeling when he was hanging out, but it lingered and made him feel foggy. He made his way quickly down the center aisle of the bus, which was a mess of empty snack containers, pizza boxes, and liquor bottles. Damn. They must have partied really hard on their last night before the tour.

In the compartment, the weed smell was a little less strong, but he opened the window anyway. When he turned back, that was when he saw the used condom.

Ugh.

He went into the lavatory and got some toilet paper to pick it up. *Asqueroso.*

He flushed it and went back into the room. He didn't want to set his bag down on the floor. He hung it up on the luggage hook. Then he looked at the bed. Did he want to sleep on those sheets?

He peeled the sheet off. It still grossed him out. He flipped the mattress over. Something about that helped. He texted Claire to ask how he might get some clean bedding.

You're in luck, Claire said. **They have housekeeping scheduled for tomorrow.**

He asked if they could bring a fresh comforter, too.

After he sent the text, Damián surveyed the bed. He took the pillowcase off the pillow and put a T-shirt on it. Then he lay down fully clothed. He could sleep in sweats and socks. He didn't want any part of the bare mattress touching his skin. It would be just one night before he got fresh bedding. He could manage one night.

And maybe he could have, if it had just been the bed. But it wasn't. An hour after he had settled in, the crew climbed onto the bus. And they weren't alone. The three guys, their entourage, and clearly a number of young white women as well.

They played loud music and talked even louder.

Damián put on his most expensive DJ noise cancellation headphones. He had almost fallen back asleep when somebody started fucking in the compartment next to his. And not quietly.

It was as if the girl was performing for the other guys outside.

"Oh yeah, Nasty Axe, do me good!" she screamed.

The two bodies thudded against the shared wall.

When they were together, Lisette had taught him how to spot a fake orgasm. Through the wall, he got to listen to that as well.

Damián vowed to always read his contracts after this. Always.

He fell asleep an hour later but woke up some time in the early morning to the sound of someone puking in the bathroom.

Had he actually landed in hell?

When he woke again at six in the morning, the bus was finally quiet. He had to pee. But one look inside made it clear that the lavatory was not an option. Whoever had puked had only gotten half of it into the toilet. The seat was covered. And no one had wanted to put the seat up after that, so there was piss splatter all over.

Damián backed out. He decided to do like the dudes who worked in the Amazon.com warehouses, where they didn't get decent bathroom breaks. He picked up one of the empty liquor bottles and peed into it. He capped it back up and was gonna leave it for the guys to find. But then he realized they wouldn't be the ones to pick it up. It would probably be some Black or Latina woman who came to clean. He took the bottle into his compartment. Besides, it was a two-liter bottle. He might need to use it again.

By ten in the morning, Damián was awake for good. The bus was quiet. They had crossed into California and were headed for the Oakland Coliseum.

Outside the bus window, the view alternated between desert and dense green forest. But he couldn't enjoy it. His mind couldn't settle. He kept returning to that moment with Deza. If he had played that right, he might be sharing a compartment with her. They might be the ones fucking in the bus, not him up here listening to this fool and some groupie faking it.

He finally got hungry and ventured outside his compartment. The lounge had two couches, each with girls sleeping on them. And at the table was the DJ for the group, Swampman. He was a dark chocolate brown, and his hair was in a wild Afro with tight kinks, a black fist pick sticking out of it. Classic.

They exchanged nods, and Damián looked in the fridge. Nothing but beer. He looked in the cupboards and saw that all the chip and pretzel boxes were empty. But a few bags of nuts had survived. As well as a lone bag of kale chips. Damián grabbed them both.

He was getting ready to go back to his compartment when Swampman spoke: "Feel free to take a seat," he said.

"Yeah?" Damián said. "Cool."

He sat and opened the bag of nuts.

"Heard about y'all show in New Orleans," he said. "That shit was fye, boy."

"Thanks, man," Damián said.

"Yeah," Swampman said. "The *Rolling Stone* article was good, too." He lowered his voice. "I been trying to get these niggas to try sump different musically, but they all bout the same old shit. You know. They more bout that party life than that musical innovation life."

Damián chuckled. "Yeah, man," he said. "I been working with the women on the tour, and it's so different. It's like a fraction of the ego."

Swampman raised his eyebrows. "I know that's right," he said.

"How do you sleep, though, man?" Damián said. "I'm dead after last night."

"You got good DJ headphones?" Swampman asked.

"Yeah," Damián said. "They didn't cancel enough of the noise."

"The trick?" Swampman said. "Put earplugs in and put the headphones over. Then get some ten-hour rainstorm track and turn it up. Somebody could be getting murdered in the next compartment and I really wouldn't hear."

"Seriously, though," Damián said. "Is it true that Trey killed a man in cold blood?"

"Ay man, I don't know nun bout that shit," Swampman said. "I just play the beats."

"How long you been working with them?" Damián asked.

"Bout a year," he said. "They went through three DJs before me. They twins. They figured out years ago how to share toys and treats. But they don't know how to share with nobody else. But me? I just wanna do my thing. Stack that paper. I got my wife and kids at home. I don't trip off these girls or this party life. I don't fuck with the gas. I like one good drink after a show, and then I'm in bed, boy. Good earplugs? And I don't give a fuck what they do."

Damián nodded. "Facts."

That night, as the bus headed from Oakland up to Seattle, he tried the earphone and earplug thing with the rain sound, and it worked. But it couldn't muffle vibrations. Somebody was having sex in the bathroom, the thumping was right against the foot of his bed

What the hell? How did they even fucking fit in there?

But by the time that racket finally died down, the bus stopped so the driver could take a smoke break.

The next thing Damián knew, there was a woman yelling and banging on the door of the bus. Then she banged on the bus wall. He couldn't make out what she was saying until he took off the headphones. She walked around to his side of the bus and banged on that wall.

"Where my daughter at?" she demanded. "Girl, I did not raise you like that. You better come out here, so I can beat your ass!"

By now, Damián had his earplugs out, and was listening. He could understand why the girl didn't want to come out. Who would?

"I don't believe in calling the police on nobody Black," the woman said. "But my daughter is seventeen. And I will do it if I have to. Because I'm not leaving this bus without my daughter."

The bus door opened and Damián heard the woman walk up the aisle.

"Shut up, bitch," came a drunken male voice. "Ain't no

twelve gonna take your daughter side if she get on a tour bus wit 'Pussy Wagon' on the front."

Damián didn't want to get involved. But he did open his door a crack so he could see out.

She was a thickset Black woman with her arms crossed across her ample chest and a stone-cold expression. "Bring yo lil punk ass out here and say it to my face," the woman said.

Which was when Trey came out with a gun. "I'll shoot you in your motherfucking face," he said.

Was this woman gonna get shot on this fucking bus?

The woman didn't back down. "Then you have to motherfucking shoot me," she said. "Because I been following this bus all the way from Oakland to wherever the fuck we at now. Oregon? Some shit. And I ain't leaving. Without. My. Daughter."

Damián wasn't sure if it was a real gun or loaded or not. But Trey didn't shoot. The two of them just stood there, staring each other down.

"If your daughter a natnat and wanna get on a pussy wagon with a bunch a niggas, then that's on you," Trey said. He held the gun casually.

The woman didn't reply.

Swampman came out of his compartment. "Trey," he said quietly. "Is the girl in there with you?"

"Nah," he said. "I got two strippers in here with me."

"Well then, let's find the girl so this lady can go on her way, okay?" Swampman asked.

"I don't appreciate her coming in and fucking disrespecting us like that," Trey said. "This is my house."

Damián wasn't going to tell him that it wasn't a house, it was a bus. But that was beside the point. He stepped forward.

"Ma'am," Damián said. "If you'll give me a moment, I'll see if I can get your daughter to come out."

"If she ain't off this bus in five minutes, I'm calling the police," she said. "It's a last resort. Black Lives Matter? My daughter's life fucking matters."

Damián nodded. Trey continued to stand there.

The woman turned and strode to the front of the bus, her back ramrod straight. She waited at the bottom of the steps, just inside the bus door.

"Were you just gonna fucking shoot her?" Swampman asked Trey in a low voice.

"It ain't even loaded," Trey said. "I don't think."

"So where this girl at?" Swampman asked.

"I think she in with Axe," Trey said. "He like the young ones."

"You know it's statutory rape whether you ask their age or not," Damián said.

"Tell that to Axe, not me," Trey said. "I like grown-ass women."

Swampman and Damián went to Axe's compartment.

Damián knocked on the door. "Hey," he said. "Uh, party's over. Somebody's mother is here to pick her up . . ." What could he say? What would a girl feel in a situation like this? He tried for levity. "I know it's been mad fun, but it's done, okay? We'll give you a piece of cake to go."

Swampman smiled at him.

Slowly, the compartment door opened. A young woman came out. She didn't look that young, but Damián would have carded her on a blind date. She had her head down as Damián walked her to the bus door.

"You take care of yourself, little sis," he said.

"Ain't no real cake?" she said.

"Nah," he said. "I was just joking."

She nodded and walked off the bus.

One of the two strippers leaned out of Trey's door. "You need to tell your brother to stop fucking those young girls. R. Kelly, Car Willis, and Bill Cosby all went to jail. Shit is changing, baby."

Chapter 24

Chicago

Chalaya had always been Deza's nemesis at school. The girl was clearly jealous of how pretty Deza was: "She think she so cute." In the hierarchy that was color in middle school, Chalaya was lighter skinned, so she should have been considered prettier. But she had bad acne, and her family didn't have the money to keep her hair done. Obviously Chalaya thought Deza was cute. Or envied the fact that other people thought she was. Deza knew people thought she was pretty. But so what? She didn't put that much stock in it. Not since Tyrese Miller, the cutest boy in third grade, had begged to be her boyfriend. He said he chose her because she was so pretty. And then a week later—after their first kiss—had dumped her to be with Vanessa Sanchez. What had pretty gotten her?

Now that she was in eighth grade, she watched her aunt Tyesha. Her auntie did well in school and now had her own room at college. That looked like a strategy that had paid off.

But since she had started middle school, her academics were slipping. She needed something different now, a new plan to get out of her parents' house, out of the hood. To be the boss.

She began to watch rap videos of girls. It seemed that a lot of the girls worked alone. They were the sexy ones. They rapped about sex and relationship drama and how cute they were and not much else. But Deza found a YouTube video of an old hip hop song by Queen Latifah and Monie Love, "Ladies First." Later, she found Queen Latifah's solo song "U.N.I.T.Y." Telling Deza that she had to let everyone know that she wasn't a bitch or a ho. It was the first time she questioned whether or not she wanted everyone to think of her as a bad bitch. It was also the first time she heard female rappers talking about anything other than their big asses and how they could take your man. She wanted that.

And at the recent talent show, Chalaya had been the only girl to rap. Her girls had backed her up with a lukewarm dance number. Deza could do without the dancers, but she needed Chalaya.

Chapter 25

"You need to put me back on Deza's bus," Damián was saying.

"There's no way anyone is going to give up a single to double up. And none of the women wanna bunk with a guy," Claire said.

"He had a gun, Claire," Damián said.

"It's a fake," Claire said. "He waves it around."

"Have you seen it?" Damián asked. "It didn't look fake."

"He has two strikes against him," Claire said. "He would be an idiot to carry an actual gun."

"You telling me Lil Trey is incapable of doing something stupid and self-destructive?" Damián said.

"I'm telling you that's not an actual loaded gun," Claire said.

"So you admit it might be a real gun?" Damián asked. "I'm not waiting around to find out if it's loaded."

"Damián, you signed the contract that you would be on that bus," Claire said.

"How's it gonna go when I publish my story on Insta that he pulled a gun on some mother who came looking for her under-age daughter who was found in his brother's compartment?"

"It's gonna look like your word against his," Claire said. "And you look like a young DJ trying to get attention."

Damián looked out the window at the gray sky and the low-slung houses. Seattle didn't really even look like a city. It was supposed to be a rainy town, but they'd been having a freakish drought season. Global warming.

"Okay then," Damián said. "And if someone does get shot later on, the label will be in a terrible position because there will be a public record that people knew about it and did nothing."

"Damián, I can't get a whole other guy bus just for you," Claire said.

"What if I could get one of the women to bunk with me?" he asked. "Or get them to share?"

"Sure," she said. "If you can do it. But I don't want anyone getting pregnant on my tour, either."

"It's not that kind of party," Damián said. "And how are you worrying about someone getting pregnant on the women's bus? The pussy wagon is what you need to be worrying about."

Claire winced. "That's not really my tour. I'm only managing them under duress."

"I can see that," Damián said. "Sorry to make your job harder."

"Me, too," Claire said. "They make everyone's job harder."

At sound check, he asked Anasuya.

"I would, Damián," she said. "We're cool like that. But my man is coming tomorrow night to our gig in Portland. You could bunk with me tonight. But tomorrow, you're back on their bus."

"I'm desperate," he said. "I'll take it one night at a time."

It was a bunk bed compartment, so it wasn't really a big deal. Like his girl cousin he'd visited in Puerto Rico.

And he was so exhausted from two bad nights on the Murda Lockk bus, he slept like a rock.

* * *

The next day at sound check, Lil Trey approached him.

"Hey boy," he said loudly. "So you didn't come home last night. Heard you was on the ladies' bus. You was getting some?"

"Nah, man," Damián said. "It ain't like that. We're just friends. Your bus was a little too wild for me."

"What's up then?" Lil Trey asked. "You gay or somethin?"

"No," Damián said. "I ain't gay, I'm just not trying to fuck every woman I see."

"If you ain't gay, maybe you a limp dick nigga then," Lil Trey said with a laugh.

"Why you up here talking bout my dick?" Damián asked.

"Ain't nobody talking bout yo dick," Lil Trey said. "But most real men would be glad for a chance to get some left-overs on the pussy wagon."

"Whatever," Damián said and started to walk away.

"What did you say?"

Damián turned around. "Trey, I said 'whatever.'"

"Nah," Trey said. "What you really tryina say?"

"I wasn't really trying to say anything," Damián said. "But if you wanna know what I think? I think your crew was mad disrespectful to every woman that stepped on that bus, including the girl's mother. And that real men are respectful."

"You tryina say I ain't a real man?" Trey demanded.

"Nope," Damián said. "I'm just gonna agree to disagree. Cause I'm not trying to get shot tonight."

"What?" Vienna said. "Did he threaten you with a gun?"

Damián hadn't seen her walking by. He had kept his focus on Trey. Now he met Trey's eye. "Nope," Damián said. "But haven't you heard his song? 'I carry a gun/I shoot niggas for fun'?"

"That's just a rhyme," Lil Trey said, looking down Vienna's shirt. "And you welcome on the bus any time, shawty. You a dancer or something?"

Vienna rolled her eyes and walked on. "You have got to be kidding me."

Damián gave Trey the side-eye and then headed to the green room.

"I can't believe you just spoke up to him like that," Deza said.

"Yeah, but I'm fucked," Damián said. "I'll be sleeping on the couch in your bus lounge tonight."

"Why?" Deza said. "I thought you were bunking with Anasuya."

"I was," Damián said. "But her man is coming tonight. They haven't seen each other in a month. They're not gonna give up their only night together."

"What if we swapped rooms?" Deza asked. "Just for tonight. They can have my double bed. And I'll sleep in Anasuya's bed."

"Seriously?" Damián said. "That would be amazing."

"Of course," she said. "We gotta show a united front against Murda Lockk."

"Anasuya's gonna love this idea," Damián said.

"Yeah," Deza said. "Just tell her to make sure my sheets get changed."

The Portland venue was nearly full, but the crowd was largely white and subdued.

"Last time I was here," Deza told the audience, "I was at Lauryn Hill's twentieth anniversary Miseducation tour. Anybody else here go to that show?"

About a third of the audience yelled that they had. "I just wanna shoutout Lauryn and all the queens in hip hop who came before me. And I hope that twenty years from now, I'll still be rocking stages like Lauryn is. Anyway, her album is all about love, and I got some love songs, too. So here's one of my favorites, and I'll dedicate it to her, because she loved hip hop, even though it didn't do right by her . . ."

Maybe it was the prospect of the sleepover with Damián, but Deza felt somehow shy on stage with him.

Meanwhile, Royal always had that funny intuition with her. Any time she was getting close to some other guy, he always seemed to call. Like a sixth sense. Her phone rang right before the show. And without even looking at it, she knew it would be Royal. They had a connection.

"Just wanted to check in before you go onstage," he said. "How you doing? Those Murda Lockk niggas ain't getting too crazy?"

"No," Deza said. "They're on a whole separate bus."

Why did she feel guilty? She and Damián were just friends. Besides, Royal didn't own her. But people did gossip. If it ever got back to him that she had spent the night in the same compartment as a guy, he would be pissed. But fuck him. He had cheated in the past. Maybe he was cheating again. Nothing was gonna happen with Damián anyway. Royal needed to trust her.

After her set ended, Deza barely registered the host introducing Murda Lockk. She just kept flipping through her mental list of clothes to sleep in. The top was obvious, her Lauryn Hill T-shirt. It was oversize and made of thick cotton. But what to wear on the bottom? Full sweats would be too hot. But the boxers she often slept in were too much like booty shorts. Maybe if she hadn't had so much ass, they would have been unremarkable. She had a pair of cutoff leggings, but they had started to fray, and sort of looked like they had a slit up the thigh. Not the message she was hoping to send. When she really thought about it, she had only prepared for the onstage part of this tour. Bringing her most glam gear. But she hadn't thought much about the time offstage. She could see now why Thug Woofer and Tyesha had encouraged her to bring someone along. The time offstage was long and lonely. She wished she hadn't messed things up with Damián by practically fucking him. It could have been perfect now that she was with Royal.

Damián could have been the homie. Or like they said in corporate America, the work husband. Instead, he was all friended up with Anasuya, and Deza spent her days wishing Royal would call more often. She had gotten a lot more done on her album, though. So there was that.

Maybe tonight they could rekindle the sense of camaraderie. Maybe it could be more like a kids' slumber party. Yes! She could grab some snacks from the green room and take them on the road. Something childish and funny.

She managed to take a bag of popcorn and several mini-boxes of junk cereal. Perfect.

She cut off another pair of leggings that was getting thin at the knee. On her way over to Damián's compartment, Anasuya came up to her.

"Deza, thank you so much," she said. "I know you know what it's like doing the long-distance thing, with your man in Chicago. You're calling and texting, but it's just not enough. You just want that private, in-person time."

"Yes, girl," Deza said. "I understand."

Anasuya leaned forward and hugged her. In the sudden embrace, Deza realized she hadn't been hugged in what felt like a long time. Since Murda Lockk had joined the tour, they had stopped hanging with the fans afterward. The vibe was bad. And she didn't have any friends who lived in this part of the country, anyway. So there was no one backstage with her. She didn't have her own dressing room anymore, so she wasn't isolated in the same way, but it was like being at a new school. Everyone was hanging out and easy with each other, while she sat on the sidelines.

She knocked on Damián's door with a laptop in one hand and a bag of goodies in the other.

"I brought supplies," she said. "I haven't had a slumber party in a long time."

"Oh so it's a party?" Damián said. "Am I supposed to be spinning something?"

"Didn't you have slumber parties as a kid?" Deza asked. "A bunch of friends over and you watched movies and ate junk food?"

"Not really," Damián said. "My family didn't have slumber parties. Just sometimes we'd go to Puerto Rico and I'd have like twenty cousins and we'd all sleep at my grandma's house."

"Was there junk food and movies?" Deza asked.

"Not really," Damián said. "But there was always sweet stuff to eat."

"Okay, well this is how we did it," Deza said. "And I bought a classic movie. *Beat Street.*"

"No way!" Damián said. "I geeked out on that so hard!"

"See?" Deza said. "I knew you could get into the slumber party spirit."

Damián had the tech: a splitter for headphones. The two of them plugged into the laptop. Damián's headphones had a long cord and they were able to sit on opposite ends of the bed. They propped the laptop on Damián's suitcase and watched a South Bronx story of early hip hop that was both corny and classic.

"I remember those dance battles," Damián said. "Before I had a turntable, I thought I might be a dancer."

"And?" Deza asked.

"Nope."

They laughed. And both would try to be the first to point out cameos of famous artists. Deza spotted Doug E. Fresh first, but Damián spotted DJ Kool Herc.

Deza hadn't remembered the romantic part of *Beat Street*. And when Kenny and Tracy had their kiss, she felt an awkward moment.

Deza explained the snacks. "You start with the popcorn and then move to the harder stuff."

"Which is cereal?"

"At a real slumber party, it would have been chocolate, but caffeine keeps me up at night."

"The caffeine in chocolate?"

"I can't mess with it after noon," Deza said.

"We Puerto Ricans would be giving the children coffee at the slumber party. And they would still be crashing out."

"Ugh," Deza said. "Give me coffee at night and I won't sleep for a week."

"You been sleeping okay on this tour?" he asked.

"Not really," Deza said. "At first I felt all this pressure to perform. Then, when Murda Lockk came on, I just felt . . . I don't know. Like I failed."

"What?" Damián asked. "Nah, sis. You've broken so many records with this tour. It's crazy."

"I guess . . . But I just thought it would feel different," she said. "Like more . . . more exhilarating or some shit."

"Like being in a music video?" Damián asked.

Deza laughed. "Right! I know it sounds crazy, but I just . . . I guess it was a pretty immature fantasy. I don't know if this tour life is all it's cracked up to be. Or maybe that's just the sugar cereal talking."

Damián laughed. "Look," he said. "We do music because we want to make other people feel things. And we want to feel them too. Nothing wrong with that."

"I just didn't realize that success wouldn't change the way I feel," Deza said. "Like with every new thing, I get excited for a minute, but then it's back to real life."

"I know," Damián said. "When I got the call for the tour, I was like, 'this changes everything!' But does it?"

"We'll see," Deza said.

"I have this friend who's a recovering addict," Damián said. "He told me something once that really stuck with me: 'I can never get enough of what doesn't satisfy me.' I kept thinking about that shit for weeks. Seems like in this business, we think if we just get more, it'll finally be enough. Maybe we just need to learn that we are enough."

"Hard to feel like I'm enough after Murda Lockk came on," Deza said.

"Yeah," Damián said. "Thank God I'm off their bus. I wish we could go on like we were before."

"What if we did?" Deza asked. "What if we just acted like the concert was over after my set?" She cracked up.

"No, Deza, for real," Damián said. "That's genius. We could just pack up and go."

"I wasn't serious," Deza said.

"Why not?" Damián said. "They're a self-contained unit. They can take their artists, their entourage, their groupies, their liquor, and their weed on a later bus. We can just roll out right after your set finishes. Like 'we out.'"

"Right," Deza said. "What are we waiting for?"

"Nothing," Damián said.

"I think that's the best idea I've had in a long time," Deza said.

"See?" Damián asked. "Things are looking up."

Damián unplugged the headphones from the laptop and carefully rolled up his cords. Then he climbed up to the top bunk.

"You okay down there?" he asked. "Got everything you need?"

"Yeah," she said. "I'm good. Damián, I just gotta say I'm so glad you came on this tour. I feel like I really needed a friend. And since I fucked up so bad with all the girls on here, I really needed a clean slate with someone. Thanks for being so . . . cool about things . . . you know, as we . . . sort of figured out how we were gonna work together."

"Yeah," Damián said. "I think when men and women are developing a . . . friendship . . . it takes a minute to find the groove. Like on the record. There's that static at the beginning and then the song starts."

Deza smiled in the dark.

"Well, we certainly found the groove tonight," she said. "Cooking up rebellions and shit."

"But that's the best part," Damián said. "We're not gonna do anything dramatic. Just leave. Like you know, it was time to go."

Deza couldn't sleep. She heard Damián's breath—heavy, but not a snore—on the bunk above her. Royal's quick call before the show had been the first time she'd actually talked to him in days. She texted him a good night, but he didn't text back. She went on Instagram, and it said he was active now. Had she made the wrong choice in getting back with Royal? When they talked, everything felt right, but he didn't call enough, and the rest of the time, he seemed to be curbing her. Every time she determined that he was an asshole, and she should break up with him, he would call and just be so sweet.

Really, there was no way to know on tour. Afterward, they would need to live in the same city for a while. See what daily life was like. She hadn't brought it up, but maybe she should ask him to move to New York with her. No, that wouldn't work. His fan base was in Chicago. Maybe she was the one who could live anywhere. Anywhere *but* Chicago. Not as long as her mama was there. Maybe they could move in together somewhere else in Illinois. Close enough that they could get to Chicago to record and perform, but far enough from her family. She was finally starting to understand her aunt Tyesha's decision to leave the city.

She fell asleep looking at suburban Illinois real estate on her phone.

The first person Deza and Damián told about the plan to leave early was Anasuya. Really, she was the first person they tried to tell. The singer-songwriter was sleepy and blissed out from her night with her man.

Anasuya agreed, but she might have said yes to hijacking the pussy wagon and leaving Murda Lockk stranded.

"Let's try someone a little more . . . invested," Damián said.

"And less postcoital?" Deza suggested. Was it too soon to joke like that with Damián? He was laughing. Good sign.

"Vienna," Deza said as they pulled into a spot to pick up their lunches. "Damián and I have an idea." She spelled it out.

"I like it," Vienna said. "I'll tell the band." And she gave Deza the first genuine smile in their entire time on tour together.

After the show, they were quiet about it. The roadies loaded the gear into the bellies of the buses as usual, Deza supervised the fill-up with the biodiesel fuel as Damián checked the fuel filter. But instead of hanging out in the dressing room or talking on the phone in the parking lot, all the artists, other than Murda Lockk, filed onto the buses like a school group at the end of a field trip. Phones away. No one taking selfies or going live.

But some of their fans were also heading out. Those who had gotten tickets long before Murda Lockk was announced. Those who loved Deza or Vienna or Anasuya and didn't want to see the toxic testosterone fest that was Murda Lockk.

By the next morning, #LeftTheConcertEarly was trending on social media.

Several days later, Deza came in from the gig, exhausted. She had been up too late the night before talking to Royal. She had asked him not to call after the gigs, because she needed to sleep.

"Seriously, Royal, I gotta get off the phone," she had said, walking to the bus.

"Come on, baby, he said. "I can't sleep tonight. I think it's because I'm so lonely for you."

So they talked on the phone for a couple of hours. He suggested they have phone sex. She wasn't interested. Maybe if they had been together for longer, but their reconnection was so recent.

"Nah, boo," she said. "The walls on this bus are too thin. I don't want everyone to hear me." Which was also true.

The next day, she dragged through the concert. The shows had become more tedious, because there were always young girls trying to get backstage to see Murda Lockk. When they couldn't get the boys' attention, they would say they were friends of one of the female acts. Security had taken to texting her photos of the girls who were there claiming to be her friends from New York. She had gotten fifteen different texts at this concert alone. She didn't want to ignore them, because someone might actually be there to see her, a journalist or someone important to network with. But none of these young girls with shiny lipstick and their titties halfway out was gonna be able to help her career.

It had been a long day. There were technical problems at sound check, she was tired, and her set had been off. She headed onto the bus to crash. But when she opened up her compartment, there was a girl in the bed. Wearing a thong and nothing else.

"What the fuck?" Deza said. "What are you doing in my fucking compartment?"

"You ain't Lil Trey," the girl said, almost indignant.

"This ain't their bus," Deza said. "How'd you even get in here?"

"Anybody could pop that lock," the girl said. She stood up and put on her trench coat. "Well, point me to the right place. I ain't no dyke."

"Fuck you," Deza said. "Take your homophobic ass outta here. I ain't pointing you any fucking where."

Damn. Everything about those guys was a nightmare.

Chapter 26

Chicago

Deza walked across the cafeteria, bold as you please, to where Chalaya was sitting with her friends. The moment she approached the table, it got quiet.

"Excuse me," Deza began in a voice that was calm and civil, but not deferential. "Chalaya, I would like to speak to you in private about something."

Then she just stood and waited. She watched while the girls all gave one another looks across the table. Chalaya didn't move.

Deza shrugged. "Okay, then. I'll take that as a no." She turned to leave, but Chalaya stood up.

"Wait," she said. She turned back to her crew and sucked her teeth. "Lemme see what she want."

Deza chose a spot out of earshot of any of the tables.

"You did good at the talent show," Deza said. "I rap, too. We should team up for the spring talent show. I think we could win. If we split the prize money, that's fifty each. Think about it."

Chalaya was clearly surprised.

"Now," Deza said. "I'm a turn and go back to my table. I'm letting you know so you can turn at the same time."

And that was it, their first piece of shared choreography. Maybe it was the offer itself that Chalaya found so inviting. Or maybe it was Deza's thoughtfulness. She knew the two of them were already onstage. The whole cafeteria watching them. She wouldn't leave Chalaya hanging. She had her back already. Was committed to making her look good. Wouldn't take a win at her expense.

Chalaya said yes.

The two girls stood side by side, waiting to go on at the spring talent show. The boy on stage was telling jokes, doing a bit from a TV comedian. The audience was laughing, mostly because he had managed to keep the rude humor of the jokes, while cutting the profanity that made them officially objectionable.

Deza's heart was jackhammering against her ribs. When they called her name, she was frozen for a minute.

"Don't tweak, bro," Chalaya said. "We got this." Chalaya took Deza's hand, pulling her onto the stage.

Deza looked out at the crowd of students, glaring and whispering. She couldn't do this. She just couldn't. But then, she heard the opening beats of the music. An instrumental track they had selected. And it all came back to her. All their lyrics. All her moves.

The two of them killed it. They won the talent show.

As she moved into high school, Deza no longer aimed for college, but she made sure to pass all her classes. She wanted to be at school all day every day. She hung tight with Chalaya and a couple other ninth grade girls who were their dancers. She finally had a crew.

Chapter 27

"So Lil Trey," Dante, AKA Dante-By-Day, the host of the nationally syndicated morning radio show said into his hanging mic. "What you think about this 'left the concert early' hashtag? I mean, it's all over the media this morning. 'Forget Boycott, is this a Girlcott? Female artists walk out of concert.' Are they making a political statement?"

Lil Trey, Axis, and Trey's girlfriend, Anaya Later, were guests via phone on this particular urban radio show that was known for stirring up controversy. Dante's co-hosts were Paco and Chantrelle.

"These bitches upset because they wasn't making no money," Lil Trey said. "So a nigga like me, who got millions of fans, came in to rescue they sorry asses. They should be fucking grateful. But instead they jealous, ya know I'm sayin?"

"Our sources seem to think that Deza was the one who started the—what did they call it?" Paco asked. "Girlcott?"

"Deza?" Lil Trey said. "First of all, Deza was they second choice. Everybody know that supposed to be Nashonna, ya know I'm sayin? Deza's was just the flavor of the week when she had that girl name in her rap. They only put her on cause, after Nashonna, she the biggest female rapper on they label. My bitch Anaya Later could headline the fuck outta that tour. But she on a different label. Then, when Deza couldn't deliver, they call us in. Here come the cavalry to rescue yo sorry ass."

"Hold up," Chantrelle said. "I heard that the venues weren't empty. They were actually pretty full, but the label got greedy and just wanted to fill every single seat. Lemme play devil's advocate. Leanne Jacobson, the white girl who's supposed to be such a phenom, didn't sell any more tickets than this tour, but nobody sent Justin Bieber to headline for her. How come the Black women are expected to fill every seat? And if they don't, they send some men to get top billing?"

"Nah, nah," Lil Trey said. "It's a simple fact of business. Paperclip know we gonna fill every seat in that stadium. Every single one. So they gonna put us in there, because everybody want they money."

"Maybe they filled every seat, ticketwise," Chantrelle said. "But have you seen some of the stuff on social media from the start of your set? It was packed in the front, but social media is full of videos showing people leaving. Folks in the back moved up to take those seats."

"Propaganda," Lil Trey scoffed.

"That's not what the fans are saying," Chantrelle insisted. "This is from DezaDazeFanGirl in Seattle by way of Chicago." She read the tweet: " 'Hell yeah, I #LeftTheConcert Early. I'm gonna act like Deza is the headliner she shoulda been from the start. Murda Lockk is okay if I'm in a super-ratchet mood, but I didn't pay good money to leave with that taste in my mouth.' "

"Bitch," Axis said, "we put what we want in yo mouth and you gon like it."

The men laughed.

"And you wonder why female fans are leaving early," Chantrelle said dryly.

"For real, though," Lil Trey said. "I'm sick of all this Deza Deza Deza. She overrated. She got no real talent. She won a crapshoot name contest. Now my bitch Anaya Later here? She got real talent, boy. Anaya, what you got to say?"

"Deza, I'm sick of you talking shit about Murda Lockk," she said. "Here's what I got for you:

> *Jenny-come-lately bitches like Deza make me*
> *   sick*
> *Naming dead girl names like a parlor trick*
> *She probably just mad cause she ain't getting*
> *   the dick*
> *Her faggot looking boyfriend from Chicago*
> *   ain't there*
> *Cause he probably laid up in some dude's sex*
> *   lair*
> *And why she tryna headline a tour anyway*
> *Cause I could rap her into the ground any day*
> *No skill and no talent and she ain't even cute*
> *You need to go do like Lizzo and take up the*
> *   flute*
> *You should be a single instrument in an or-*
> *   chestra*
> *Because your solo career is really torturous*
> *Since people don't wanna hear you but you're*
> *   forcing us*
> *We gotta sit through your set to get to the sor-*
> *   cerers.*
> *Lil Trey got the magic. Lil Trey got the rhyme.*
> *Lil Trey get out and slay em every time.*
> *So sorry that you lost your headline spot*
> *But it looks like you ain't a prophet like we*
> *   thought*

We regret the inconvenience but there's been a
*   mistake*
The number one spot was never yours to take
So step back to heavy hitters who can make the
*   earth quake*
Cause you never deserved it, yo ass was always
*   fake.*

"Yeene-enno my bitch could spit like that!" Lil Trey said. "That's what I'm talking bout, boy. That's fye! She slick rhymed it straight off the dome! She finesse that shit!"

"Seriously?" Chantrelle asked. "Straight off the dome?"

"I got bars," Anaya Later said.

"Straight off the dome?" Deza said to Claire. She was fuming in the bus lounge with the tour manager. "Didn't you say Lil Trey begged to have Anaya on the show? You think she didn't prepare that ahead of time?"

Claire shrugged. "Don't worry about it," she said. "The controversy is good for us. It raises our profile. They offered for you to come on the show tomorrow morning and respond."

"You're damn right I'm going on their damn show to respond," Deza said.

A few hours later, she got a text from Tyesha to both her and Thug Woofer.

I heard the radio show. Whatever you do, don't respond.

Woof added his thoughts an hour later.

Seriously, don't respond.

"So Deza," Dante asked. "This is a big break for you."

"Come on, Dante," Deza said. "Don't act like this is a regular interview. You had Lil Trey and his crew up here not twenty-four hours ago talking trash about me. That's why I'm here. So let's pick up where this beef left off."

"See?" Chantrelle said. "That's what I'm telling you about Deza. She doesn't play."

"Okay," Dante said. "If you don't play, then what did you think of Anaya Later's little freestyle about you?"

"Here's what I think," Deza said. "I've asked Jimmy, your engineer, to play something. Jimmy, can you roll that clip, please?"

Woof had taught her to learn the names of anyone who did the tech for her. Always be polite and thank them.

"What clip?" Dante asked.

"Deza's producer said she would be bringing a couple of clips," Paco said. "You gotta read the emails, Dante."

"So this," Deza said, "is what Anaya Later said about me."

> *You should be a single instrument in an orchestra*
> *Because your solo career is really torturous*
> *Since people don't wanna hear you but you're*
> * forcing us*
> *We gotta sit through your set to get to the sor-*
> * cerers.*

"I was there," Dante said. "So tell me something I don't know."

"Okay," Deza said. "Well, this is Anaya Later's mixtape from a few years back."

> *You're as weak as the triangle in the orchestras*
> *With a rhyme scheme so bad it's really tor-*
> * turous*
> *Don't nobody wanna hear you but you're forc-*
> * ing us*
> *But me and my crew are the true sorcerers.*

"This is why a lot of the old heads are saying hip hop is losing its edge," Deza said. "If you wanna be a recording artist and rhyme on the beat for money, do that. Celebrate it. Stack your paper. Live your best life. But don't come up here pretending to be somebody you're not. Anaya Later, you ain't a emcee. You don't freestyle off the top of your dome for a live audience. Or even a radio audience. You're a recording artist. Stay in your lane."

"So would you battle Anaya Later?" Dante asked.

"Look," Deza said. "I'm on tour. I'm doing six concerts a week. Press. Fan events. Right now, I'm working on my next album. And I'm not gonna come on this show acting like I can do a spontaneous dis rap. I mean I could, but it wouldn't like—poof!—magically be the best rhymes of my career. When I was battle rhyming, I'd be up in my head freestyling all day. Making the best word combinations I could imagine. That's why it's called flowing. You get it started and it just flows. I'm not in that headspace right now. Trying to pretend like you're just flowing when you already wrote that shit is a foul. And if Anaya Later said, 'I wrote this dis rap about Deza,' I could respect that. But she don't deal in respect. Because her man is one of the most disrespectful artists out there when it comes to women. I don't understand what these women see in him, but these chicks are up here throwing themselves at him. Like the girl who broke into our bus by mistake and was lying on my bed in a thong talking about 'surprise, Lil Trey!'"

"You're saying there was a naked girl in your bedroom?" Chantrelle said.

"Not for long," Deza said. "I threw her out. And she left talking about how she wasn't gay. And while we're on the subject, calling my boyfriend gay is a weak-ass dis, Dante. Ain't nothing wrong with being gay. My sister is gay. My boyfriend, on the other hand, is not gay."

"I have to say, Deza," Paco said. "I'm surprised. You didn't grow up in a hood where you were gonna let people just talk about you like that. Those are fighting words."

"That's right," Deza said. "I fought a lot. In middle school. In high school."

"Is this the new Deza?" Chantrelle asked. "The 'woke' Deza? The Urban Prophet?"

"I'm not even gonna touch that 'prophet' label," Deza said. "But it's not about being 'woke,' it's about being grown. I'm not fifteen anymore. I'm a grown-ass woman, and beyond that, I'm a professional. Anaya Later has everything to gain by gunning for me, and I have nothing to gain by firing back. My song has been in the top ten spot for the last fifteen weeks and she's not even on the chart."

"Then why'd you come on the show?" Chantrelle asked.

Deza laughed. "Because your producer called before Woof and my auntie called to tell me not to take the bait. By the time they got to me, I had already said yes. And I'm a professional. So I keep my word and honor my commitments."

"Okay, Miss Professional," Chantrelle said. "So what do you have to say about the recent tragedy with your endorsement deal?"

"What tragedy?" Deza asked.

"Oh girl," Chantrelle said. "There was a fire in Indonesia where Rock.it athletic apparel is manufactured. Over a hundred people were killed. There's been an ongoing campaign about child labor and sweatshop conditions. And some folks have been fighting to raise awareness among celebrities that when you lend your name to those enterprises, you legitimize slavery. It's one thing when Murda Lockk does it, they've made it clear that they're just out for self. But I thought you were about more than just that money."

It hit Deza like a sock to the stomach. Damián had been right. Damn.

On the way back from the radio show live taping, she tried calling Tyesha, Woof, and Royal. No one picked up.

She scrolled through Instagram only to find someone had posted a photo of Royal.

It was a candid at the club. Several artists posing for the selfie. But Royal wasn't looking at the camera. He was sort of leering at a dancer who was mostly out of the frame. But you could see her shoulder, her cascading red hair—probably a weave—falling across her neck. One breast half-exposed in the low-cut black dress. And her tiny waist and big ass. It curved into the frame at an angle, a sphere of influence.

"Maybe Deza don't got it all the way locked down," someone commented.

And Royal's eyes were unmistakably glued to it. He was looking at her ass. Her. Ass.

A younger Deza would have posted something like "LoL. Brothers gonna look." But she thought back to what she had said on the show. She was a professional. A grown-ass woman. What the fuck was she doing with a man who acted like a teenager? Was undermining her like this. Looking at other women's asses when he should be calling her. Should be fucking giving her the least bit of goddamn support when she was out on this tour with her debut album.

She felt a knot in her stomach. What did folks keep saying, when people show you who they are, believe them? Royal had shown her. Was still showing her. Yeah, maybe he looked at women's asses. It wasn't a crime. But to get caught doing it on Instagram? Really? It was humiliating.

A few minutes later, her phone rang, and it was Royal. She didn't pick up. He kept calling and she didn't pick up his calls for the rest of the day.

Woof called about the Rock.it disaster. "Deza, my bad for real," he said. "I never shoulda said to take it. I'm sorry. Your auntie said don't do it, but I thought I knew better."

"It's not your fault," Deza said. "Damián also said not to fuck with it. He told me all about their shady factories. I made my bed on this one. But what do I do now?"

"Nothing yet," Woof said. "Wait for a chance to do damage control."

"Okay," she said. "Speaking of damage control, did you see that other shit on Instagram today?"

"That shit with Royal?" Woof asked. "I ain't getting in that one. Your need to ask your auntie."

"I know," Deza said. "But I can't seem to catch her."

"Her work crazy right now," Woof said. "I barely see her and we living together. I'll tell her to call you."

After Deza hung up with Woof, she didn't know what to do with herself. These were the worst moments on tour. When hard shit happened and there was nobody to tell. Nobody to comfort her. She couldn't call Royal because he was the one who she was mad at. She kept trying her aunt, but she was busy. Deza realized that this must be the place where people called their mother. That's what a mother was supposed to be. That person who put their kids first. Who made the time. Who put everyone else to the back of the line. Deza needed that now. And she wasn't gonna get it.

There was a knock on her compartment door. "Fifteen minutes till sound check, Deza," Claire said.

Deza pulled out her makeup case. She swallowed all the rage and humiliation and put on a full face of makeup. She wore it to sound check like a mask.

Chapter 28

Brooklyn

After her parents' big blowout at the Brooklyn hotel, Deza and Amaru moved in with Tyesha for the rest of their family's New York trip.

It was like those days at the dorm, except better. Tyesha was grown now. She had a car. Money. A big flat-screen TV. They ate takeout every meal. Tyesha took them out to hip hop shows. Including Cardi B in an intimate show at MoMA PS1. Deza never wanted to leave New York.

She was sitting around the apartment with her aunt and sister playing spades when there was a knock at the door.

"Are you expecting Thug Woofer?" Deza asked, jumping up off the couch and putting on a fresh coat of lipstick.

"No," Tyesha said.

Deza opened the door to find her mother.

"Okay now," Jenisse said. "Babysitting time with Auntie Ty-Ty is over. So pack up your shit because we going back to Chicago."

"What?" Amaru said. "School doesn't start for another month. I'm just getting into a workout rhythm here."

Tyesha went over and put her arm around Amaru.

"Yeah, Mama," Deza said. "Auntie Ty's gonna get me the

hookup in my music career." If her mother wasn't going to respect their wishes, maybe she'd be excited about the prospect of Deza making money.

"I know y'all think your auntie can work miracles, but I'm sure she's tired of your little slumber party. Especially when she can't just send you back. Like I said, we're goin home to Chicago. I got your plane tickets. Now go get yo shit."

Deza could feel herself getting hot. "Mama," Deza said. "This is some bullshit. We came to New York with no notice, nothing. You were just like, pack yo shit, Zeus is going to New York. So we get something going here, and now you're like 'Pack your shit. Let's go.'"

"Don't you cuss at me, little girl," Jenisse said. "And when you pay the bills, you can make the rules."

"It's not like you pay the bills," Deza muttered. Deza hadn't consciously intended for Jenisse to hear. But being on her aunt Tyesha's turf had emboldened her. So she hadn't quite whispered.

Jenisse turned her head sharply. "Excuse me?" Jenisse asked pointedly. "What did you say?"

"Nothing," Deza mumbled.

Even in Tyesha's apartment, Deza was cowed by the tone that often preceded a slap.

Jenisse put her hands on her hips, and any pretense at politeness fell away. "Now you listen here, you ungrateful little bitches," Jenisse said. "That motherfucker doesn't just pay for shit out of the goodness of his heart. Just because he got money don't mean we got money and it certainly don't mean you got money. I been fucking that nigga and stroking his overblown ego for decades to make sure his ass is in a good mood when it's time to throw down money for y'all. So yes, I do pay the bills. Now get yo asses ready and let's go."

Deza stood her ground. "We ain't going," she said. "You

and Zeus have a fucked-up relationship, but that ain't our fault. Auntie Ty said we could stay and we wanna stay."

Amaru swallowed hard and nodded.

"You think Auntie Ty is ready to take on a pair of no-job little bitches like you all?" Jenisse said with a laugh. "Think again."

Tyesha looked directly at her sister. "They can stay if they want." Her voice was gentle, but not apologetic. "It's up to them."

"Oh so now you want em," Jenisse said. She turned to her daughters. "You about fifteen years too late. Just so you know, it was your precious auntie who told me to get an abortion when I was pregnant with Amaru. And when I told her I wouldn't, she said she was sorry I had Deza. That's right. I gave you life. Life, you ungrateful little bitches. And she thinks you both a mistake. So I'll be at the hotel and our flight leaves day after tomorrow. But if you don't come tonight, you can get back to Chicago on your own."

Jenisse turned on her heel and slammed the door behind her.

Deza was stunned. Neither she nor Amaru could meet their aunt's eyes.

"Is it true?" Amaru asked quietly.

"It's not how it sounded," Tyesha said, curling her arm tighter around Amaru. "I love you both. It's—I was just worried about the kind of mother Jenisse was. And I thought . . . she was having kids for the wrong reasons. To keep your father. I mean, when she got pregnant with you, Amaru, your brothers were in high school and running the streets and getting into trouble and—"

As her aunt spoke, Deza sank down until she was sitting on the floor against the front of the couch, her arms wrapped around her knees.

"Deza," her aunt said, turning to her. "You were barely in kindergarten and Jenisse seemed to think she could just keep having kids and give them to Mama—your grandmama—and Mama would handle it, but I knew Mama's health wasn't good. Auntie Lou had just died. It was only a matter of time before Jenisse was gonna have to actually take care of you, and that looked like a bad plan. The only people Jenisse seemed to be able to think about were herself and Zeus."

"You're right, I guess," Amaru said. "When we lived with Grandmama, it was cool. But since we been living with Mama, it's been all bad."

"But now you got me," Tyesha said. "And getting to know you both these past days, I'm nothing but glad you were born. I love you both so much. And if it's one thing Jenisse did right, it's having you. Not that she knows how to raise kids, but fortunately, you're old enough to decide. So you can stay with me as long as you want."

"For real?" Deza asked.

"For real," Tyesha said. "Amaru, should I be looking at schools for you in the fall?"

Amaru shook her head. "I gotta go back to Chicago," she said. "But one of the girls on my team says I can stay with her when school starts."

"Deza?" Tyesha asked.

Deza sat quiet for a long time. Finally, she spoke, this time her voice little more than a whisper. "Ain't nothin for me in Chicago but two crazy parents and an ex who broke my heart," she said.

"What ex?" Tyesha asked. "Do I need to go to Chicago and kick his ass? Where do I find this motherfucker?"

"He's one of the most famous DJs in Chicago," Deza said. "Everywhere you go, you'll see his picture, hear his mixes on the radio. It's like I couldn't get away from him. I'm so glad to be in New York. I can go three or four days without hearing this motherfucker's name."

"Tell me about it," Tyesha said. "When I stopped seeing

Thug Woofer that last time, I had to leave the country to get away from reminders of him."

"But how am I gonna get back to Chicago in the fall?" Amaru asked.

"Mama gonna calm the fuck down before then," Deza said.

"And if she doesn't," Tyesha said, "I got you covered. For plane fare and whatever else you need for the start of the year."

"Thank you, Auntie Ty," Amaru said, and threw her arms around Tyesha's neck.

"So we got a plan," Tyesha said. "Amaru, you're staying for the summer, and Deza, you're here indefinitely."

Deza smiled. "More like temporarily," she said. "I'm just staying till Thug Woofer discovers me and sends me out on tour."

Book 3

Chapter 29

KeeKee Samuelson, All My Ladies Femcee Blog

So the Face To The Sky tour is a little bit of a mess, right? They've made it to the West Coast and have stops next in Southern California. After that, they'll stop in Las Vegas, where the tour's head-liners will attend the Billboard Music Awards, and Deza is nominated in three categories.

Deza seems to be all over the news these days. First it was the disaster of her sportswear endorse-ment deal with a factory fire, then it was the #WhoseAssIsThat meme on social media.

If Beyoncé can lemonade it out with Jay-Z, then anything is possible. Especially since it was just announced that Royal will play a small role in a blockbuster movie about the growth of hip hop in Chicago.

So both of their stars are rising. Deza and Royal might still be the "it" couple from Chicago at the Billboard Music Awards.

Voice mail from Royal: Hey baby, it's me. What's up baby? Call me back. We need to plan everything for the Billboard Music Awards. Do you all have a hotel room already in Vegas? Do I need to get it for us? How do you wanna link up? We got stuff to figure out, girl. Let me know wassup. I love you baby.

The tour had just arrived in Los Angeles. They were staying an extra day, because so many of them had business in town. The label had put them all up on the same floor in a four-star hotel. Deza was thrilled to have a bed that wasn't moving. She crashed and took a nap.

After she woke up, she pulled herself together. Got cute, actually. She was going to invite Damián to go to the Billboard Music Awards as a friend. As her work husband. But it didn't hurt to look good.

She put on a cute top and a tight pair of jeans and knocked on his door.

He opened it with a huge smile.

Hey," she said. "How are you settling in?"

"Good," he said. "It sure beats the bunk bed."

Deza smiled. "I was thinking—"

"Who is it?" a woman's voice asked from inside the room.

"It's Deza," Damián said. "Let me introduce you."

A pretty Latina girl came into Deza's sight. She was an almond brown, with hourglass curves. She had that kind of obvious African heritage that some Latina girls claim proudly and other girls play down. This girl wore her auburn hair pulled back in untamed, springing curls.

"Deza, this is Lisette," Damián said.

"Hey," she said and put out her hand, smiling. "I'm Damián's girlfriend from New York."

Deza's smile was only a fraction of a second late. "Nice to meet you," Deza said.

"I have family in San Diego, so I thought I would visit them and surprise Damián," she said. "Surprise!"

"So what's up?" Damián asked.

"Just work stuff," Deza said. "Don't let me interrupt. We can talk at sound check."

"Okay," Damián said, still with that big smile.

On her way back down the hall, she passed Anasuya, who introduced Deza to her man, Nicasio. He had a young Lenny Kravitz look.

"Did you meet Damián's girlfriend?" Anasuya asked. "She seemed really sweet."

"Yeah," said Deza. "The sweetest."

Later, in her hotel room, she realized everyone seemed to be paired off. Vienna lived with her man in LA, so she wasn't even at the hotel.

Well, that was that with Damián. She had decided after Jyron never to mess with anyone else's man. But why did it keep happening to her? Were all men just cheaters? Or was it some kind of psychological thing where she kept repeating what her parents did? She thought she was so different from Jenisse because she dumped Royal the minute she caught him cheating. And she stayed away. For years. But how different was she really if she took him back a couple years later and he just did it again?

Damián and Lisette had begun making out the moment she showed up at his hotel room.

"What about protection?" he asked.

"Don't worry," Lisette said. "I'm on the pill."

Which made Damián feel uncomfortable. Was she using the pill with other guys? Had she been planning this for a while? Didn't it take a few weeks for the pill to be effective? Or what if . . . He didn't want to think about Lisette trying to trap him, but . . .

"Extra safe," he said, and he fumbled in his backpack for a condom. With a pang, he realized he had bought them the day after he and Deza had almost . . . But that was obviously never gonna happen. He was glad that the package was closed. He made a show of opening it in front of Lisette, so it didn't look like he had been fucking around a lot on the tour. For whatever it was worth.

He had some misgivings, but nothing he was going to let stop him from having sex for the first time in months.

Afterward, they lay in the big bed with the clean sheets.

"You know what, baby?" she asked.

"What?" He had missed this. Not just the sex but the intimacy. The ease with someone.

"I've been thinking about it, and we could have a five-year-plan that would have us back on track. We could get married and have a baby by the time I'm thirty-six."

"Can we just . . . I don't know . . . be a little more in the moment?" he said.

"I just want you to know that we can take our time," she said. "You can have it all. A family and your music career. We can make it work."

But easy as it sounded, it didn't sit easy with him. Would she expect him to stop touring? Only work in the City? That the family would tour with him? He liked the fantasy of that life with her, but also felt constrained by the pressure. He was just starting to figure out who he was artistically. He had projects planned with Anasuya, Deza, maybe even Vienna. Would they all be completed in five years? Would he be able to work on them from New York?

He didn't know quite what to say. So he said nothing. And the silence just stretched. And her words ended up being a sort of final say on the subject. Damián didn't exactly agree. But he wasn't sure he *didn't* want that. Besides, it was nice having Lisette in his world. Seeing him in this context as a successful artist. Despite his friendships on the tour, the road still got lonely. He wanted her to stay as long as possible.

Anasuya wanted to maximize her time with Nicasio in LA, so she stayed with him. Which meant that Damián had their compartment all to himself. He invited Lisette to ride along to Las Vegas. He didn't have a ticket to the Billboard Awards, but they could go to some of the pre-awards events and watch it on the hotel TV.

Royal was calling every day now. More than once a day. Twenty-four hours into her silence, he finally spoke about the photo.

"Baby, I realize that I should have spoken up earlier," he said to her voice mail. "I just didn't realize something so trivial would get to you. I mean, you know you're the only one for me. I really hope you're not gonna let a little thing like this spoil our future together. Baby, we gonna have it all."

It wasn't an apology. The next morning, he got it right.

"Baby, I was wrong," he said. "I'm sorry. Even though that moment didn't mean anything to me, I didn't think about how it would affect you. And I been looking at some of the memes and comments. I shoulda known better. I talked to one of my boys, and he let me know how disrespectful that behavior really is. I just—you know, I grew up with uncles and cousins just always checking girls out. And I didn't really question it for a long time. Like, if I wasn't actually cheating it was cool. But really, you deserve better. I know I've said it so many times now, but I'm sorry. I hope you can forgive me. I got this plane ticket to Vegas. So . . . should I be trying to get my money back? Come on, girl. You gotta tell me something, okay?"

Deza couldn't bring herself to call. It felt like too little too late. But she couldn't let it alone, either. They had so much history together.

She finally called Tyesha to ask for advice. While she was waiting for Tyesha to call her back, her sister Amaru called.

"Hey, sis," Amaru said. "I just wanted to see how you're holding up with all this Instagram drama."

Deza had never really confided in her younger sister, but Amaru was older now. And she had no idea when Tyesha would call her back.

"I don't know," Deza said. "He came to my show in Chicago, and was all woo-woo, I'm so sorry. Then woo opp de bam, gimme another chance. And the next thing I knew, I jumped back into it with him, but now I have no idea if he's for real or just on some bullshit."

"Facts," Amaru said. "And that photo was fucked up."

"I know you never liked Royal," Deza said.

"I never did," Amaru said. "But I'm not the one fucking with him. And it sounds like you want to forgive him. Do you still want him back?"

"Maybe," Deza said. "But is he just using me?"

"I don't know," Amaru said. "Is he still making all the power couple videos on Instagram?"

"No," Deza said. "But to be honest, I think maybe he just doesn't want to look stupid. In case I'm really through with him."

Amaru was quiet for a minute. "I know it's not the same," she said. "But in my little, girls school lesbian world, the big gay captain of the basketball team is like . . . the shit . . . someone girls wanna be seen with. So sometimes, to see if a girl really likes me, I'll give her the option: does she wanna go with me to some big school function or does she wanna go out one-on-one. If she picks the big school function, then I know she just wanna be on my arm for the status."

"But how does that help me?" Deza said. "I'm not in Chicago. I can't invite Royal out for pizza or whatever."

"So why don't you go to the Billboard Music Awards

without him?" Amaru suggested. "If he's still trying to get with you afterward, then it was always about you."

"Go to the Awards all alone?" Deza asked. The prospect of walking the red carpet without a date was awful.

"Figure out someone to go with," Amaru said.

Just then, Deza's phone lit up with a call coming in from Tyesha.

"That's Auntie Ty," Deza said.

"Cool," Amaru said. "Catch you later."

"Amaru, wait!" Deza said. "I love you, sis."

"Love you too."

Deza caught Tyesha up on the drama.

"Amaru knows what's up," Tyesha said. "Go with someone else."

"But who?" Deza asked.

"What about your work husband?"

"He's got a girlfriend," Deza said.

"Too bad," Tyesha said. "He was cute."

Deza didn't want to get into it. "I can't go all by myself," she said.

"Maybe you can go with Woof," Tyesha said.

"You'd let me go with your man?" Deza asked.

"Of course," Tyesha said. "I'm sick of those things by now. Plus, I've got work in New York. So damn much work. The more I think about it, the more I like the idea."

"I like it, too," Deza said. "And I can call Royal afterward. If he's still interested, I'll know he wasn't just using me. It's like Amaru said, a test."

"And here's the other thing," Tyesha said. "He might be embarrassed or whatever. But if he really understands what he did wrong, he won't hold it against you. He embarrassed *you*. You're just saving your own face. Never trust a man who shows a different face in public than in private."

* * *

Royal left five more voice messages that night. Each one increasingly desperate.

"Seriously, Deza, what's up? Am I getting on this plane? Are you telling me that it's over? How you gonna just ghost on me after all we been through? Baby, please? I love you. I can't live without you. You gotta let me know."

It took everything for her to stick to the plan. But she stuck. By the time the bus crossed the state line into Nevada, it was three in the morning. Royal had stopped calling, and Deza had finally fallen asleep. Despite the fact that Damián and Lisette were still awake and having sex in the other compartment.

Chapter 30

Chicago

It was senior year in high school and Deza seemed to have everything. She and her crew, the Fierce Ones, were making a name for themselves around town. She was seventeen and a half, and Amaru was on a girls' basketball team at the community center. Her coach was like a second mom, which was good because their first mom continued to be faulty.

But Deza had started to do hair, and now she always looked good. Chalaya's acne had cleared up some, and with Deza keeping everyone's hair done, their crew always looked great.

Also, with the money Deza made doing hair in the neighborhood, she had money for food, for Lyft rides, to get her nails done, for jewelry, for cute clothes, even beyond what Zeus provided.

Zeus was out of town a lot these days, trying to expand his territory into other states. Of course, Jenisse went with him. With Amaru at the center till late and her parents gone, Deza had the house to herself a lot of the time. And "to herself" meant to share with her girls and her boyfriend, Jyron.

When they first met, she thought he was steady playing. He said he wanted to be her boyfriend, but she knew boys said all kinds of things to get it. She made him take her to a show and buy her dinner. Then she waited a whole month before they had sex.

He was her first. She had learned from her aunt and her great-aunt, *don't get pregnant*. She had gone to Planned Parenthood and gotten the birth control shot.

Chalaya was worried at first that Jyron would put Deza off her game. But it seemed to just enhance her rhymes. Tyesha had told her to rap about what she knew. Now she knew about having sex. She had more range, rapping about sexy stuff as well as her usual girl braggadocio. When she and Jyron got in a fight and broke up temporarily, she also developed a *fuck you* anthem that she would deliver with gusto at shows where he was in attendance, but then give him a little wink afterward. Like *fuck you* was really about fucking you after the show. Sort of taking a page from her parents' playbook.

"How come yo nigga always gotta be around?" Chalaya complained. Her bestie and her boyfriend didn't seem to get along, but it was nothing Deza couldn't look past. She wasn't gonna let it get her down. Other than that, everything was perfect.

During one of her parents' extra-long trips to Detroit, Deza gave Jyron the spare key to her house. He had dropped out and wanted to chill at the house while he waited for her to get out of school.

Today, she would need to ask for it back. She had gotten a text that her parents were coming home earlier than expected. She needed to clean the house, too. And while Jyron was cute and funny and sex was exciting, he wasn't great at cleaning up after himself. In just three days, he had managed to trash the house more than she and her girls had done in three weeks.

When she got home, it was obvious that she wasn't alone. Damn! Her parents had beaten her? How was that possible? Her mother was going to kick her ass. But she didn't smell the cloud of her mother's signature perfume. Had Amaru gotten home early?

She was texting Amaru that they needed laundry detergent. Would she pick some up at the store on the way home? She had the phone in her hand as she walked into her bedroom to put away her backpack. The cleaning needed to start now.

And that was when and where and how she found them. Chalaya and Jyron. Fucking. In her own bed.

When she walked into the room, Chalaya was on top. Jyron lay back beneath her, his hands gripping her ass. Chalaya had her head tilted back, the long, auburn weave Deza had sewn in brushing the tips of Jyron's fingers.

Deza had always thought she would fight in a situation like that. Would rip the tracks right out of Chalaya's head. She would be justified. The two people in the bed definitely thought she would fight. She had every intention of rearing up and losing her shit. But she had the phone right in front of her. The text open to Amaru. And it had the little camera icon. She pressed the button and snapped the shot. Several of them, catching Chalaya turning her face to see. The photos were all soundless on Deza's silenced phone.

She sent them to Amaru with the random message about laundry detergent. Like that still mattered.

Deza didn't say a word. She just stood at the door in complete silence as the two of them climbed out of bed and got dressed. Neither one could look at her.

"My keys," were the only words she had for Jyron.

He fished them from the pocket of the jeans he had halfway up. His eyes stayed glued to the keys as he set them in her palm.

Chalaya huddled into her jacket and headed out the door behind him.

At school on Monday, their two dancer friends could tell things were not cool. Deza rolled up to Chalaya and asked to talk.

"I'm kinda busy right now," Chalaya said.

Deza started to laugh. "You sure?" she asked.

"Yeah," Chalaya said. "Maybe later."

"Okay," Deza said. "You know I wanted to show you a picture I took yesterday," Deza said. "It was so funny. It really makes me laugh."

"I wanna see it," one of the other girls said.

"No," Deza said. "This is for Chalaya's eyes only. She's in it. I figure she should decide if anyone else sees it. Whenever she can find the time."

Suddenly, Chalaya looked like she had swallowed a stone. She jumped up from the table.

"Deza," she said. "Wait!"

Chalaya ran after her.

"Gimme that damn phone," she said, taking it from Deza's pocket.

"You really think I got the only copies of you, ass out, fucking your best friend's man? I already texted it to somebody."

"To who?"

"Somebody I can trust."

"Tell me who!"

"Give me my fucking phone, Chalaya, or I will have photos of your naked ass all over this school," Deza said.

With a shaking hand, Chalaya returned the phone.

Deza scrolled through it.

"What do you want, Deza?"

"Don't you want to see the picture?"

Chalaya shook her head. "Just tell me."

"You drop out of the big show. We do it without you."

"What?" Chalaya asked. "We been working toward that all year."

"Bitch," Deza hissed. "There is no way I'm gonna enter that show with you."

"And the paperwork says there are four girls in our crew," Chalaya insisted.

"Then I'll get someone else to dance or just fucking stand there," Deza said. "Girls in crews don't fuck their best friends' boyfriends."

For a moment, Chalaya looked like she might cry. But she pulled it together.

"What you gonna tell them?"

"Not a damn thing," Deza said. "You gonna be the one to tell them."

"What do I say?"

"That you're dropping out of the group," Deza said.

"They gonna ask for a reason," Chalaya said.

"Then give them one," Deza said. "I don't give a fuck."

"What the hell is going on?" one of their other friends asked, walking up to them.

"I'm quitting the group," Chalaya said.

"What?" the other girl asked. "Why?"

"Yeah," Deza said. "Why?"

"Because," she said. "Because I just quit, that's all."

"Does this have anything to do with some photo Deza took?"

"Does it, Chalaya?" Deza asked.

"No," Chalaya said. "I'm just sick of rap. I'm sick of all y'all bitches. I'm sick of all this shit. Fuck The Fierce Ones. I ain't with the shit no more." Chalaya stalked off.

"What the hell is her problem?" one of the girls asked.

"I don't know," Deza said. "But we better start practicing if we gonna enter that show without her."

*　　*　　*

When Deza had fought in middle school, it always made her feel better. Even the few times she got her ass beat, it just felt so good to release all that anger. This time, she was all pent up. The rage, the betrayal, the bitterness. It had nowhere to go. Until the night of the show.

Years later, it would become clear that that had been Deza's first big break. She was on fire that night. She wanted to wound the audience with her words, make them feel all the hurt she felt. Her performance scorched the stage. She won the contest. And got the attention of one of the hottest up-and-coming DJs in Chicago. A wavy-headed pretty boy named Royal.

Chapter 31

Las Vegas

Deza had never done an awards show performance before. Of course, she had been a guest on *The Daily Show* and a couple other spots like that, but never this big, splashy performance. She was supposed to do a sort of medley number with Anasuya and Vienna. Anasuya would start out with the singer-songwriter vibe, and then it would shift into Vienna, with Deza doing the finale. The producers were doing a tribute to Big Mama Thornton and wanted them to do a cover version of "Ball and Chain." Anasuya knew the legendary blueswoman's work best, and suggested they do "I Feel the Way I Feel" instead. Deza was the one who had the most pull, so she advocated for it, and the producers agreed.

But doing a Big Mama song meant that Deza had to write some new material. Of course Murda Lockk only had to perform the clean version of their big hit. But still, they weren't nominated in any category, and Deza was nominated in three.

She rolled up to the venue, tired and struggling to focus. The decision was made. It was too late to tell Royal to come now, but she kept wondering if she had done the wrong thing. Men had egos. Royal certainly did. Maybe Tyesha was wrong. Not all men started therapy like Woof. Some were more like fixer-uppers. You had to hold their hands through this a little bit. Maybe Royal had suffered enough. Maybe she should have just punished him by making him wait. Maybe she should have called him last night and told him to come on the red-eye from Chicago. Everything Tyesha said was right, but maybe he wouldn't be able to get past this public humiliation. Maybe there was some middle ground. She regretted taking her aunt's advice. But it was too late now.

"Deza?"

She looked up at the director. "Huh? Sorry," she said. The director was a British woman with dyed black hair and an aging rock-and-roller look.

"Your mark is a bit to the left," the director said. "We want you in the light."

Deza stood in the center of the stage. The spotlight shone harsh in her face. The theater wasn't as big as the stadium shows, but it was more intimidating. Partly because it was so upscale, with the velvet curtains and fancy upholstered seating. But also because these people hadn't come to see her. A lot of the audience would be people who didn't even like hip hop.

"We need you right in this spot at the end of the song," the director said.

There was a neon yellow X on the stage to indicate the place where Deza needed to stand.

"Try it again, please," the director said.

Deza tried it again.

Four hours later, Deza was at the Paperclip tribute to women in hip hop event. Paperclip had not signed that many female rap artists, and prior to Nashonna, all of them had left the label. They did, however, have many female artists they never signed, but had been featured on different tracks—both hip hop and R & B—or had otherwise collaborated on projects with Paperclip.

Woof's plane was delayed and he had just landed. She wouldn't have to walk the red carpet alone, but she would need to walk into this party by herself.

She stood outside the door and took a deep breath. Then the elevator dinged and someone else was headed her way. She couldn't be caught just standing there. She pulled out her invitation and walked in.

The first person she saw was Damián with his girlfriend. Both of them cleaned up nicely. They were talking to another female artist Deza recognized from her time in New York. La Bruja, a Puerto Rican emcee from the Bronx.

Should she go over and say hello? But before she could decide, Nashonna came and swooped her into a conversation with her and Noname, another rapper from Chicago. They only had a brief moment to catch up before the photographer pulled all the women up front for a photo. Deza squeezed in between Nashonna and Chika on one side and two emcees from California on the other. Nashonna had introduced them as Mystic from the Bay Area and Medusa from LA. All together, there were almost three dozen female rappers, from eras dating back to the '80s. MC Lyte, CMG from The Conscious Daughters, Foxy Brown, even Yo-Yo. Despite the many beefs over the years, they were all smiling that night.

After the photographer got the shot, everyone pulled out phones to take selfies and go live on Instagram.

"I'm here live with my girl Deza," Nashonna said. "Who's nominated in three categories. Y'all better tune in tonight to watch her win!"

Deza hugged her, and hoped Nashonna would be proven right.

Three hours later, Deza was backstage with Anasuya and

Vienna. They had just announced the category of best foreign language album. A group of Dominican artists were on stage saying thank-yous in heavily accented English.

Anasuya stood in the middle and squeezed Deza's hand. Deza assumed she was squeezing Vienna's also.

When they called Anasuya's name, Deza looked over at her. The girl's face was luminous, delighted.

Anasuya sort of floated forward onto the stage. She moved into the spotlight, where her guitar was waiting. In a clear, strong voice, she began with the lyrics of Big Mama Thornton's "I Feel the Way I Feel."

Anasuya's voice rose through the building:

> Lord I feel the way I feel, I see the way I see
> And my love all the way belongs to me . . .
> Everything in this world—and I know my
>   love is mine
> But I feel everything belongs to me . . .

"I remember being that girl," Vienna said. "Being so excited about performing."

"I know," Deza said. "It's not that I don't enjoy it anymore. It's just that it's work. These days it's always work."

"Yeah," Vienna said. "I came on to this tour pretty burned out. I told my manager I didn't want to do it, but he said that if I just pushed through, I would have saved enough to take a year off. A *year*. I couldn't say no. But after the mess it's been, I probably should have."

Deza also wanted to maybe apologize, or at least empathize, but a production assistant was cueing Vienna in their headsets. The blonde stood up straight and marched forward onto the stage.

Then Deza stood alone in the wings.

The music tempo sped up, and Vienna did an electronic

cover of the melody. Anasuya sang over it at a slower tempo, and somehow, it worked.

Deza adjusted her jacket. She was the only one who had to change backstage. Anasuya and Vienna could wear their Award Show gowns, but Deza couldn't rap in a floor-length Dilani Mara golden velvet dress.

She had performed in miniskirts when she was just starting out. But now she only wore pants. Shorts if she wanted to be extra sexy. But tonight, she wanted armor. A pair of pants that had horizontal zippers every few inches going down, like stripes. The sides slit open to make it just a little bit sexy. A jacket with torn, studded belt fringes that whipped back and forth as she walked. Deza liked movement in her clothes.

She wore combat-style boots with only a slight heel. She never performed in stilettos. It took too much of her focus to make sure she could balance. She wanted to be grounded, firm.

"Fifteen seconds, Deza," the British voice sounded in her ear.

She checked her wig. She had decided to do something different with her hair for tonight, but redoing all the tracks took too long. She had a lace front blond wig that was extra-glamorous, a sort of updo. She carefully wound her long black weave around her head and covered it with a wig cap. Then there were an army of pins. In addition to the lace front, she used glue. Ugh. So much glue. To keep the blond wig in place while she danced. It was like the damn thing was welded onto her head. But when she admired herself in the mirror, the edges looked natural, and when she shook her head, it stayed in place.

She took a deep breath and moved to the edge of the curtain.

When the music changed and played her intro, Deza exploded onto the stage. The fringes flying wildly.

Usually, with a headset mic, she didn't know what to do

with her hands, but she had worked on the choreography, and gestured to punctuate the song.

> We not beginners
> We award-winners
> But some would have you believe that we
>   original sinners
> Blame women for everything that goes
>   wrong
> Then take the credit when we write the song
> You ain't nothing but a thief for stealing her
>   art
> You ain't nothing but a racist with a plagia-
>   rist's heart
> You ain't nothing but a dog just scratching
>   ya fleas
> And we'll never forget about your theft and
>   your greed
> But Big Mama believed that the world was
>   hers
> And she made it that way with the strength
>   of her words
> I feel how I feel and I feel like it's time
> To take down the statues that commemorate
>   your crime
> All over the world, icons toppling down
> Cause we rocking like kings and we coming
>   for that crown

It was an awards show, so the audience was too far back to touch physically. It was hard to see them, but she could feel them. Thousands of people. Thousands of eyes and ears. She gave them everything. Three nominations? She would show that she deserved every single fucking one. That she should still be the headliner of her tour.

It reminded her of the show she had performed after Chalaya had fucked her boyfriend. All the anxiety about Royal, second-guessing herself, wondering if she'd done the right thing. She took all that angst as fuel. She tore up the stage. Lit it up. And it transported her. By the time she was done, she didn't feel uncertain anymore. This was her time. This was her power. Royal would need to come to her. On her terms. Fuck running behind him. She almost strode off the stage in victory. But then she recalled the little X of tape on the stage. Her ending mark.

She stood in place and the audience's applause was thunderous.

The director had told her not to move until the lights changed. They weren't changing.

But then there was a collective gasp from the crowd. They were looking up. She was looking up.

And someone was coming down. On a wire. Some guy was whizzing down toward the stage. Wow, they had really done it up for her exit.

It all happened so fast. She saw the bottom of the guy's dress shoes. Then the dark flash of his suit, and finally the light brown of his face.

That was when she realized it was Royal.

She stood stunned, as the host introduced him: "Welcome Chicago's number one DJ and featured artist in Galaxy Studio's upcoming feature film, *Elevated Tracks*!"

Royal wore a high-watt grin and stood beside her in a second spotlight.

"Give it up one more time for the Queen of Urban Prophecy, Chicago's very own Deza!" Royal commanded.

The audience exploded in cheers.

"Although two of the categories that you're nominated in haven't been announced yet," he said. "You'll always be a winner to me. Deza, I've loved you since the minute we met.

I know we've had our ups and downs, but my life is better with you in it. You're the only one for me."

She looked up at him, totally confused. Why was he doing this? Why was he even here? She had never called him back.

But he was looking at her, intently. The cameras were on them. And then he reached for her hand. She didn't resist, letting him take it. But then he got down on one knee and the audience screamed.

To Deza, it seemed like she was suddenly underwater. What was happening?

Royal knelt in front of her. She felt light-headed. Disoriented. Unsteady.

"Deza Starling," Royal asked, "will you marry me?"

There was only one answer to the question. The answer was yes. The audience was starting to murmur it. Then say it out loud. Then it became a chant. Yes! Yes!

Deza stood there with her mouth open. She looked at the ring. It was the same ring he had given her before. The one she had thrown out the window in Chicago. How had he even found it? She recalled his first proposal. Just the two of them. In that awful apartment. How hopeful they had been. The life they were going to build. Together.

"So what do you say, baby?" Royal asked. "You gonna make me the happiest man in the world?"

Deza couldn't quite get her internal balance. He was proposing? Had just proposed? She was supposed to respond now? Deza opened her mouth, uncertain of what she was gonna say.

The moment stretched beyond suspense. Beyond awkwardness.

Royal knelt in front of her, the ring box aloft. His once hopeful smile now frozen in place. His lips still drawn back, but every second his expression was turning into more of a grimace.

Deza stood there with her mouth open. She needed to get

it together. She needed to say something. Everyone was watching. A few nervous giggles went up in the audience.

She tried to say "I—" but her throat was tight. It came out as almost a cough. And then she tried again, but what came out wasn't a word but a sound, a beat. Then another.

Her voice made the association before her mind did. She suddenly found herself beatboxing the intro to one of her old songs. She wished she had a DJ, but she wasn't prepared for this ambush.

> From the very beginning, your love was fake
> Rode in like a stallion but you were really a
> snake

She had gotten through the first verse when the DJ put on the actual version, the instrumental track.

Royal was the last one on the stage to get the memo. His face fell as he realized he was being turned down. He got up off the stage floor.

As Deza rapped to the audience, talking about him in the third person, he stood on the stage, both hands, including the one gripping the ring box, buried in his pockets.

Deza finished the song. She didn't appreciate being used like this. The director, the producers, everyone must have been in on it. They'd all counted on her being startled into saying yes. Making it a night to remember.

It still would be. Maybe they didn't care, either way. But Royal cared.

She stalked off. Leaving him standing alone on the stage, right next to an empty neon yellow X.

Damián and Lisette came back to the hotel after the Paperclip party to watch the show. It was familiar, comfortable between them. They always watched award shows. He would jokingly pick up one of her mermaid statuettes and give improvised thank-you speeches while she laughed and clapped.

And yet, this year, it felt a little like a step back. He was actually closer to this now. Was DJ for the only artist nominated in three categories this year. He was a good sport, but part of him wanted to be there, *in it for real*.

When Deza came on, he had to keep looking away from the screen. He couldn't let Lisette witness how much Deza entranced him. If he watched her for more than five seconds at a time, Lisette would see. Lisette would know what it meant.

His eyes kept moving back to Lisette to keep from giving himself away.

He was looking at Lisette when the cameras cut to the audience, to the wild applause and then the gasp. That was what brought his attention back to the screen. Someone was coming down onto the stage.

It was that fucking DJ *cabrón*. And when he went down on one knee, Damián almost cursed at the TV.

But then, in an instant, Deza was telling him no? Was disrapping him? Damián's mouth fell open.

Lisette was laughing and pointing. "That's right, girl," she said. "You tell his ass."

Damián was laughing too. And then the show's DJ mixed her song in right on the beat.

"Nooooo she didn't!" Damián jeered at the TV.

Then Lisette was hugging him. "I wonder what it'll be like when you propose," she said.

Damián stopped laughing. Deza had turned the DJ down. Presumably, she was single now. No guy was gonna come back from that. Being turned down on national TV. Deza and Royal were done for good. And he was back with Lisette.

On a five-year plan.

* * *

Backstage, Deza had just gotten her mic taken off when she turned to exit and put her gown back on. Royal was standing there.

"You couldn't have at least said you'd think about it?" he asked. "You had to leave me there on my knees? With a ring in my hand? Did you enjoy making a fool out of me?"

"Making a food out of *you*?" Deza asked. "You don't get it. Did you ever actually listen to any of my music?"

"This ain't a song, Deza," Royal said. "This is real life."

Deza saw he still had the ring in his hand. Then she realized she was still wearing his necklace. The diamond D. She had still been hoping that maybe they'd get through this. Until the moment he came down on a wire to ambush her. She took off the necklace and put it in his other hand.

"Here," she said. "Look like you gon be keeping all your jewelry tonight. I wore this tonight because I still love you, Royal. I still wanted it to work. But you don't get to pull a stunt to force me to say yes, because it's what you want. You need to actually ask, and be ready for me to say yes, no, maybe, or I don't know. Or say yes with some conditions, some shit that would need to change. If you don't wanna be embarrassed, don't propose in public. Especially when you knew I was mad and wasn't calling you back."

"I counted on you, Deza," Royal said, "to at least show me a little consideration."

"You counted on me to put you above myself," Deza said. "Which is why I can't fuck with you no more. Ring or no ring."

From deeper in the backstage, they heard a commotion.

"Come back here!"

A paparazzo appeared from the darkness of the backstage, his camera had a bright light, and he was filming.

Deza stepped back.

"In the end, you did me a favor," Royal said loudly. "You're at your peak, Deza. Unless you can magically predict some other shit, it's all downhill from here. But not me. I'm on my way up. Hollywood, baby. I'm probably better off starting my movie career as a single man. Just like the *Rolling Stone* reporter said: first me, then this new DJ on your tour. Without the music, you got nothing."

He walked away, leaving her standing there. She realized that the cameraman was filming her shocked face.

A security guard grabbed the paparazzo and hauled him out.

Deza stood there, stunned. She had lost in one of the music award categories already. Maybe Royal was right.

She stood backstage, shaking. Why did it seem like everyone left her? Hurt her? She couldn't count on anybody. And here she was in the spotlight. Alone. Motherfuckers coming at her, and no one had her back.

Chapter 32

Brooklyn

It was in the first few months that Deza was living with Tyesha. The honeymoon was wearing off. Three of them living in close quarters had started to grate. Thug Woofer hadn't called and offered her a record deal. Deza was going to open mics in New York and having to prove herself as an out-of-town emcee. She didn't seem to be on a rocket trajectory to stardom. It was just a new version of real life. Deza didn't want to impose too long on Tyesha. What if her mother had been right? She worried that Tyesha would get tired of them before Deza's big break. She couldn't afford to live on her own in this city. Going back to Chicago to live with her parents would be the worst possible outcome. A daily chorus of "I told you so" to "ungrateful bitches" who didn't know how to stay in their lane.

That night in Brooklyn, Amaru was asleep and Deza was oiling Tyesha's scalp in the bedroom.

"Auntie," Deza said quietly. "Why'd you move to New York?"

Tyesha sighed. "Too much family drama," she said. "I thought I might never finish college."

Deza took a deep breath. "You didn't need to get two

degrees and move to New York to run a health clinic. Auntie Lucille's clinic in Chicago been waiting for you since the day she died. It was supposed to be you there running it. Not some old white lady from Hyde Park who got cultural competency."

"I couldn't—" Tyesha began. She absentmindedly began to straighten one of the pillows that was slumped down. "It was barely the funeral and already people were talking about how I was gonna take over the center. I was only fourteen. Besides, it was Auntie Lou's dream, not mine. All those boys. Like I was supposed to be able to be their leader? They were all trying to fuck me. She was the caring mother figure they never had. Not me."

"Mama said you saw her get shot," Deza said quietly into the back of her aunt's head.

Tyesha nodded.

Deza pulled a fingerful of hair grease from the jar and slid it down the line between the tracks in her aunt's scalp.

"But I still don't understand why you had to leave," Deza said. "You didn't have to take over the damn center if you didn't want to. But why you had to leave?"

"I told you," Tyesha said. "I had to get out of Chicago."

"Stop talking about leaving Chicago," Deza said. "You didn't leave Chicago, you left us. One day you were there and the next day you called to say you were moving." Deza began to cry.

Tyesha turned around. She opened her mouth like she wanted to protest, but then she closed it. She leaned toward Deza and put an arm around her, but Deza pushed it away roughly.

"You fucking left us," Deza spat, furious. "You knew Mama was crazy and Grandmama was no help, and our brothers were in jail. Zeus was useless and his 'like-a-son-to-me' bodyguard was around all the time, and Auntie Lou was dead, and you left us. How could you leave us? You were the only one who could help. The only one left we could trust." She threw herself down on the bed and began to sob in earnest.

From the other room, they heard the springs of the couch creak, like maybe they had woken up Amaru.

Tyesha crept toward the door.

"What?" Deza said. "You bout to leave again?"

"No," Tyesha said. "I was just gonna check on—" She broke off and sagged down onto the bed. "I'm sorry I left. I'm sorry I didn't think about how it would affect you. I'm sorry it was so hard."

Deza curled into Tyesha's lap and sobbed hard. And apparently Amaru slept through all of it. The howling sobs, the hiccupping as Deza caught her breath.

When Tyesha opened the door to get some tissue for Deza to wipe her face, they heard Amaru's heavy, even breathing from the couch.

Tyesha handed Deza a wad of tissues and sat down beside her again.

"I was twenty when I left," Tyesha said. "Your age now."

Deza turned sharply. "No you weren't," she said.

Tyesha nodded. "I had just voted for the first time, but I couldn't drink legally."

"You were really just twenty?" Deza asked, incredulous.

Tyesha nodded.

"Somehow I thought you were older," Deza said. "Damn, it's hard enough trying to take care of Amaru, but at least she's fourteen. I would have been what? Twelve? Amaru would have been in elementary."

"I couldn't ever say no to your mama, because it meant you all were vulnerable. But I also knew that if she didn't have me to call, she would have to step up."

"Yeah," Deza said flatly. "It didn't really work out that way."

"I know," Tyesha said. "But if I had flunked out of college, then I wouldn't have anything to give you girls. I would've been back at Mama's in the projects or struggling to keep a studio apartment in Chicago on minimum wage."

"Amaru and I spent a lot of nights alone," Deza said. "We would've rather be on your couch or Grandmama's couch than on our own."

"I know," Tyesha said. "I can never make that up to you. But I finished college. And I got myself together so now I can be there for both of you. For real. I can support you in getting your rap career going. And I can help Amaru. When that big opportunity comes up for you, you won't have to worry about your little sister. I got her. You can just rise and shine."

Chapter 33

At the Billboard Awards, Deza was back in the velvet gown. She sat between Woof and Anasuya. Deza's chest was still tight from Royal's verbal attack. Her smile was a little frozen. It was good to be with friendlier faces, but what she needed was to cry it out on her aunt's shoulder.

On her way out through the backstage, she had run into Cardi, who was on her way to announce one of the categories. She was paired up with RM, one of the rappers from the K-pop group BTS. Cardi hand-pulled Deza into a hug. In her ear, Cardi whispered, "Girl, you did the right thing."

Deza squeezed her hard for a second, then let go. They took a photo together that they each posted on their Insta accounts, and Deza hustled back to her seat.

"Damn, girl," Anasuya said when she sat back down. "That was crazy."

Deza could only nod. A production assistant had rushed her out front, because they were announcing another category she was nominated in.

Anasuya was sitting there, smiling. Was that a backstabbing smile?

Deza found her voice. "Did you know?" she asked Anasuya. "Did they tell you he was coming to surprise me?"

Anasuya shook her head.

Deza wanted to say something else, but then they were announcing the category of top new artist.

Nicasio Louis was the favorite. Anasuya's man. His song, "Honeysuckle Girl," was the love anthem that America had been waiting for. Paperclip had all their machinery behind him.

"Good luck," Anasuya whispered to her.

Her face was so open. Deza's suspicion dissolved.

"Good luck to your man," Deza whispered back. She didn't know if Anasuya heard, because she was leaning over to put her arms around Nicasio.

Which was good. Because the Afropop queen called Deza's name.

She was stunned.

"Top new artist!"

Deza stood, shakily. She had to figure out how to walk and not fall in the heels, the long dress. She grabbed a fistful of gold velvet skirt and strode to the stage, applause thundering all around her.

She hadn't really practiced a speech. She thought it would jinx it.

"Wow," she said. "I just—want to thank Thug Woofer, first of all, for believing in me."

She looked out at him. He was clapping and pointing back at her.

"I need to thank my family," she said. "My mom and dad. My sister Amaru." God, they sounded so normal. When did she ever call them that? "And my auntie. Really both of them. My aunt Tyesha, and this is for my aunt Lou. If you Black from Chicago, you know who I mean. And this is for all the female emcees. Who think there's only one way to make it big in hip hop. I hope this lets everyone know, you can just do you. Thank you."

*   *   *

Lisette had fallen asleep. Damián stayed up watching the videos and all the post show analysis. Then he started on the less official videos on social media.

His breath stopped when he came across an interview with Deza.

Deza was talking to an older African American woman when an entertainment reporter interrupted them. The reporter was a light brown woman with a bone-straight weave that she kept having to tuck behind her ear to keep it from slipping into her eyes.

"Excuse me," she said to the older woman. "Can I just ask Deza a few questions?"

"Of course," the woman said. She stepped back, but Deza held on to her.

After the typical exchange about how Deza must be so excited to win, the reporter asked, "So what's next for you, Deza?"

"I want to put together a series of remixes with my DJ, Damián Castellano," Deza said. "I love what he's doing in terms of local and regional hip hop from different parts of the US."

"Will these be dance remixes?" the reporter asked.

"If Damián is doing them, they'll definitely be danceable," Deza said. "But also serious. Joanne here is a music producer, and we've just started discussing a collaboration about hurricanes and climate."

"I used to be in Houston," Joanne said. "But I'm a refugee from Hurricane Harvey. I've been following everything that Deza and Damián were doing, and I want to do a special project with them."

"So you all just started talking about it right now?" the reporter asked.

"Right here, right now," Deza said. "Next, I'll be talking to my folks at the Paperclip label to get them to sign off."

"So I guess this is a live exclusive," the reporter said. "Multi-award-winning artist Deza just revealed her next project right here on *Entertainment Live*."

My DJ, Damián Castellano.

Damián couldn't get the sound bite out of his head. He scrolled through the internet to get all the reports as Lisette slept, her beautiful face only a few feet from him on the bed.

When Damián said goodbye to Lisette in front of the hotel, it didn't feel right. Or maybe it felt too right. She was kissing him goodbye ten times and telling him how much she would miss him. He was saying the right things, but wasn't totally feeling it.

Of course, he had offered to go with her to the airport to see her off, but she said no, save his money. And he agreed to put her in a shuttle from the hotel, it was practical. But he realized that if he didn't really want to go to the airport, he wasn't hungry to extend his time with her. To wait in the ticket line with her. To hold hands at the security gate till the last possible second. To watch her and wave when she got through. He realized that as much as he'd enjoyed the company and the sex and the connection, he didn't have that in-love feeling with her.

But maybe that was realistic. They had lived together. Had gotten up and gone to jobs every day. Had fought about whose turn it was to clean the bathroom. It was usually his. She did it without needing to be reminded. Maybe it was that. It must be that, right? You can't expect a guy to snap back to the honeymoon phase after they'd gotten so familiar, right?

But what if it wasn't?

There was this way that he had felt about her in New York. Whenever they went out. At clubs. Walking down the street. Just on the subway in between things. This is my girl. My woman.

When he saw her off, he didn't feel that way. When they had been alone, it had been . . . warm. Comfortable. Familiar. But the minute she left, it was as if the spell broke.

And how had he agreed to this five-year plan if . . . if he wasn't really in love with her? Which was fucked up, because she had come all the way out here to see him. To try to get him back. It was kind of like Royal with Deza. But no, that was totally different. Royal proposed in public. Lisette showed up privately. They talked about it. But first they had sex. Right. They had just sort of fallen back into things. Picked up where they had left off. But it wasn't the same.

As he packed up his few belongings in the Las Vegas hotel room, he realized that while he had enjoyed Lisette, he wasn't excited to get back to New York and start their life together. But that might be him just taking her for granted again. It was hard to know. He grabbed up his backpack and closed the hotel door behind him.

Deza had spent the morning on the phone with her manager, her producer, two different execs from the label. She should have talked about this with them before putting it out in the media. She had deadlines on this sophomore album. She was behind.

Yes, but she was unblocked. She was writing again.

They liked the tracks, but it wasn't enough to get them back on schedule for the album release date.

Deza promised to get all the rest of the work in on time.

This wasn't how it worked. Deza didn't just get to go out and set up projects with anyone she wanted and inform the label after the fact. She couldn't keep them in the dark.

"Hold on a minute," Deza said, her voice rising. "I just won you all two awards. And before that, I was just on national television and my ex, who is a fucking cheater and a hustler, proposed to me out of nowhere. And I was standing there stuck on stupid, till I figured out a way to get myself out of it. Only to have him disrespect me in a clip that has gone viral. Do you really mean to tell me that every single person at this label was also in the dark about that? Nobody from Paperclip approved that? When you all wanted to know what I was wearing and what I was doing with my hair. When we argued about the height of my heels. I'm still washing glue out of my baby hair. So don't tell me about being left in the dark. I'm willing to meet all your deadlines, but I want a little creative freedom to work with this producer on a couple of tracks. The last thing we argued about was putting 'Almost Home' on the album. And it wasn't me but Woof who got you to agree to that. I think we can all agree that my last idea worked out pretty well."

The moment the words were out of her mouth, she regretted them. Shaqana's life wasn't a bargaining chip with her label. Monique's grief wasn't something to use to her advantage.

But it hit home with the label.

"I don't want you to misconstrue my actions here," the exec said. "I am approving this collaboration because you are still new to this business. Still able to get caught up in the moment. I'll chalk it up to that. Please run any new collaborations through us first." He let it hang in the air for a moment. "Are we agreed?"

"Yes," Deza said. "We're agreed."

So it was official. Deza would go to Austin after the tour was over, and she invited Damián to join her on the project.

"Austin?" Lisette asked. She had called him that night to check in.

"Yeah," Damián said. "With this Black producer who's a refugee from Hurricane Harvey."

"But I thought you were coming back to New York," she said.

"I will," Damián said. "Paperclip will only let her do one

song. But if the producer likes what I'm doing, they might let me do the whole album. We have this vision of different local and regional hip hop styles from different parts of the country that are being affected in different ways by the climate crisis."

"That's great, Damián," Lisette said. "But what about our five-year plan?"

He felt like an ass. He couldn't really back out of it. Not when they'd woken up in Las Vegas together and had sex that very morning.

"I know," Damián said. "I have five years to get my music off the ground to support our family."

"Right," Lisette said. "And I thought it was understood that you would stay in New York."

"Yeah," Damián said. "But I expect to be free to travel until after we get pregnant."

"It's not like everything just magically falls into place," she said. "There's a lot of work. In setting up a house. All of it. I don't expect to be doing all of that on my own."

"Lisette," Damián said. "You're talking about particulars for year five. I'm talking about year one. Month one, really, and you're already trying to keep me from doing my music."

"I'm just saying that you've been on tour for over a month. Couldn't you come back to the city before you start the next thing? Can you think about us and not just about your music career?"

"It'll only be a couple of days in Texas," Damián said. "It's practical. I can save like five hundred dollars if I travel to Austin by bus and then just buy a one-way ticket to New York. It's so much cheaper to come back a few days later." He felt like a punk, hiding out behind the math of it. But he needed time to process.

"But what if she wants you to do the whole album?" Lisette asked. "That's more than just a few days."

"I know," Damián said. "And we'll cross that bridge

when we come to it. Mami, I'm trying to build up my career so I can make a living when I come back to New York."

Lisette didn't back down, though. "You want to have it both ways," she said. "You build this life without me that takes place all over the world. And then promise you'll give it up to have a family. But will you really? Am I supposed to just trust you? What if you resent it? Guys like you *think* you want a family. But it's a lot of fucking responsibility. I'm not gonna end up divorced and single parenting while you decide that the family life you only fantasized about isn't what you really want. What the hell do you really want, Damián?"

"I want you to stop fucking pressuring me, Lisette," Damián said.

"Ugh," she said. "Here we go again."

"No," Damián said. "Actually, here we don't go again. You came and surprised me, but you had this plan already, didn't you? You were gonna come out and fuck me and then be like 'I have a plan for us.'"

"Right," she said. "A plan for *us.*"

"No, Lisette," he said, his voice rising. "You don't get it. You may think it's for us, but it's your plan."

"And here comes the *macharón*," she said, her voice rising, too. "You act like planning is something women do to control men. Planning is fucking work that I take on because you never do it. You never planned a fucking thing when we lived together. Not a meal, not a color scheme of a room, not a system for the house, not an evening with friends. Nothing. You just go with the fucking flow. It's not a flow, dude, somebody else is actually rowing the boat. But then, when I share the plan after doing all the work, you're like, 'you are not the boss of me!' I'm not trying to fucking control you, I'm trying to make our life happen."

"I don't want you to make our life happen," he said. "My life is already happening. This is like the most exciting shit that's ever happened in my career and it seems like you can't wait for it to end so I can get back to New York and get back on track with your plan for us."

"Everyone isn't doing their dream job, bro," Lisette said. "We don't all have that privilege."

"Why the fuck not?" Damián asked. "I don't mean everyone, I mean you. Why aren't you doing what you love? Or figuring out what you really love and going after it? You used to love your teaching job. But then you said you should go into administration, because it paid more. And ever since then, you've been miserable at work."

"I'm not miserable," she said.

"You're definitely not happy," Damián said. "When we met, you were singing backup for your girl on a dare. You were gonna take that acting class. You used to make all your jewelry. You were teaching part-time and you were happy. Since you turned thirty, it seems like all you can go after is the idea of having a family."

"What's wrong with wanting a family?" she demanded. "Or being willing to sacrifice to have one?"

"Nothing," he said. "But I don't think that the way to a happy family life is to do some shit you hate every day. Our parents did it like that and they didn't seem very happy. And then they kept saying they were working so hard so our lives could be different, and now we're trying to make our lives the same."

"That's ridiculous, Damián," Lisette scoffed. "We're nothing like our parents."

"Maybe that's because we're not parents yet," he said. "I seen pictures of my folks when they were young. They looked so much happier. *Coño*, Lisette, my papi is like a shadow. Like a goddamn ghost. I don't want to fucking end up like him!" Damián banged his fist against the wall of the bus.

"You're not gonna end up like your father, Damián," Lisette said quietly.

"Damn right I'm not," he said. "I'm gonna build the life I

want. And then I'll have kids later, once I've set it up so I know I can keep my creative life going. Yeah, I want kids, but I'm tired of being the bad guy because I don't want them as much as you do. I don't want to be the bad guy because for me, a family isn't the *only* thing I want."

"No, Damián," Lisette said. She didn't sound as angry anymore. She sounded tired. "I don't want to be your fall-back plan if you can't make your dream happen of traveling all over the world as a DJ. I need a man who wants the family life first. I should have known. I should never have come out to see you. Goodbye, Damián."

"Lisette, wait—" In the moment he was losing her, he still knew he wasn't in love. But he didn't want it to end like this.

"No," she said. "I'm clear about this. I shoulda known that first night on the bus. When I told you I was on the pill and you pulled out those fucking condoms. You think I wanna trap you? No. I'm looking for a man who wants this as much as me. Who's gonna work as hard as me to make it happen. And then who's gonna stick around and enjoy it. You didn't need to use those damn condoms, Damián."

He didn't know what to say to that.

"I just—" he began.

"Have fun in Austin," Lisette said. And she hung up.

The next day, Damián sat in the bus lounge with Anasuya, working on beats, unable to get his call with Lisette out of his mind.

"Damián?" Anasuya said. "Are you even here, dude? You seem a million miles away."

"My bad," Damián said. "Lisette dumped me last night."

"I'm sorry," Anasuya said.

Damián waved the empathy away. "It was my fault," he said. "I feel like such a dick. I played house with Lissette for a little while, but part of me knew I didn't really want what she wanted. She said I was using her as a fallback plan. In case DJing didn't work out."

Anasuya furrowed her brows. "Yeah," she said. "That is kind of fucked up. You invited her all the way out here and played along, but you didn't want it for real."

"No," Damián said. "I didn't invite her. She just showed up. But then things started to happen. And I just went along with it."

"Oh," Anasuya said with a shrug. "That's totally different. If she came to get back with you, then she's the one who put herself out there. You tried it on and didn't like it. Nothing wrong with that."

"Are you sure?" Damián asked. "So why do I feel like such an asshole?"

"It's just the cultural hype," Anasuya said. "There's nothing wrong with not wanting kids. Unless you already happen to have them." She made a wry face. "Shoutout to my father."

"Right?" Damián said. "I don't wanna ever be a deadbeat dad."

"Well that's the good news," Anasuya said. "Men can be one hundred percent in charge of whether or not they have sex with birth control. But it's okay that you don't know if you want kids. I don't know if I want kids. So it's good you all broke up now. Save everyone a lot of heartache."

"Part of me feels like if Lisette really had a passion of her own, she wouldn't want kids so much."

"Maybe," Anasuya said. "But some people just really want that. Like Nicasio. If I popped up pregnant this month, he'd be up here doing the happy daddy dance. Even though it makes no sense. I'm on tour. He's in the studio. Nobody has time for a baby. But he feels like family love will conquer all. Since when can we trust that to work out?"

Damián shook his head. "Maybe you're right. Maybe it's

good that we broke up. It's fucked up that I might have gone along with her for a life that would be second best."

"What would be first best?" Anasuya asked.

He looked at the closed door of Deza's compartment.

"If I'm honest about it," Damián said. "She's who I want."

Anasuya smiled. "Then you should go for it."

"But now it would look like I was rebounding," Damián said.

"Are you?"

"No, I'm starting to think the second try with Lisette was the rebound from Deza."

Chapter 34

Outside Las Cruces, NM

When Deza woke up the next morning, she expected to feel heartbroken about Royal. But she didn't. Deep inside, she had known that it wasn't going to work since Oklahoma City. The girl's ass was just the final straw. No. He could have come back from that. The proposal was the final straw.

Mostly, she felt relieved. She had been swimming in anxiety from wondering whether she should forgive him or dump him. Aaaand we have a winner! The move was dump, and she had done it. She felt relieved to know she was rid of him.

She looked out at the desert landscape. She had heard that it was carved from ancient times, when it had been the bottom of the ocean. Only an underwater landscape could explain the outcroppings of rock. Nothing could develop in those shapes if it were subject to the aboveground gravity that made hills and mountains.

But it was so damn hot here. Temperatures staying in three digits. Anyone who still doubted global warming needed to spend some time in the Southwest right about now. Or maybe these corporations didn't care. They would just keep turning up their air conditioning as long as they were making a killing.

She was already feeling pessimistic about corporations when she got an update about the fire in the Indonesian sweatshop factory where they made Rock.it sportswear. She was horrified by some of the details that the corporation had been attempting to suppress.

An investigation of the fire revealed not only the dangerous working conditions, but in digging through the burned building, they brought out several small corpses, confirming that there had been children at work.

The photo showed a pair of brown-skinned men carrying a stretcher with a small shape under the white cloth. The caption said the victim was seven.

Her breath caught. How had she let herself be part of this? Deza could feel her eyes fill with tears. So small. She remembered when Amaru was that small. Even as a child, she had the urge to protect her little sister from everything. Who was gonna protect these kids? She took a deep breath and the tears passed. Then she went to knock on Damián's door.

"Can I talk to you for a minute?" Deza asked when he opened the door.

"Sure, what's up?" he asked, leaning against the doorjamb. "I been working on something new for you. I was gonna wait till it was more done. Do you wanna take a listen, though?"

Deza shook her head. "I just read the news out of Indonesia," Deza said.

Damián sighed. "You thinking about the fire?" he asked.

"It's fucked up," Deza said. "I should have listened to you about the Rock.it endorsement."

"Yeah, it's fucked up," Damián said. "But that fire would have happened with or without your endorsement."

"I know, but it just feels so irresponsible to have gotten on their bandwagon when you warned me that they were shady. At this moment when my face is everywhere, I gave them a signal boost."

"You can use your visibility to talk about it," Damián said. "Write a rhyme about them. Fight fire with fire."

Deza's eyes lit up. "Yes!" she said. "That's it!" She leaned forward and hugged him.

Deza stood in the parking lot in El Paso, Texas. The desert air was dry and crisp in the early morning. The sun wasn't up yet, but the temperature was already in the eighties.

Damián set up his laptop and a speaker as she set up two tripods, one with his phone and one with hers. Behind her was a metal clothing rack with three Rock.it sweatsuits. Red, white, and blue.

She pressed Record on Damián's phone to videotape the whole thing.

Damián had made her a track, and he pressed Play on his laptop. It looped for twenty minutes, so she could take her time getting into the groove.

She felt awkward, nervous performing for just him and Anasuya. She had written the lyrics in a rush, just that morning. Anasuya had composed the hook and chorus in fifteen minutes.

"You got this, Deza," Damián said. "Just do you."

She nodded, then she went live on Instagram on her phone.

> *Leather, mohair, cashmere, wool*
> *Corporations fiending for the dollars they can*
> * pull*
> *Cotton, rayon, linen, jute*
> *What about human life? It doesn't compute.*
> *The fabric of murder is itching my skin*
> *I'm sweating in the suit that I got dressed in*

After the first verse, Anasuya's voice came up on the track, singing the hook.

Fight fire with fire.

Deza reached into her pocket and took out a lighter. She flicked it twice and the flame leaped up. She touched it to the hem of the pants on one of the sweatsuits, and it bloomed into flame. She had poured lighter fluid on the three suits before she hung them up. The white one in the middle blazed first.

> *Thought I was blessed and ready stock it*
> *The money from associating with Rock.it*
> *Till I saw their stock options led to the dead*
> *And the plan I had began to burn in my head*

At the second chorus, she lit up the red one.

> *Fight fire with fire.*
> *It's too hot for this fabric, too hot for this gear*
> *Too hot for the conditions of workers in here*
> *We want the hottest, the latest, the bargain the*
> *   steal*
> *But children are dying so we can get a cheap*
> *   deal*

By the time she got into the third chorus, other artists had seen the blaze and started to come out of the buses to watch. Deza motioned to Anasuya to come join the shot.
Fight fire with fire, the vocalist sang, harmonizing with her own recorded voice, as Deza lit the blue sweatsuit on fire.

> *We used to pick cotton from dawn to dusk*
> *Now we just wear it cause someone picks it*
> *   for us*
> *Here's the question to my Black folks in the*
> *   USA*
> *Are we gonna let slave labor clothe us today?*

Two of Vienna's backup singers joined in from the crowd, making it four-part harmony. Deza motioned for them to join in the shot. The Black girl shook her head but kept singing. Neither of them had their hair or makeup done. But the Latina girl came up. She had on a torn sweatshirt and her hair in a sloppy ponytail.

> *Burn it all down, the corporate greed*
> *Burn it all down, spend on what people need*
> *Good jobs and unions and justice and edu-*
> *   cation*
> *Where children are safe, not victims of*
> *   exploitation*

The empty parking lot was filled with flames and smoke and harmonies and rhythm, and Deza kept repeating the final line:

> *Fire brings light to expose the truth*
> *Fire burns bright to reveal the proof*
> *Hip hop nation I hope I can trust*
> *That Rock.it is fired from speaking for us*

Within fifteen minutes, #FireWithFire was trending on social media. Hundreds of individuals, including several other celebrities, burned their sweatsuits in livestreams.

For several hours that day, #FireWithFire was trending at #1. Paperclip rushed some paperwork to Deza and Damián to make the song available on iMusic.

@RatchetRapActivist:
That's what I'm talmbout. All you haters were like, "Almost Home" is a fluke. Deza can't really predict the future. What's she gonna do next? She gonna help

shape the future. Shape it for justice. That's what
Deza's gonna do, motherfuckers. Watch.
#FireWithFire
#BurnTheRockit

Then the conversation on Clubhouse devolved into an argument about whether people should burn their Rock.it sportwear or just sell it and donate the proceeds to the families of those killed and injured.

The next morning, Deza got a nasty letter from Rock.it. Her sponsorship was being terminated. But not only that, they were going to sue her to get the money back.

"You did the right thing," Damián said. "And you managed to make a bigger statement by taking the sponsorship and burning the clothes than you would have made by turning it down."

"You're right," Deza said. "But I wish I could keep the money."

"You haven't spent it yet, have you?" Damián asked.

"I haven't even gotten it yet," she said. "Now I probably never will."

Chapter 35

Brooklyn

There was a cadence to their parents' fights. Like a familiar song. There was an intro, when her mama had a particular tone. Then a first verse of Zeus denying whatever Jenisse had accused him of. Her mama then, like the woman singing a catchy hook: *you cheated, you lyin ass, no-good nigga.* Then a second verse. More denials. Gaslighting. Then her mama, singing the hook again: *you cheated . . .* Maybe it should have given Deza some compassion for her mother, but it didn't. He was so obviously lying. Why didn't she just leave?

But this fighting dance was the agreement. His penance. He let her verbally abuse him and maybe land a few blows on his chest, and then they made up. Like the rich guys who cheated and publicly embarrassed their wives, and then went out and bought them diamond jewelry.

But that time in that hotel in Brooklyn, it was the wrong song. The intro was off-key. Zeus wasn't the confident rapper, throwing down his bars. There was no hook. Just voices back and forth.

"You gon tell me how to run my business?" Zeus demanded. His own voice singing tenor instead of bass.

It was the wrong fight.

"I been watching you do this shit for almost thirty years. Don't act like I don't know what I'm talking about."

"Stay outta this, Jenisse," he growled, his voice a warning. "It ain't yo business."

"Nigga, you gon get yourself killed," she said. "And that's definitely my business."

Zeus's eyes glanced to the front door of the suite. His bodyguard, Reagan, was right outside. Given the volume of the fight, he could hear everything.

Deza was in her late teens now. She could piece the information together. Zeus had been trying to move into new territory in New York. Had some brushes with the Ukrainian mob.

He was in over his head. Reagan had been blowing smoke up his ass. "You got this, boss," Reagan said. "These white boys can't hold a candle to a real nigga like you. These Ukrainians don't know nothing about Chicago."

Reagan was ready to put Zeus in the line of fire. If anything went wrong in New York, Reagan would inherit Zeus's entire Chicago empire.

Jenisse knew it. She was right to warn her man, but she was drunk and not thinking. She had said it too loud and caused Zeus to lose face in front of Reagan. And his kids. Deza and Amaru sat frozen on the couch. Teenagers now, but feeling like scared kids.

Then Jenisse took several steps toward the bedroom.

"Where you going?" Zeus demanded, grabbing her arm. "I ain't through talking to you."

"To get my purse to go shopping for a black dress," Jenisse said. "I wanna look good when I go from common-law wife to common-law widow."

She yanked her arm free and tried to enter the bedroom, but Zeus grabbed her by the hair and dragged her back into the living room.

Jenisse started cussing and tried to fight him off.

Up until now, the two girls had sat frozen, listening. But upon sight of their father grabbing their mother, Deza screamed and Amaru started crying.

With a shaky hand, Deza made a call on her phone. "Auntie Ty, you need to come get us."

"Your mama and Zeus fighting again?" Tyesha asked.

"Come now," Deza said. "Please."

"On my way."

Fifteen minutes later, Tyesha texted that she was headed up in the elevator. Deza threw the last few things into her bag and stepped out into the hallway.

The nondescript hallway was beige, with forgettable, muted watercolors on the wall. Outside the door stood the unwelcome figure of a tall Black man in a long gray coat. Reagan.

The deep bass of Zeus's voice blasted into the hallway, his incomprehensible rant, into which Jenisse interjected sharply: "Well, I don't give a fuck—"

"Amaru, come on!" Deza shouted into the suite, adding another layer of noise.

"I can't find my gym bag," Amaru said. Through the door, Deza could see her sister looking around wildly, brows knit, nearly in tears. "I'll be in trouble if I miss my workout tomorrow."

"I can get you new stuff," Tyesha offered.

Deza walked in and stood in the middle of the room. Then she picked up a pair of basketball sneakers from beside an armchair and led her sister out into the hallway.

Tyesha pulled both girls into her arms. "Let's just go, okay?"

Zeus's baritone voice sounded from inside the suite: "No, bitch, just shut your ass up, okay?" His words gained in clarity and volume as he came closer to the door.

Deza felt Tyesha pull her and her sister to the other side of the hall and out of the way.

"That's right, nigga," Jenisse's voice came, shrill and contemptuous. "Run off like you always do. Can't stand up to your own woman, no wonder some pussy white boy mobsters kicking yo faggot ass. You betta get back in here!"

Zeus tore out of the hotel room with his fists clenched. "Either I'm leaving or I'm a kill yo ass. Right in front of yo kids. You put one hand on me and you made your choice."

Deza felt Tyesha's arm close around her tightly. Her aunt marched her and Amaru toward the elevator.

Zeus strode past, towering and regal in a long black trench coat. Reagan was right on his heels, like a pale shadow.

The two men took the elevator car down.

Just before the door closed, an empty liquor bottle flew out of the suite and hit the hallway's opposite wall.

"That nigga ain't shit!" Jenisse slurred from inside the room. "Ain't even dog shit."

Deza started pulling Tyesha toward the elevators.

"Is she gonna be okay?" Tyesha asked.

"I think so," Amaru said. "As long as he's gone."

"I don't give a fuck about her one way or the other," Deza said.

As they waited for the elevator, Jenisse began a loping walk toward them. She had an empty brandy glass in her hand.

"I don't fucking believe it," Deza muttered. "We almost made it out."

"What the hell you think you doing, Tyesha?" she asked. "You taking my kids outta my house?"

"It's not your house," Tyesha said. "It's a hotel. That Zeus paid for."

"And nobody invited you, bitch," Jenisse said.

"Deza called me," Tyesha said. "So I guess that was my invitation."

Deza cocked her head to the side, punctuating Tyesha's claim.

"She an ungrateful little bitch, too," Jenisse said. "Just like you."

Even with Tyesha's arm around her, the words still stung.

"See?" Jenisse said. "Bitches always trying to take you down. Take yo man. Take yo kids."

"And I shoulda taken them that time in Chicago," Tyesha said. "But I wasn't grown enough to know what to do. But now I know. I'm letting them decide. Girls, you wanna come with me?"

"Hell yeah," Deza said. Her mother wanted an ungrateful little bitch? She could have one. Amaru didn't answer, but she stayed close to Tyesha.

"You know where to find your kids," Tyesha said. "When you're sober and not ready to brawl with their father right in front of them."

"That nigga deserve it."

"Maybe," Tyesha said. "But they don't deserve to have to watch it."

"What you gonna do, Amaru?" Jenisse asked. "You gonna be a little traitor bitch like yo sister, or you gonna stay with yo mama?"

Amaru said nothing, but tears started to fall down her cheeks.

That was when Deza was ready to lose her shit. It was one thing for her mama to bully her. But her sister? She was ready to go off when the elevator arrived.

"Actions speak louder than words, baby," Jenisse said. "You get on that elevator, and it's just like you spat in my face."

Deza was so furious, she could barely speak. She wanted

to break out of Tyesha's grip and jump on their mother. Jenisse was tough, but she was also drunk. Deza could probably take her.

Tyesha tried to move toward the elevator, but Amaru stood frozen, her arms cradling the pair of lilac and turquoise basketball shoes.

"You ain't the one here who's fucked up," Tyesha murmured in Amaru's ear. "Jenisse always been a mean drunk. You ain't gotta put up with her shit."

Deza felt Amaru reach behind Tyesha and grip her own arm. Tyesha backed into the elevator with her arms around both of them.

"Fine!" Jenisse spat. "Ungrateful, spoiled motherfuckers."

She threw the brandy glass at them, but it swung wide and broke against the wall as the doors closed.

The three of them rode the elevator down to the parking garage in silence. Amaru cried noiselessly. Deza kept clenching and unclenching the fist of her free hand.

In the parking garage, the three of them climbed into Tyesha's silver sports car. Her aunt fished a tissue out of the glove compartment and handed it to Amaru. She wiped her eyes and blew her nose.

When Tyesha turned on the car, the Bluetooth began automatically playing the last music Tyesha had listened to: Deza's CD.

"Do you want me to turn it off?" Tyesha asked.

"I don't care," Deza said.

Tyesha let it play.

Young Black women barely got a chance these days
Brothas act like they the only target but plenty bullets shooting my way
On the other hand, we got Sandra Bland
I don't understand why folks act like just the Black man is being destroyed

say Rekia Boyd
Yeah, say her name
Cause the reaper came
We gonna have a roll call
for Mya Hall because you can't deny
the fact of Spring Valley High

As they drove across Brooklyn, Deza burst out: "Why couldn't she stay in Chicago? Why she gotta chase a man all over the fucking country? She afraid he gonna fuck somebody else? He already does that in Chicago. He stayed with her crazy ass for thirty years. Why she gotta stick to him like some kind of crazy bitch Velcro? I'll tell you why. Because he's her job. Looking cute for him. Fucking him. Nagging him. Fighting with him. That's all she does. That's all she's ever done. She has his babies, then can't be bothered with us except for us to become new subjects for her to bitch at him about. I hate her. I fucking hate her."

Tyesha turned the music off.

"I'm sorry, baby," she said.

"But she's never sorry," Deza said. "Never. Not once. I fucking hate her."

Chapter 36

Austin

Their next tour stop was in Dallas. Murda Lockk had a concert that night in San Antonio, something they had previously booked, so the rest of the artists got a night off. Deza spent the day in the studio on a collaboration with Megan Thee Stallion about protecting Black women. Megan's people had reached out after the Music Awards drama, and Deza had eagerly agreed.

Deza rolled in with a few ideas. She expected a writing session, but she didn't realize just how much Megan liked to freestyle in the studio. And Meg was so good! Deza hadn't freestyled like this since her early years in hip hop. In the process of working with Megan, they fed off each other's energy. Meg's bars were consistently strong, but Deza had a few standouts, too:

> *You're sittin in your dodgy car*
> *Spittin that misogynoir*
> *No progeny provided for*
> *When you fuck, it's an act of war . . .*

By the end of the session, Deza felt good about the tracks she'd laid down. Afterward, she got a night off, but she couldn't stop the muse. The day with Meg had inspired her, and it was like when she was in high school, lyrics just flowing from her mind like a spool of words unravelling.

In the limo ride back to the tour bus, she couldn't stop writing. For dinner, she walked by herself to a café with just her phone, her wallet, and a notebook.

It was First Friday in Austin. All the businesses were open, and the streets were strung with lights. She wandered into a pastel-colored Victorian house that had been remodeled into a café. They served her a delicious dinner of black bean soup, rice, and corn bread on their patio. The air was humid and warm. She lingered after the meal and wrote.

She'd had a call the night before with her aunt Tyesha. When the conversation turned to Deza's usual complaints about her mother, Tyesha surprised her.

"I been thinking, you might need to cut your mama some slack."

"Excuse me?" Deza had asked. "Is something wrong with this connection?"

"No for real," Tyesha said. "I've never sugarcoated anything with you. Your mama is abusive. Plain and simple. But she definitely comes by it honestly."

"So you're making excuses for her?" Deza asked.

"No," Tyesha said. "Abuse is abuse. But I'm over fifteen years younger than your mama, and it's like we had two different mothers. My mama was saved, and her mama was out in these streets."

"I've heard all the stories," Deza said. "Grandmama was still young and running around, leaving Jenisse home alone."

"Not just that," Tyesha said. "When Jenisse came up pregnant with your oldest brother, Mama put her out in the street. She might as well have just thrown her at Zeus."

"Really?" Deza asked. "Grandmama always acts like Jenisse left to be with him."

"Your grandmama has created a whole new version of what went down," Tyesha said. "One that fits the saved version of herself."

"But what her mama did when she was fifteen doesn't justify what she's done for the next thirty years," Deza said.

"Of course it doesn't," Tyesha said. "But she was fifteen. She had to drop out of high school. She had no skills. Wasn't even old enough to get a job. Of course she had to go to Zeus. She would have been homeless, Deza. She was totally dependent on him for survival."

"Okay, fine," Deza said. "But she could have left later. After she had the baby. She didn't have to cling to him for the rest of her fucking life."

"No, she didn't," Tyesha said. "But it just seems like some part of your mama is stuck at fifteen. Still clinging to this father-figure boyfriend that feels like her only hope."

"Auntie Ty," Deza said. "That was a long time ago."

"Girl, slavery was a long time ago," Tyesha said. "But we were treated brutally and learned to treat each other brutally. That shit doesn't just go away. You gotta heal it. You gotta make a choice to unlearn those lessons."

Deza didn't buy it. But for the next few days, the phrase "stuck at fifteen" stayed in her head.

That night, at the café, she began a new rhyme called "Fifteen," a story about a pregnant teenage girl.

As she walked through the streets, her head was still buzzing with rhymes. Her mind was rhyming "amniotic" with "caustic."

As she got back to the bus, she was distracted, and it was dark. She saw a guy standing outside the bus, looking her way. His face was in shadow.

Dang, she had asked Claire to keep the fans in check.

But she put on her performance face.

"How you doing?" she asked cheerfully. She hoped she could give a quick autograph and move on. Not have to extricate herself from a story about when he had first heard her music. And would she date him now that she was single, having turned down Royal on national TV.

But the moment she thought of Royal, she realized—maybe by the man's silhouette or his stance—that he actually *was* Royal. Standing there waiting for her.

She pulled out her phone to text Claire when Royal advanced toward her.

He was pulling something out of his pocket. For a moment, Deza thought it might be a gun, but she saw that it was just his own phone.

The next thing she knew, he was filming it all.

"So, I'm standing here outside Deza's tour bus. It's not that plush, as you can see, Murda Lockk actually has a much nicer bus. But Deza isn't really the headliner anymore, is she?"

He was drunk. She could hear it in the hint of a slur in his diction. "Is she" came out as "ishi." Unbidden, her mind rhymed it with "itchy." That was how he looked. Itchy, agitated.

Some situations triggered Deza's fight instinct. But this felt more like how it had with her mother. When Jenisse was angry, especially when she was drunk, Deza got quiet. Tried not to make any sudden moves. She kept her eyes on Royal, looking for her chance to get around him.

"So what you got there, Deza?" he asked. "Your notebook? You got a new prediction? Who you think gonna win the big game this weekend? What's the next lottery number? Come on, Prophecy Queen."

"I never tried to predict anything," she said.

"Oh, I see," Royal said. "Got your notebook, huh? You writing a little rhyme there, girl? We live, baby. You wanna spit something for the fans?"

"Nah, Royal," she said. "The fans will have to buy a

ticket to the concert. We got a couple more shows in the Southwest. They can go to—"

"Shut up," Royal said. "This is *my* Instagram live. I ain't signal boosting your shit."

"What are you even doing here?" Deza asked. "I thought you had gone back to Chicago." He had a huge, iced-out pendant of a crown hanging around his neck.

"Nah, baby," he said. "I start filming in LA next week. I got time to hang out. Time to set things right between us."

"Okay," Deza said. "If you wanna talk, then please turn off the video so we can talk privately."

"Oh, so *now* you want privacy," he said. "On the stage you gonna turn me down and do some rap about me? On the motherfucking television? But now it needs to be private?"

"Royal," she said. "You're drunk. You won't like the way this ends up looking on social media. If you wanna talk, why don't you call me later?"

"Because you don't call a nigga back," he said.

"You wanna talk about not calling back?" Deza said. She felt herself getting heated and realized she was just about to put way too much of her business in the street.

Royal was grinning, pleased to have gotten a rise out of her.

She took a breath. "Okay, fine," Deza said. "You wanna do this on social media, let's do it. My name is Deza Starling. I'm from Chicago. When I lived there, I dated Royal from the time I was almost eighteen. He cheated on me and I dumped his ass. Recently, when I went back to Chicago, he asked me for a second chance, and I gave it to him. But while he was on Instagram telling all of you how much he loved me, he wasn't calling me to actually talk to me. He would call at times he knew I was performing, or send texts. Until he got busted on social media looking at some girl's ass, and then he wanted to act all attentive. Which led me to believe he was full of shit and just using me to get into the spotlight."

"Using you?" Royal said, outraged. "To get into the spotlight? Girl, I put you in the fucking spotlight. I made you, Deza. Thug Woofer wanna take credit? You were *my* protégée! You were just a dark girl with a nice ass till I put my stamp on you. That should be *my* Grammy nomination. Those should be *my* Billboard Music Awards."

Anasuya walked up to get on the bus. She looked from Deza to Royal.

"Smile," Deza said. "We're live on Instagram."

"Yeah," Royal said. "With ten thousand people watching. I got followers, bitch."

"Is everything okay here?" Anasuya asked.

"Back off," Royal said. "This ain't your business."

"You okay, Deza?" Anasuya asked.

"I said back off," Royal said. "Before I knock you over."

"Are you threatening my friend?" Deza asked.

"I'll knock both you bitches over," Royal said.

"Good night, Royal," Deza said, and attempted to get on the bus.

But he stepped in front of the door and blocked their way.

"I'm not finished yet," Royal said.

Anasuya stepped around him and tapped on the bus window.

"Come on, Royal," Deza said. "It's late. We just want to go to bed."

"Face To The Sky tour? Should be Face My Dick tour. You remember that, Deza. How you sucked my dick on our second date."

"Fourth date," Deza muttered to no one in particular.

Royal gave a leering laugh. "Everyone knows dark-skin girls are freaks."

Deza opened her mouth to speak, but she was drowned out by Anasuya banging on the bus door.

"Claire," Anasuya yelled. "We have a situation."

Royal advanced on her and pushed her away from the window. Anasuya fell and scuttled back, away from him.

Royal was still blocking the door, but Claire opened the window.

"Hey!" she called to Royal. "Get out of here. I'm calling the police!"

"No!" Deza and Anasuya said it at the same time.

"These bitches trying to call the cops on me?" Royal said.

"They'll just make it worse," Deza said. "Royal," she turned to him. "We're getting on the bus and heading out. Good luck in Hollywood."

"I'll go when I'm good and ready, bitch," Royal said.

Deza attempted to push past him to get on the bus, and Royal took a swing at her. He was drunk, so his blow glanced off her cheek.

Deza was pissed now and pushed him back. Before Claire could open the door, he came at her again. Deza landed a punch on his jaw.

As he came at Deza a third time, Anasuya body slammed him out of the way of the bus door. Claire opened it and Anasuya jumped on. Deza was right behind her, but Royal grabbed the hood of her sweatshirt and swung her away from the bus. She tried to board again, but Royal kept putting himself between her and the bus door. He was bigger and stronger, and ready to do more damage, but the liquor had slowed him down.

When he charged at her again, Deza tried to knee him in the groin, but she missed the spot between his legs and hit his thigh. His eyes flashed a boiling rage, and he flew at her. He nearly had her pinned when an arm came around his throat.

"Leave her the hell alone," Damián said.

"Get the fuck off me," Royal said.

As he struggled to twist out of Damián's grip, Deza slipped past him, and Claire let her on the bus.

Royal turned around so that he and Damián were face-to-face.

"This Afro nigga again?" Royal asked.

"Get on the bus, Damián," Claire said.

But Damián stood and faced Royal.

"I saw this shit on Instagram," Damián said. "You think you made Deza? You didn't make her. Thug Woofer didn't make her. She made herself, *cabrón*. When a man finds a powerful woman who's on her way to the top, he needs to have her back and let her shine. But instead you cheat on her? Make her look bad in public? She doesn't fucking want you, man. You had your chance, and you fucked it up. Twice. Now you want her back? But you can't even ask like a man: face-to-face, asking for forgiveness. You gotta propose like a stunt and put her on the spot? Chase her bus like a stalker? You need to listen when a woman says no. Fucking pathetic."

He released Royal and walked toward the bus. For a minute, Deza thought Royal was going to let it go, but then Royal pulled out a knife.

"Damián!" she yelled. Damián turned just in time. He ducked, and Royal's knife hit the side of the bus. They struggled for a minute, Damián's hand clamped over the wrist of Royal's knife hand.

The two men tussled back and forth below the open bus window. Deza picked up her metal water bottle and found it half-full. Royal was below the bus window, but not quite in range. Then Damián surged forward, and she couldn't hit Royal without risking hitting Damián. But then Royal got a foot against the bus's back tire that gave him leverage. He pushed forward and managed to pin Damián against the bus.

But he also leaned into Deza's range. She clocked him in the back of the head with the bottle. She didn't hit him hard enough to knock him out, but stunned him for a second.

Damián rushed onto the bus, and Claire shut the door behind him.

"Where's the driver?" Damián asked.

"Smoke break," Claire said. "We'll scoop him up later."

Claire started the engine, and they pulled out, with Royal banging his fist against the bus.

"Now I really am calling the cops," Claire yelled.

"No!" Deza, Anasuya, and Damián all yelled back.

The bus rolled forward and then Royal was running behind them. He had recovered the knife and was trying to slash the tires, but he was too slow.

Claire pulled the bus in to a nearby supermarket parking lot and texted the driver to meet up with them. Deza, Damián, and Anasuya sat, shaken, on Deza's bed.

"Are you okay?" Anasuya asked Damián. There was a bright stripe of blood on his arm.

"He cut you?" Deza asked.

"No," Damián said with a laugh. "I must have scratched my arm on that stupid ass crown pendant of his. I didn't realize I was bleeding."

Deza laughed. "I always hated that fucking pendant."

"I have a first aid kit somewhere," Anasuya said. "I'll get it." She left to find it.

"What did you see in him?" Damián asked Deza.

"I don't know," Deza said. She didn't want to admit that he was pretty and knew how to charm her.

"I think I know," Damián said.

"Really?" Deza asked, a little mortified that he might see her shallowness.

"He was the perfect mix," Damián said. "He believed in you, but he also . . . took credit. It was sort of like training wheels on a bike. Kept you upright. But sometimes you can ride without the training wheels. You just don't realize it."

Deza laughed in recognition. "I think you're right. For a

long time, I was just . . ." Deza searched for the words. "I was just too scared to be out there on my own. Some part of me knew he was cheating. I mean, I suspected for a while before I knew for sure. But I just needed someone to be out there with me. Sometimes I feel so alone in the spotlight."

"You shouldn't have to settle for being mistreated just to keep from being alone," Damián said.

"That's easy for you to say," Deza said. "Male artists have it different."

Anasuya walked back in with a small canvas pouch. She handed it to Damián, who pulled out an antiseptic wipe.

"Is somebody playing my song?" Anasuya asked. "About how male artists have it different?"

"Girl," Deza said.

"They live in a whole different world," Anasuya said. "They got a line around the block of women who wanna be their cheerleader, girlfriend, wife, baby mama, nanny, cook, secretary, maid. Women artists are out here by ourselves."

Deza recalled how Coco had said basically the same thing.

Damián finished wiping his cut. He crumpled up the trash and put it in his pocket.

"Thanks," he said to Anasuya.

"Do you need anything out of here?" Anasuya asked Deza, holding out the first aid kit.

Deza shook her head. "Nothing bruised but the ego," she said. "I'm so sorry to pull you all into my drama." She couldn't quite meet their eyes when she said it.

Anasuya squeezed her hand. "Girl," she said. "That's not on you. You told him no. That's on some toxic masculinity. I'm just glad we were there to help."

"Yeah," Damián said. "He was totally out of line."

"I just—" Deza began. But then Anasuya's phone rang.

"It's Nicasio," she said. "I'm gonna take it," she said, and went across the hall into the compartment she shared with Damián.

"Thanks," Deza said when she and Damián were alone. "For what you said out there."

"That was nothing but the truth," Damián said. "These men out there trying to claim credit for you. Or give some dude credit for you. Even the *Rolling Stone* thing. It's fucked up. Royal is just the messiest version."

"Facts," Deza said.

"But you know," Damián said. "There are men out there who know how to back up a strong woman. I'm one of them."

Deza shrugged. "Then Lisa is lucky," she said.

"Lisa?" Damián said. "Who's Lisa?"

"Your girlfriend?" Deza said.

"Lisette?" Damián said. "We broke up."

"Oh. Sorry," Deza said. Although she didn't exactly feel sorry. "For getting her name wrong. And the breakup."

Now it was Damián's turn to shrug.

"What happened?" Deza asked.

"I wasn't honest about what I wanted," Damián said.

"Which is what?"

"I want to be a musician," Damián said. "I want to follow the music and see where it takes me. She saw it as some immature dream I was supposed to get out of my system." He pantomimed scratching a record, then flung his hand as if throwing it away. "But the more I do it, the more I want to do it. I feel like I'm catching up. But you," he said. "You been doing this so seriously since your teens. That's why you're so good at it. It's like you just own it. Every night."

"I know it looks like that," Deza said. "But nights like this, when we don't perform. I mean, in general outside the spotlight. It's just a mess. My whole life is a mess . . ."

"No way," Damián said. "It's just a few speed bumps. You'll figure it out."

But it felt like she never would. She kept making the

wrong choices. Inviting the snakes into her life. Rock.it.
Royal.

Deza shook her head. "I just—" She couldn't manage to
get the sentence out before it all came back to her. Royal's
tone, the rage, the sense that he had made her, owned her, demanded her gratitude. It was ugly in and of itself, menacing,
dangerous. But somehow—now that she was safe—it still
maintained its most vicious sting from the way it reminded
her of her mother.

Yet, at the same time, Damián's face, his empathic pres-
ence, undermined her armor. She always had to be tough
with her mother, but this time, she was protected?

Most of the time, she was supposed to be the strong one.
She felt weak. Exposed. How could she impose this on him?
She was that selfish brat her mother had accused her of
being. But she looked at Damián's face, and he didn't look
put-upon or impatient. He looked . . . concerned. His eyes
were wide, his brow furrowed. He cared about her. Had de-
fended her. Was here comforting her. His body felt solid
against her back.

Him standing up for her gave her an inch to let her steel
core melt a little. And then the tight spot in her throat loos-
ened. The memory of Royal, of her mother, her father, all the
rage she had ever absorbed.

A yelp of a wail escaped her. She tried to swallow it, but
she couldn't. She managed a ragged inhale, and found her
body releasing a moan of grief that didn't end until she ran
out of breath. And then she gasped and wailed some more.
So many unspilled tears. She crumpled onto Damián and
sobbed.

This time the hurricane was also human-made. The way
her mother defied natural law in trying to tear down her children, the unnatural way the wind that was her father blew
steadily toward his sons and not his daughters. All the gusts

that had ripped at her sense of herself, the torrential downpours that had soaked her in the feeling that she didn't deserve. But in that moment—when she began to cry—the storm reversed course. Now water streamed from her eyes. The gusts of wailing blew out of her. She would send this storm back where it came from. She had carried it inside too long. It was not her, not hers to hold anymore.

And then it began to subside. Rain dripped down off her edges in rivulets, flowed down into the red dirt of Damián's shoulder. But then the storm lifted. Turned to drizzle and mist.

As Deza came back to herself, a wave of shame began to boil beneath her skin. Had she just ugly cried for the whole bus to hear? Was that snot and tears all over Damián's Mos Def shirt? Deza sat up. But her eyes stayed downcast.

"Oh my God," she said, wiping her eyes on her own shirt. "I am so sorry."

Damián smiled at her. "No need," he said. "It's okay. Everybody gets to rest sometimes. Take a night off from being the girl boss."

"Ha," Deza said. "I'm a rapper. I gotta eat wack emcees for breakfast."

"I always liked that line," Damián said.

"You knew that mixtape?" Deza said.

"Of course," Damián said. "One of my boys gave it to me a few years ago. He said you'd go far. Look at you now."

"Please don't," she said. "Here's one for Instagram live: 'Rap diva melts down.'"

"You're not a diva," Damián said. "You're a star, Deza. There's a difference. What is it Erykah Badu said?"

"'I'm an artist and I'm sensitive about my shit,'" Deza said with a laugh.

"That's you," Damián said. "You can't be hard all the time."

"It just makes me feel like a fake," Deza said.

"Nah, Deza," he said. "You're the real thing. Everybody can see it. I can see it. I feel it every time I see you onstage." He looked down. "Which is another reason I broke up with Lisette."

"Because you wanted to be onstage with me?"

"Because I realized it wasn't just the music, it was you," Damián said. "Because I realized if it was you asking me to stop traveling and raise a family in New York, I'd say yes. Because maybe we'd just be making beats for the songs we sang to our kids, but it would be enough. It would be enough if I was doing it with you. I'd know we'd always have the music with us. No matter where we did or didn't go."

"Oh shit," Deza said.

"I'm in love with you," Damián said, grabbing her hand and putting it to his chest.

"You're what?" she asked. In love? She thought maybe he liked her. Maybe he wanted to have sex with her, but in love?

"I'm so sorry," he said, standing up. "I shouldn't have said anything. I cannot believe I fucked this up, too. I knew I shouldn't. I just—can we rewind? I'm glad I was able to help with your ex. You're amazing, Deza, and you deserve backup from your crew. Call on me anytime. And I'm gonna head over to my—"

But she stood and wrapped her arms around his neck. She pulled close to him and kissed him.

He was startled at first, his lips weren't quite ready. But then he sank into the kiss. She slid her arms around him, pulled him closer. It felt different from the last time. Not frantic. Not urgent.

Damián put his arms around her neck and his fingers crept up to the nape.

She pulled back. "Hold up," she said. "Here's the thing with Black girls—"

"I know," Damián said. "Don't touch the hair."

The two of them laughed.

"I won't," he said. But then he remembered the consent workshops he taught. "But wait. I wanna make sure . . . I mean—you had a rough time with your ex. I don't want to take advantage . . ."

She silenced him with a kiss. "Just don't touch the hair and we're good."

With each kiss, they warmed to each other. Different pieces of their bodies locked together. His hands under her shirt, sliding into the waistband of her pants.

She, of course, could play in his hair, and she ran her hands from his Afro to his belt, unbuckling his jeans.

They lay back on the bed, exploring each other's bodies. She kept hearing his voice in her head. "I'm in love with you." She didn't need to rush. He would be there. He was there now.

It was different than with Royal. Her man had always been a performer. Like when he went down on her, it was for an imaginary audience.

Everywhere Damián touched her, he looked into her eyes. To see if she liked it. She did. She liked all of it.

And then he was pulling a condom out of a pocket at the knee of his cargo jeans.

Deza laughed. "Looks like somebody learned his lesson."

Damián laughed too. "I told God if I ever got a second chance with you, I'd be ready. Been carrying this around like a good luck charm."

She rolled it on him and he gasped.

When he entered her, she had to muffle her cry of pleasure. It wouldn't do to be crying all loud on this bus one minute and then fucking all loud the next.

He started out slow, gentle, but then sped up. They both did.

When she came, she bit into his forearm to muffle her screams. Her teeth dented his Puerto Rico tattoo. Top teeth in an arc from San Juan to Guayaba. Bottom teeth in an arc from Isabela to San Germán.

* * *

Afterward, the two of them lay in the double bed. Damián ran a gentle finger up and down Deza's arm. His skin was café au lait to her chocolate. His nails cut short, so the pads of his fingers made full contact with her skin.

"One of these days," he said, "you need to wear your hair like that night we met in the club. Just cornrows. Nothing fancy. I mean, it all looks good on you. But when your hair was back like that, I could really see your whole face."

"Maybe after the tour," Deza said.

"You're so beautiful," he said. "Everything about you. Your skin, your face, your body definitely. But it's—it's who you are. You're just amazing."

"Stop it," she said. "You're making me blush."

He laughed. "What we just did doesn't make you blush. Performing in a stadium doesn't make you blush. But a compliment does?"

"I guess so," Deza said.

"So, one thing you need to know about me is that when I know what I want, when I'm really sure, I'm ready to lock it down," he said. "I want you to be my girlfriend. You don't need to say nothing on Instagram. I'm sure it boosts your record sales or whatever if guys think you're single. I know it was a lot to say I'm in love with you, and I'm not taking it back, because that's how I feel. I know you might not be there yet, but that's cool. But if we're ever gonna have sex again—and I really hope we do—I need to be in a committed relationship. I'm a grown man. If you don't want that, I'm a put my jeans back on and go cry on Anasuya's shoulder, then be ready to DJ your next gig like a total professional. But I hope you say yes."

This was the ask she'd been hoping for. A real ask. A man who wanted her but wanted her to be happy more than he wanted to own her.

"Yes," she said, half-laughing and half-crying. "Yes, I'd love to be your girlfriend."

"Does that mean I can touch your hair?" he asked.

"Definitely not," she said, and then it was all laughing.

Trina: Welcome back to the Bad Attitude podcast.
Gina: Dayum! Did you see that motherfucker Royal? "Baby, I love you. Marry me." Then that nigga turn around talmbout, "Bitch, you ain't shit." And then wonder why she said no. Cause you passive aggressive as fuck, nigga.
Trina: Deza, you know you did right. And got two awards to prove it.

The next morning, Deza had over fifty missed calls and her voice mail was full. Everyone had seen the video on Instagram or had heard about it and was calling to see if she was okay. Even her mother.

Deza started with a mass text that she was fine, and then called her aunt.

"I'm fine, Auntie Ty," she explained. She wanted to tell her aunt about Damián, but he was lying next to her, scrolling on his phone. She'd tell her aunt later.

"By the way," Tyesha said. "I have a little business to discuss. Woof sent over the contract, the one with the sportswear company. One of the women I work with, Eva, is an attorney. I'm gonna put her on the phone."

From the sound of her voice, Eva sounded like an older woman. The voice was white but not quite white at the same time. Pure New York accent, though.

"You should fight to get paid here," Eva said. "Your aunt showed me the 'freedom of speech' clause in the contract that was designed to protect the company from responsibility for the misogyny of some of their other artists. But it will likely protect you."

"Really?"

"Burning your clothes while rapping as a political statement is definitely in the realm of protected speech," she said. "If you want, I can draft a letter demanding payment, now that they're the ones who dropped the sponsorship."

"Hell yeah," Deza said. "Have Tyesha send the bill to my accountant."

"Will do," Eva said.

She and Damián celebrated the good news in her bed.

@LilTreyLockk
Deza leaving the concert early for 1 reason only. She don't wanna battle my bitch. She know if they get down Deza gon be the 1 gettin knocked out.

@AnayaLaterHipHop
Deza you a chicken. Deza you a fake. Deza having you headline a tour was a mistake
One that the label had to rectify . . .

@Deza4Everr
Deza you a bad bitch. Deza you a boss. Haters like Anaya Later need to step off . . .

@LuvvieLuvLuv
Deza you a prophet. Deza you a jewel. Queen of Urban Prophecy. Girl, you came to rule . . .

Different DJs had Deza vs. Anaya Later segments on their shows or in clubs. But Deza had a lot more songs to choose from.

"So who do you think would win in a Deza vs. Anaya Later battle?" one influencer asked. Most of the answers were for Deza, but Anaya Later had her fans, too.

@ThatRealRealNiggaJoe
Deza got that ass, but she don't wanna show it. I wanna see some ass vs. ass showdown.

@Deza4Everr
If you want porn, go look at porn. This is rap, fool. Not every female rapper is tryna show her ass. No disrespect to those who do. It's just that women need to be more than one note, ok?

Chapter 37

Dallas

The tour's final stop was their massive Dallas-area concert. Deza was tired but satiated from all the lovemaking with Damián.

Her set was more languid than usual. She didn't have her usual frenetic energy, but instead there was a calmer sureness in the body of a woman who is well-loved. She had to stop herself from grinning every time she looked at him.

Only when she closed with "Almost Home" did she get serious, somber. But even in telling that story, she felt more hopeful than ever before. Black people would keep fighting until justice finally became their reality.

"Thank you, Dallas!" she said. "You've been an amazing audience. What a perfect end to my first big tour. Thank you from the bottom of my heart—"

"Nah!" a man's voice interrupted her, booming through the speakers. "Nah, that's not how the story end." It was Lil Trey. "Deza still ain't step up to battle my bitch Anaya Later."

Deza was stunned. The audience perked up. Some cheered, some booed.

Deza tried to pull off a smile and a laugh. "Hey, Lil Trey," she said. "Somebody's extra-excited to perform for y'all tonight. Give it up for the fifty percent of our next act, Murda Lockk, Lil Trey!"

The audience applauded, but Trey didn't take the bait.

"Nah, Deza," he said. "You need to battle my bitch. If you a true emcee, you gonna step up to the battle when an up-and-coming emcee come for your crown. That's the rules of real hip hop. Unless you on some fake-ass studio rapper shit."

"Lil Trey," Deza said. "The challenge ain't legit. She fake freestyled on the radio, and I clocked those rhymes in her old mixtape."

"You chicken," he said.

"Nah," Deza said. "I'm reclaiming my time. Good night, Dallas!"

"See?" Lil Trey said. "I knew this bitch was fake."

Deza swiveled. "Who you calling a bitch?"

"You," Trey said. "You a chicken-ass-bitch."

Deza could feel her heart pounding. "Damn," she said to the audience. "I started this tour taking off my earrings. It looks like I'm a end it the same way." She pulled the bamboo hoops off and placed them in Damián's palm. He squeezed her hand.

"Baby, you sure?" he murmured.

Deza nodded. "Okay," Deza said to Lil Trey. "You want me to battle?"

"Yeah," he said. "That's what I been motherfucking saying."

"Fine," Deza said. "I'm ready." In one hand, she cocked the mic up, emcee style. With the other hand, she pointed straight at him. "I'm ready to battle you."

"Me?" Lil Trey said. "Nah, I don't battle females."

"You seem to do everything else with us," she said. "You rhyme about fucking us. Pimping us. Killing us. Drugging us and fucking us without consent. But you're scared to battle one of us?"

"I ain't scared of nothin."

"Fine, then," Deza said. "What'd you just say? 'If you a true emcee, you gonna step up to the battle when an up-and-coming emcee come for your crown'? That 'That's the rules of real hip hop. Unless you on some fake-ass studio rapper shit'? Well, I'm coming for that crown tonight."

"Nah, little girl," Trey said. "You need to get off the stage. You ain't no Prophet Queen. You straight fake."

Deza circled him, emcee style:

> I didn't buy a ticket to your coronation
> because since your first album it's been pure
>   masturbation
> You got your dick in your hand/all your raps
>   are planned
> You can't freestyle to even save your reputation.

She turned to the audience. "Google those lyrics and you won't find them. Because this is off the dome, children. Watch and learn, Anaya Later. That's how you freestyle."

She turned back to Trey. "So what you got to say now?"

Trey was mad, she could see it in his eyes. He took off his jacket and tossed it on the ground. Then he stepped toward the stage.

> Ain't got my dick in my hand, I got my dick up
>   your ass
> and you be barking like a dog because I'm
>   rhyming so fast
> You're only good for a fuck, never good for a
>   rhyme
> Although I busted a nut, it was a waste of my time.

The image stung. Deza's chest felt tight, her stomach boiled.

> *Rape is a joke to you? Something to rap about?*
> *Go call your mother and your sister and check*
>   *it out*
> *Black women are precious*
> *We deserve protection*
> *Not to be targeted by men like you with zombie*
>   *erections.*

She put her free arm forward and began to stumble around the stage like the walking dead.

> *Fuck a girl here, rape a girl there*
> *catch a case when they find your jizz in under-*
>   *age underwear*
> *It isn't fair that women go through this shit*
> *Then tryna chill at the club with you rapping*
>   *about it*
> *Anaya Later in fake freestyle talked about my*
>   *ex*
> *said he didn't satisfy when we had sex*
> *It's the only thing that wasn't in her old rhyme,*
>   *boo*
> *All those lyrics are new, I think she's talking*
>   *bout you.*

"Nah," Trey said.
Nah. I handle business in bed.
Whether I hit it from the back or she's giving me head.

Still dead! Deza jumped in. *Same old shit.*
About fucking women. It's a tired-ass bit.

You got nothing to say about our world today.
When George Floyd died you had a concert that night.
You didn't mention his name because you're blinded by
fame.
You can't relate to the streets, folks out here tryna survive
but you're bragging about how you're living the good life
Nine minutes and twenty-nine seconds on the brother's neck
You didn't bother to mention in your concert set
Say his name! George Floyd. Say her name. Breonna
Taylor
Rap is bigger than you. Rap has work to do.
But you're sitting on your ass waiting for rap to enrich you.
Maybe you are the pimp, you treat hip hop like a ho.
Making money off her but now you got to go.
You ain't the king, you're just a low-level underling
I bit that from Latifah, but here's the thing
Our people deserve better than date rape party anthems
We need to reach for the power of the Black Panthers
So when you're ready to join the fight
DM me on Insta. But for now, good night.

Deza literally dropped the mic and strode off the stage.

Trey stood there, stunned for a second. "Nah," he said. "Nah . . ." and tried to get his groove back, but then he looked out at the audience and saw that about half the people were leaving.

"Fuck this shit," he said, and walked off the stage.

From the DJ stand, Damián said: "Ladies and gentlemen, Deza Starling. And that's our time."

Backstage, Trey was standing over Anaya Later. "Bitch, I told you to come out!" he yelled.

"But she said she wanted to battle you, not me," Anaya Later said.

"You do what I say, not what she fucking say," he spat at her.

"A little extra for your money tonight," the announcer was saying. "And now, representing the Skranky South, that crew out of Atlanta, Murda Lockk!"

Trey grabbed one of the guys from his entourage. "Gimme a shot," Trey commanded. "Gimme two."

"Sure thing," the guy said, and pulled out a flask with a metal shot glass for a cap. He gave two shots to Trey in rapid succession.

The rapper slugged them back and turned to Anaya Later. "Wait for me in the bus!" he said.

"You said you was gonna bring me onstage tonight for the final show," she said.

"Not no more," Trey said. "Not since you fucked this up." He turned away and swaggered back onto the stage.

Anasuya looked at Anaya Later. "Hey, girl," she said quietly. "It wasn't your fault."

Anaya Later shrugged. "Niggas."

"You don't have to get on that bus," Anasuya said. "The rest of us are going to the hotel. Then the bus is taking us to the airport in the morning. We could help you get wherever you need to go."

Anaya Later looked at the stage. Trey was all agitated motions and spitting on the mic. She nodded.

"I left my purse in their dressing room," Anaya Later said.

Anasuya looked around. All the guys from the entourage were in the wings watching the show.

"Come on," Anasuya said. "Let's get your purse."

"You okay?" Damián asked Deza when she got off the stage. He handed her back her earrings.

Deza was jangled from all the adrenaline. She felt rattled, but still victorious. She tried to put the earrings back on, but her hands were shaking. She put them in her pocket instead. She hadn't had this feeling since middle school. Fighting. But even when she won, she never felt quite right afterward.

"Let's go," Deza said. "I'm ready to leave the concert early."

"So glad this is our last stop with this motherfucker," Damián said. "You have no idea how hard it was for me not to try to step on stage and fuck him up."

"I'm glad you resisted the urge," Deza said. "Is it true he has a gun?"

"Yeah," Damián said. "We might wanna switch hotels."

When they told Anasuya, she agreed, and said she had Anaya Later with her.

"Damn," Damián said. "She jumped ship?"

"I'm surprised," Deza said.

"I'm not," Damián said. "Anasuya's like that. She helps people. She helped me. I moped around for so long talking about how I fucked up with you."

"You fucked up with me?" Deza said. "I was the one who fucked up with you. Ready to have sex without a condom. I had lost my damn mind."

"How about sex with a condom?" Damián asked. "Tonight?"

"Yes, please," Deza said.

The next day, she and Damián met up with the producer from Houston on the climate album project.

As they sat in the reception area, they both got a text from Anasuya. **Anaya Later heard from Trey this morning and he said he was sorry. She said he never apologized before, and she went off to meet him. Apparently, he did come to the hotel last night. Looking for both her and you, Deza.**

Good luck to her, Deza texted back. It reminded her too much of the push-pull of her own parents. At least Anaya Later had a career. Hopefully, it would outlast Trey.

She and Damián sat in the producer's waiting area with their fingers intertwined. They were a contrast in shades.

"Man," Damián said. "Look how pale I'm getting." His

skin was a caramel compared to her milk chocolate. "When I get some sun, I'm practically your color."

"My color?" Deza said.

"*Mas o menos*," Damián said.

"You Puerto Ricans be tripping," Deza said laughing. "You be light-skinned and thinking you straight-up Africa."

"Are you denying my Blackness?" Damián asked. "Are you up here questioning my Negritud?"

"You a goofy for that," Deza said.

"I'm what?" he asked.

"You're tripping," Deza said.

"I'm tryna tell you," Damián said. "I'm so much darker when I get in the sun. I'm a take you to Puerto Rico, and you'll see."

"Is it questioning your Blackness to say that you're delusional?"

Damián was about to answer when the producer's assistant came and interrupted them: "Joanne will see you now," she said.

The wall behind Joanne's desk was covered in gold and platinum albums. The producer had three Grammys and several other awards. Some of the biggest names in the business.

"Something different about y'all since Las Vegas," she said.

Deza shrugged.

"Are y'all a couple?" the producer asked.

Damián looked at Deza. She still hadn't decided whether to disclose it publicly.

"Yes," Deza said. "Definitely. But still keeping quiet about it."

"Yee-ah!" the producer said. "Me and my wife had a bet on it. I saw you two in New Orleans and said, 'they a couple.' She didn't think so."

"We weren't together back then," Deza said.

"Yeah, but the chemistry was already there," Joanne said. "Working together can be hard. My wife and I met at work. By the end of this album, y'all either gonna be bonded for life or not speaking."

Deza and Damián smiled at each other. "I'll put my money on bonded," Damián said.

Deza laughed and reached for his hand under the desk.

Author's note:

I came of age in the Golden Era of hip hop, and was deep into the music for a few years in the '80s on the East Coast. But I am not an emcee. And even though I was a hip hop theater artist in the mid-00s, I was never even a true hip hop head. I have freestyled on a public stage exactly once. In the Midwest. It was with a Bay Area group called Company of Prophets. There is no video, so you will have to take my word for it.

I grew up in the Bay Area as a lefty feminist activist Black girl, who just kept getting pissed off at sexism in hip hop, and tuning it out. And my time spent as a performer in the hip hop community was more like a transfer student from spoken word. Plus, I was already out of college and had dropped out of an MFA program when I moved into that world. I never was that young female in the game trying to win. I had a job in social services, and I was living on my own.

So many of us seek the spotlight because we have early trauma in our lives, and I was no exception. But by the time I was engaging in hip hop, I was in therapy. I was in a support group for Black people healing from racism. I didn't drink or smoke. I didn't have the insecurity, either emotional or economic or social, that makes young women so vulnerable in those scenes. I was mostly anchored in the spoken word and slam community, which was a much more nurturing space for women artists, and it nurtured me. I could be an artist who dabbled in hip hop when it was convenient. I could skate in on my cred from an adjacent scene. I could be in hip hop but not of it.

Also, I was in the Bay Area hip hop scene where there were noncompetitive spaces for women. Sisterz of the Underground and the strong community of queer women meant that there was much more room for powerful female voices in hip hop. Of course, there was a ton of sexism in the broader hip hop scene. But we had spaces of refuge and shelter where we could rap about our lives and vent our rage about hip hop's misogyny. Young female artists could come of age in those spaces without hip hop gaslighting them, and we didn't have to form ourselves under the approval or dismissal of the male gaze.

Back in the day, I recall doing a talk at the Yerba Buena Center with DJ J9 about women in hip hop, and we were testifying about the challenges of facing sexism in the hip hop community. A fellow artist, Will Power, acknowledged the trauma that women faced, but (as a male ally) also challenged us to articulate a vision for hip hop as well. Out of that challenge came my spoken word piece "If Women Ran Hip Hop," and the larger theater show "Thieves in the Temple: The Reclaiming of Hip Hop," which I worked on from 2001–04. This book is a continuation of that conversation—how do women find power in this cultural conversation called hip hop? And when we have power what do we do with it?

In addition, this book came out of a question I posed to myself in 2016. Could I write a romance that wasn't also a thriller? What type of situation would be compelling for me to explore? I liked the idea of two people sort of awkwardly stuck together. How about a tour bus? How about a diva emcee and her DJ? I had outlined it as a straight-up romance in 2019, but thank goodness my editor, Esi Sogah, said she wanted it to fall in line with the social justice novels I had been writing, even if it wasn't a thriller. From there it was easy to bring in the issues of misogyny and corporate control of hip hop that I have been shouting about for the last twenty years. Finally, in the 2020 blossoming of the Movement for Black Lives, I landed the novel in that struggle as well.

That draft was finished and submitted to my editor in November 2020. Then I began reading Sofia Quintero/Black Artemis's *Explicit Content*. This groundbreaking novel about female emcees in New York really shook me up about the book I had just turned in. I still loved my premise and plot, my characters and writing. But I could see that I had written Deza without context. She was missing the world of hip hop. The drama and *bochinche*.

I had been dying to read *Explicit Content* for years. But I am a working mom, with a full-time teaching load, who also publishes a novel every year. If both my hands are free, I am writing a book. Which means that I can only "read" in audio. Because then I can read while I clean, drive, fall asleep, lay in bed awake at night trying not to worry about everything on my to-do list, my kid's mental health in the pandemic, and the state of the world. *Explicit Content* was written in 2004 and only became available in audio in 2019. I am so grateful for the days in late November 2020, when I immersed myself in Quintero's work. She so fully realized the context of her characters, it showed me where mine was threadbare.

And I did what I have had to do so many times in my artistic career—I asked for help. Enter Coco Peila. Coco Peila is my family, is my sister in struggle, is my favorite emcee. With her permission, I had already included her as a character in the book, because witnessing her journey as an emcee is one of the biggest inspirations and foundations of this book. She served as a consultant on this book. She is the reason that all the characters don't sound the same, speaking a dated mash-up of unspecified, regionless slang. She also may be the only reason this book would resonate with a younger generation.

It takes a village to raise a book. So, if you feel compelled by the hip hop milieu that Deza moves in, you have Coco Peila and Sofia Quintero to thank. Prior to their influence, my book only had Deza, her high school crew, Nashonna, Murda Lockk, Anaya Later, and three DJs. But now, I think we have a much more fully realized hip hop world. And thanks to Moya Bailey for coining the term "misogynoir."